ABANDONED
FRAGMENTS

SUN VISION
PRESS

ABANDONED FRAGMENTS
UNEDITED WORKS 1897–1917
Franz Kafka
ISBN 978-0-9838842-0-0
Published 2012 by Sun Vision Press
Copyright © Sun Vision Press 2012
All World Rights Reserved
www.sunvisionpress.org
Design: Curtis Albrecht
Originally published as *Nachgelassene Schriften und Fragmente I* (S. Fischer Verlag, 1993)
Translated by Dr. Ina Pfitzner
The translation of this work was supported by a grant from the Goethe-Institut, which is funded by the German Ministry of Foreign Affairs.

CONTENTS

ABANDONED FRAGMENTS

UNEDITED WORKS 1897–1917

FRANZ KAFKA

[1]

There is a coming and a going
A parting and often no – homecoming

Prague, 20 November.

Franz Kafka.

[2]

How many words there are in the book! They are meant to be reminders! As though words could ever be reminders!

For words are poor mountaineers and miners. They collect treasures neither from the mountain heights nor from the mountain depths.

But there is a living remembrance that gently brushed across everything memorable as if with a coaxing hand. And when the blaze arises from these ashes, glowing and hot, massive and strong, and you stare into it as though under a magic spell, then–
But into this chaste remembrance, one cannot inscribe oneself with a clumsy hand and blunt implement; one can do it only in these white, unassuming pages. I did this on September 4, 1900.

Franz Kafka

[3]

<u>a</u>   One must not say: only the new idea arouses aesthetic pleasure, but rather every idea that does not fall into the sphere of the will arouses aesthetic pleasure. Saying it regardless, however, would mean that only a new idea could be perceived in such a way that leaves our sphere of the will untouched. It is certain, however, that there are new ideas that we do not judge aesthetically; then which part of a new idea do we judge aesthetically? The question remains.

<u>b</u>   It would be necessary to explain "aesthetic apperception" – an expression that may not have been introduced as of yet – in greater detail, or, really, from scratch. How does that pleasurable sensation arise and in what does its peculiarity consist; in what way does it differ from the joy of a new discovery or news from a foreign land or area of knowledge.

<u>c</u>   The main proof of this new view is a general physiological, and not only aesthetic, fact – and that is fatigue. Now, on the one hand it follows from your numerous restrictions on the concept "new" that everything, really, is new; for since all objects are caught in a constantly changing time and light, and the same goes for us observers, we must therefore always encounter them in a different place. On the other hand we tire not only of enjoying art but also of studying and mountain climbing and eating lunch, but we still wouldn't be allowed to say, veal is no longer a dish that agrees with us, just because we are tired of it today. Most of all it would be unwarranted to say that there is just this double relationship with art. Better: the object hovers above the aesthetic edge, and fatigue (which really exists only in the form of fondness for the time that has just gone by), thus: the object has lost its equilibrium, and in a bad way at that. And yet your conclusion calls for arranging this contradiction – for apperception is not a state of being but rather a movement, and hence, it must complete itself. There will be a little noise, with this harried sensation of pleasure in its midst, but soon everything must come to rest in cavernous retreats.

<u>d</u>   There is a difference between aesthetic and scientific persons.

<u>e</u>   What remains uncertain is the concept of "apperception." In the sense that we know it, it is not an aesthetic concept. It might be represented as follows. Let us say I am a person with no sense of place whatsoever, and I come

9

to Prague as to a foreign city. So I want to write to you but I don't know your address, I ask you, you tell me your address, I apperceive that and never have to ask you again. Your address has become something "old" for me; this is how we apperceive science. But if I want to visit you, I must keep asking at every street corner and intersection, I will never manage without passers-by, apperception is fundamentally impossible here. It is possible, naturally, that I get tired and step into a coffeehouse on the way, so as to rest a bit there, and it is also possible that I give up the visit altogether, and yet I still have not apperceived...

"This easily explains..." this should not come as a surprise, for straight from the beginning, in anticipation, as it were, everything is obliged to hold onto apperception like a handrail. "The same theory explains..." this is quite a feat. From what I can see, this line is followed by the sole proof – which you had to learn first, then, rather than at the end. "One is instinctively wary–" this line is a giveaway.

[4]

As Eduard Raban came through the hallway and stepped into the open doorway, he saw that it was raining. It was not raining much.

On the sidewalk in front of him, many people were walking with varying gaits. Every now and then, one of them would step forward and cross the road. A little girl was holding a weary puppy in her outstretched hands. Two gentlemen were making announcements to each other, the one holding his hands out with their insides up and moving them steadily as if he were balancing a load. Then a lady came into view whose hat was laden with ribbons, clasps, and flowers. And a young person rushed past holding a thin cane, his left hand, as though paralyzed, laid flat on his chest. Now and again came men who were smoking and carrying small upright longish clouds in front of them. At regular intervals, three gentlemen – two with light overcoats in the crook of their forearms – walked from the building to the curb, observed what was transpiring there, and then pulled back, talking all the while.

Through the gaps between the passers-by, one got a glimpse of the neatly joined bricks of the road. Horses with long outstretched necks were pulling carriages on delicate high wheels. The people reclining on their padded seats silently took in the pedestrians, the shops, the balconies, and the sky. Should one carriage pass another, the horses would press against each other, their bridles dangling. The animals would pull on the shaft; the carriage would roll, swaying in haste, until the arc around the preceding carriage was completed and the horses would then spread apart again, only their narrow tranquil heads tilted toward one another.

Some people quickly approached the front door, stopped on the dry mosaic tiles, turning around slowly. And then gazed into the rain that fell in confusion, trapped in the narrow street.

Raban was feeling tired. His lips were as pale as the faded red of his fat tie, which displayed a Moorish design. The lady sitting by the doorstep opposite was gazing in his direction now. She did so indifferently, and she may also have been gazing at the falling rain in front of him or at the small nameplates affixed to the door above his hair. Raban felt she was gazing in wonderment. "Well," he thought, if I could tell her, she wouldn't be astonished after all. One worked excessively at the office, to the point of being too tired to even truly enjoy one's vacation. But all the work in the world doesn't entitle one to be treated with love by everyone; rather, one is a complete stranger to everyone. And as long as you say "one" instead of "I," it's nothing and one can recite this story, but as soon as you admit to yourself that it's you, then it virtually bores right through you, and you are horrified.

He set down his valise with the sewn-on checked cloth, bending his knees. At the edge of the road, the rainwater was already running in streaks that extended to the lower-lying gutters.

But if I myself make a distinction between "one" and "I", how dare I complain about others? Likely they aren't unfair, but I'm just too tired to accept everything. I'm too tired even to walk the distance to the train station without effort, which is, really, not far. Why, then, don't I stay in the city this short holiday break, to recover? I'm being unreasonable. This journey is going to make me ill; I know it well. My room won't be sufficiently comfortable; in the countryside, there's simply no other way. And we're barely in the first half of June, when the air in the country is often still quite cool. I'm prudently dressed, to be sure, but I'll have to join other people on late-night walks. They have ponds there; so one will likely take walks along the ponds. I'm surely going to catch a cold there. However, I won't distinguish myself much in the conversations. I won't be able to compare that pond to other ponds in faraway lands, for I've never traveled, and – talking about the moon and feeling blissful, rapturously clambering up a pile of rubble – I'm too old not to get laughed at for that.

People were passing with slightly lowered heads, above which they were loosely holding their dark umbrellas. A freight cart also went past, a man sitting in the straw-filled driver's seat with his legs stretched out so carelessly that one foot was almost touching the ground, while the other one rested on straw and rags. It looked as if he were sitting in a field in nice weather. But he held the reins alertly, so that the cart, its iron-rods clanging, rolled smoothly through the crowd. On the wet ground, one could see the reflection of the revolving iron-rods slowly sliding from cobblestone row to cobblestone row. The young boy opposite, next to the lady, was dressed like an old vintner. His pleated garb formed a large circle at the bottom and was held together only by a leather strap almost up around his armpits. His semispherical hat came down to his eyebrows, and a tassel hung from its tip to his left ear. He was pleased about the rain. He ran out of the gate and looked up at the sky his eyes wide open, to catch more of the rain. He jumped up frequently, which made the water splash a great deal, and passers-by admonished him severely. Then the lady called him to her and held him by the hand from then on, but he did not cry.

Raban was startled then. Wasn't it too late already? His overcoat and jacket were open; he swiftly reached for his watch. It had stopped. Morosely, he asked the time from a neighbor, who was standing somewhat further down the hallway. The neighbor was having a conversation and replied, through the laughter that was part of it: "Just past four, you're welcome," and turned away.

Raban quickly opened his umbrella and picked up his valise. But as he was about to step onto the street, his path was blocked by some women in a rush, so he let them pass. In so doing he found himself gazing down upon a little girl's hat, woven from red straw and with a green wreathlet on its undulating brim.

He still remembered it when he was already in the street, which ascended slightly in the direction he was headed in. But then he forgot, for now he had to make some effort; his valise felt heavy, and the wind was blowing straight at him, flapping his jacket and pushing in the umbrella ribs in front.

He took deeper breaths now; in the distance a clock in a nearby square sounded a quarter to five; from under his umbrella he could see the short, light steps of people coming his way, braking coach wheels were grinding, turning slower, the horses were stretching their skinny front legs daringly like chamois in the mountains.

Then it appeared to Raban that he would weather the long bad period of the coming two weeks as well. For it was only two weeks, a limited time, and even if his troubles were growing ever more serious, the time during which one had to deal with them was waning. In turn, the courage would be waxing, no doubt. All those who wish to harass me and who are now occupying the entire space around me will be pushed back little by little by the kindly passing of those days, without my helping them in the least. And, as a natural consequence, I can be meek and quiet. They can do whatever they want to me, and yet everything must turn out well, merely due to the days passing.

And what's more, can't I just do things the way I did as a child in dangerous situation? I don't even need to go to the countryside myself; that won't be necessary. I'm simply sending my clothed body. So I'm sending this clothed body instead. If it stumbles out the door of my room, its stumbling is not an indication of fear but of its insignificance. And it isn't nervousness, if it

13

trips on the stairs, if it goes to the countryside sobbing and eats its supper there weeping. Because I, I will be lying in my bed in the meantime, smoothly covered with a tan-colored blanket, exposed to the air blowing in through the slightly opened window.

Lying in my bed, I have the shape of a large beetle, a stag beetle or a cockchafer, I think.

He stopped before a window display of small men's hats hanging on rods behind the wet panes of glass and looked inside, his lips pursed. Why, my hat will do for the vacation, he thought, and walked on, and if no one likes me on account of my hat, then it is all the better.

The large form of a beetle, yes. I then pretended that I was hibernating and pressed my little legs against my bulbous body. And I lisp a small number of words, instructions to my sad body, which is standing close to me, bent over. But soon I'm done, it takes a bow, walks off swiftly, and it'll do everything as well as it can, while I'm resting.

He reached a freestanding archway at the top of the steep street, leading to a small square bounded by myriad shops that were already lit up. In the middle of the square, partly obscured by the light around the edges, was a low monument of a man seated in contemplation. People were moving in front of the lights like narrow blinds, and as the puddles spread all the luster far and wide, the view of the square was constantly changing.

Raban advanced rather far onto the square, but avoided the passing vehicles in spasms, leapt from one dry rock to other dry rocks and held his open umbrella in his hand raised high so as to be able to see everything around him. Until he stopped next to a lamppost – a trolley car stop – which was mounted on a small, square, paved base.

I'm expected in the countryside, though. Aren't they already wondering? But I haven't written to her the whole week since she has been in the country, just this morning. So they may imagine me looking different, after all. They might think that I would pounce when I address someone, but that isn't my custom. Or that I embrace upon arriving, but I don't like doing that either. I will exasperate them when I try to placate them. If only I could perfectly exasperate them, in the attempt to placate them.

Just then an open carriage was passing, not quickly, two ladies sitting behind its two shining lanterns on a small dark leather bench. One of them was reclining, her face covered by a veil and the shadow of her hat. But the other woman's upper body was upright; her hat was small, lined with thin feathers.

14

Everyone could see her. Her lower lip was slightly tucked into her mouth.

Just as the vehicle passed Raban, some sort of pole obstructed his view of the lead horse of the carriage, then some driver – wearing a big top hat – on an unusually high box seat moved in front of the ladies – this was much farther on now – and then their carriage turned around the corner of a small house, which now emerged and then disappeared from sight.

Raban gazed after them with his head bent, pressing the handle of his umbrella against his shoulder so as to see better. He had put the thumb of his right hand into his mouth and was rubbing his teeth against it. His valise was lying next to him, overturned.

Coaches rushed from street to street across the square; the horses' bodies flew horizontally as though thrown, but their nodding heads and necks suggested the momentum and effort of their movement.

All around, on the curbs of the three streets meeting in the square, there were loafers tapping on the cobblestones with small sticks. Between these groups, there were little towers in which girls were serving lemonade, then heavy street clocks on thin stilts, then men wearing large placards on their chests and backs advertising amusements in colored letters, then porters in yellowish armchairs with an evening—

[1 page missing]

a small party. Two stately carriages, which drove across the square into the descending street, separated several gentlemen from the party, but after the second carriage – they had already made an anxious attempt after the first one – these gentlemen reunited with the others into a group, with whom they then stepped onto the sidewalk in a long line and crowded into the door of a coffeehouse, inundated with light from shining bulbs hanging over the entrance.

The large cars of the electric trolley rolled past nearby, others stood vaguely still far back in the streets.

"How stooped she is," Raban thought as he looked at the picture now. "She is never really upright, and perhaps her back is rounded. I will have to pay much attention to that. And her mouth is so wide and, without doubt, her lower lip juts out, yes, I remember now, too. And the dress. Of course, I don't know anything about dresses, but those tightly sewn sleeves are ugly for sure; they look so much like a bandage. And the hat, its rim elevated all around her face in varying curves. But her eyes are beautiful; brown, if I'm not mistaken. Everyone says that her eyes are beautiful."

When an electric trolley stopped in front of Raban now, many people around him pushed toward its steps, with slightly opened, pointy umbrellas they were holding upright in their hands pressed against their shoulders. Raban, holding the valise under his arm, was pulled off the sidewalk and stepped heavily into an invisible puddle. Inside the car, a child kneeling on the bench pressed the fingertips of both hands to his lips as if saying goodbye to someone who was leaving. Some passengers alighted and had to walk a few steps alongside the car to escape the crush. Then a lady mounted the first step; the train she was holding with both hands barely covered her legs. A gentleman held onto a brass rail, and, his head raised, told the lady a thing or two. Everyone trying to get on was impatient. The conductor shouted.

Raban, now standing at the edge of the waiting group, turned around, for someone had called his name.

"Ah, Lement," he said slowly and extended the little finger of the hand holding the umbrella to an approaching young man.

"So this is the groom, on his way to see the bride. He looks terribly in love, " said Lement and then smiled with his mouth closed.

"Yes, you must forgive me for going today," said Raban. "I wrote to you this afternoon, too. Of course, I would have loved to go with you tomorrow, but it's Saturday tomorrow; everything will be overcrowded, it's a long trip."

"I don't mind, really. You did promise me, but when one is in love–. I'll just have to go by myself." Lement had placed one foot on the sidewalk, the other on the cobbles, and supported his upper body now on the one and now on the other leg. –"You were about to get on the trolley car; now it's leaving. Let's walk, I'll come with you. There's still time."

"But isn't is too late, I beg you?"

"It's no wonder that you are anxious but you still have time, really. I don't keep track of the time, so that's why I missed Gillemann just now."

"Gillemann? Isn't he staying out there, too?"

"Yes, he and his wife; they are going out there next week, and that is precisely why I had promised Gillemann to meet him today, when he gets out of the office. He was going to give me some instructions on their home furnishings – that's why I was supposed to meet him. Now for some reason, I was late; I was running errands. And just as I was wondering whether I shouldn't go to their place, I saw you, was first astonished about the valise, and started talking to you. But now it's too late in the evening to pay visits; it is quite impossible to go see Gillemann now."

"Of course. So those are some acquaintances I will have out there. I've never seen Mrs. Gillemann."

"And she is really beautiful. She is blond, and pale now, after her illness. She has the most beautiful eyes I've ever seen."

"Tell me, what do beautiful eyes look like, don't you think that the eye itself cannot be beautiful after all? Is it the gaze? I've never found eyes beautiful."

"Well, I may have exaggerated a little bit. But she is a pretty woman."

Through the glass pane of a ground-floor café, one could see a few gentlemen reading and eating around a three-sided table close by the window; one of them had lowered a newspaper onto the table and was holding up his little cup, glancing into the street out of the corners of his wide eyes. Behind those tables by the window, all the furniture and equipment in the large room was blocked from view by customers, sitting next to one another in small circles. They sat hunched over in the back of the room where

[1 page missing.]

Besides, this is not an altogether unpleasant business, is it. Many would be glad to take on that burden, I believe."

They stepped onto a rather dark square, which started first on their side of the street, for the opposite side protruded farther. On the side of the square on which they continued to walk, there sat an uninterrupted row of houses, from the edges of which two rows of houses initially far apart extended into the indiscernible distance, where they seemed to join one another. The sidewalk was narrow in front of the mostly small houses, there were no businesses to be seen, no car drove along the street. An iron post adorned with caryatids in grasses and under leaves, near the end of the street from which they came, held a few lamps attached in two rings hanging horizontally above one another. The trapeze-shaped flame burned between joined glass sheets under the tower-like wide cover as if in a small room and left intact the dark, which was only a few steps away.

"But now it's surely too late; you kept it from me, and I'm missing my train. Why?"

[2 pages missing]

"Yes, Pirkershofer at the most, and, well, you know him."

"His name is mentioned in Betty's letters, I think. He's an aspiring railway clerk, isn't he?"

"Yes, an aspiring railway clerk and an unpleasant person. You'll agree with me once you've seen that tiny knobby nose. Let me tell you, walking through those boring fields with *him*. As it happens, he has already been transferred, and so I think and hope that he'll be leaving there next week."

"Wait, you said earlier that you advised me to stay here tonight. I've thought about it; it wouldn't work too well. After all, I wrote that I was coming tonight; they must be expecting me."

"But that's easy – you send a telegram."

"Yes, that would work – but it wouldn't be nice, if I didn't go – also, I'm tired, so I'll be going anyway; if a telegram came, that might just frighten them. –And what's the use, where would we go, really?"

"In that case you'd better go – I was only thinking – Also, I wouldn't be able to go with you today since I'm sleepy, I forgot to tell you that. Let me say goodbye now, then, for I don't want to accompany you through that wet park – I still want to look up the Gillemanns. It's a quarter to six, so one can still pay a visit to good acquaintances. Addio, then, have a safe journey, and say hello for me to all!"

Lement turned to the right and offered his right hand to say goodbye so that, for a moment, he was walking toward his own extended arm.

"Adieu," said Raban.

From a short distance, Lement shouted again: "You, Eduard, do you hear me, close your umbrella now, it stopped raining long ago. I didn't get around to telling you."

Raban did not answer, shut his umbrella, and the pallid, darkened sky closed in above him.

If at least, Raban thought, I got onto the wrong train. Because then I would have the impression that the endeavor had begun, and if I later, having cleared up the mistake, came through this stop upon my return, I would feel so much better. But if it's dull out there, as Lement was saying, that cannot be a disadvantage, not by any means. Rather, one will stay in the rooms and never know for certain where everyone else is, for if there is a ruin in the surroundings, everyone will likely go on a joint stroll to this ruin, just as one had probably agreed to do some time before. In that case, one must look forward to it; one shouldn't miss it. If there is no such landmark, there will be no prior plan, for one expects that everyone will gather easily – if suddenly, against all custom, one fancies going on a larger outing, for one need only send the maid to the other's apartment, where they will sit in front of a letter or books and be bowled over by the news. Well, it isn't hard to protect oneself

18

against such invitations. And yet, I'm not sure if I will be able to, for it isn't as easy as I think, for I'm still alone, and I can still do anything, I can still turn back if I want to. For I won't have anyone to visit there when I want to, and no one to go on more demanding outings with who would show me the way his crop is growing or a quarry he owns out there. For one cannot even be sure of old acquaintances. Hadn't Lement been friendly to me today; he explained a thing or two, and he described everything the way it will present itself to me. He had approached me and then accompanied me, although he didn't want to find out anything in particular from me and had some other business to attend to. And now he left suddenly, and yet I cannot possibly have hurt him with anything I said. I did refuse to spend the evening in the city, but that was only natural; that cannot have hurt him, for he is a reasonable person.

The train station clock rang out the hour; it was a quarter to six. Raban stopped because he felt his heart pounding; then he quickly went along the park pond, came onto a narrow, poorly lit path between large shrubs, tumbled onto a square where many empty benches were leaning against the little trees, then, more slowly, walked to the street through an opening in the fence, crossed the street, leapt through the doors of the train station, found the ticket window after a while and had to tap on the metal latch for a bit. Then the clerk looked out, said it was high time, took the bill, and tossed the requested ticket and change noisily onto the counter. Now Raban was about to quickly count the change because he felt he should have received more in return, but a valet who was walking nearby pushed him through the glass door onto the platform. There Raban looked around, shouting "Thank you, thank you!" to the valet, and since he could not find a conductor, he climbed the closest set of stairs to the car by himself, setting his valise on the next higher step and then following himself, one hand resting on his umbrella, the other on the valise's handle. The railway car he entered was bright from the many lights in the station concourse in which it stood; in front of some of the window panes, all of them completely closed, there hung a hissing arc lamp visible from close up, and the many raindrops on the glass were white; some of them moved frequently. Raban could hear the noise from the platform, even after he had closed the car door and sat down on the last remaining end of a light-brown wooden bench. He saw backs, and backs of heads, and between them the reclining faces on the benches across from him. In some places, smoke spiraled from pipes and cigars and languidly trailed past the face of a girl. The passengers frequently changed seats and discussed those changes, or they moved their bags, which were sitting

19

in the narrow blue netting above a bench. If a cane or the iron-fitted edge of a suitcase protruded, the owner was alerted. He would then go and restore order. Raban, too, reconsidered, and pushed his valise under his seat.

On his left, next to the window, two gentlemen sat across from each other and discussed the prices of merchandise. "They're traveling salesmen," Raban thought, and breathing regularly, he looked at them. The merchant sends them to the country, they follow, they go by train, and they go from store to store in every village. Sometimes they take a car between villages. They can never stop for long, for everything must be done in a hurry, and they must only ever talk about merchandise. What a joy it must be to exert oneself in such a pleasant trade!

The younger one had yanked his notebook from his rear pocket, leafing in it with his index finger quickly wet on his tongue, and then read a page while drawing the back of his fingernail down on it. He gazed at Raban when he looked up and, even now, as he was discussing the prices of yarn, he did not turn his face away from Raban, the way one fixates on something so as not to forget what one meant to say. In so doing, he drew his eyebrows against his eyes. He held the half-closed notebook in his left hand, his thumb on the page he had read so as to easily look it up again if necessary. The notebook trembled, for he was not resting his arm anywhere, and the rolling car struck against the rails like a hammer.

The other traveler was leaning back, listening and nodding his head at irregular intervals. One could see that he by no means agreed with everything and that he would give his opinion later on.

Raban cupped his palms over his knees and, leaning forward, he saw the window between the travelers' heads and, through the window, lights flying past and others flying back into the distance. He did not catch any of the traveler's talk, and he would not catch the other's reply. That would have required a lot of preparation, for those are people who have been dealing with merchandise since they were young. But if one has held a spool of yarn in one's hand and handed it to a customer every so often, one knows the price, and one can talk about it. One can talk about it as villages rush toward and past one, while at the same time turning into the depths of the country, where they must disappear for us. And yet, those villages are inhabited, and there may be travelers in them going from store to store.

In the corner of the car at the other end, a tall man holding playing cards in his hands stood up and shouted: "Hey, Marie, did you pack the zephyr shirts, too?" "Of course, I did," said the woman, who was sitting across from Raban. She had been sleeping a little, and when the question woke her up, she answered softly, as if she were speaking to Raban. "You are going to the market in Jungbunzlau, aren't you?" the animated traveler asked her. "Yes, to Jungbunzlau." "It's a large market this time around, isn't it?" "Yes, a large market." She was sleepy; she propped her left elbow on a blue bundle, and her head rested hard against her hand, pushing through the flesh of her cheek into her cheekbone. "How young she is," said the traveler.

Raban took the change he had received from the cashier out of his vest pocket and counted it again. He held each coin upright between his thumb and index finger for a long time and twisted it back and forth with the tip of his index finger on the inside of his thumb. He gazed at the emperor's image for a long time, then noticed the laurel wreath and the way it was attached at the back of his head with knots and bows of ribbons. Finally, he decided that it was the right amount and placed it in a large black wallet. But as he was about to say to the traveler: "They are a married couple, don't you think?" the train stopped, the travel noise abated, conductors called out the name of the place, and Raban said nothing.

The train started moving so slowly that one could picture the wheels revolving, but soon it chased down a depression and, without warning, the long railings of a bridge were being torn apart and pressed together in front of the window, or so it seemed.

Raban enjoyed the fact that the train was speeding now, for he wouldn't have wanted to stay at the last place. When it is so dark there, when one doesn't know anyone, when it's so far from home. It must be terrible there during the daytime, then, as well. And will it be different at the next stop, or at the previous or the later ones, or in the village I'm going to?

The traveler suddenly spoke more loudly. It's still far, Raban thought. "Sir, you know as well as I do that the factory owners send their people to the smallest hamlets, they creep to the filthiest grocer's store, and do you think they give them different prices than us merchants? Let me tell you, sir, exactly the same prices. I saw it in black and white just yesterday. That is what I call drudgery. They're crushing us; it is simply impossible for us to do business in today's conditions; they're crushing us." He looked at Raban again; he was not ashamed of the tears in his eyes; he pressed the knuckles of his left hand to his mouth because his lips were quivering. Raban leaned back and weakly pulled at his mustache with his left hand.

The grocer woman opposite him awoke and smilingly brushed her forehead with her hands. The traveler spoke more softly. The woman straightened herself once more as if for sleeping, leaned half-prone across her bundle and sighed. Her skirt stretched taut over her right hip.

Behind her sat a gentleman with a traveler's cap on his head, reading a large newspaper. The girl opposite him, who was likely a relative of his, asked him – tilting her head against her right shoulder – to open the window, for it was very hot. Without looking up he said he would do so in a moment; he only needed to finish reading a section in his newspaper, and he showed her which section it was.

The grocer woman was unable to go back to sleep; she sat up straight and gazed out the window; then she gazed for a long time at the kerosene flame, burning yellow at the ceiling of the car. Raban closed his eyes for a little while.

When he looked up, the grocer woman was biting into a slice of cake covered with brown jam. The bundle next to her was open. The traveler was silently smoking his cigar, and continually pretended to tap the ash off its end. The other was moving the point of a knife back and forth inside the works of his pocket watch, in such a way that it was audible.

His eyes almost closed, Raban vaguely saw the man with the traveler's cap pulling at the window belt. Cool air burst in, a straw hat fell off a hook. Raban thought he was waking up and that was why his cheeks were so refreshed, or that someone was opening the door and pulling him into the room, or that he was somehow mistaken, and he swiftly fell asleep.

The steps of the car still trembled somewhat as Raban descended. His face, emerging from the air inside the car, was struck by the rain, and he closed his eyes. –Rain thundered on the tin roof in front of the train station, but in the vast countryside it rained just in such a way that one thought one was hearing a steady blowing wind. A barefoot boy came running – Raban had not noticed whence he had come – and asked Raban, breathlessly, to let him carry his valise for it was raining, but Raban said: Yes, it's raining, that is why he was going to take the omnibus; he had no need for him. At that, the boy grimaced as though he thought it more elegant to walk in the rain and have someone carry one's valise rather than taking the bus, turned around, and ran off. So when Raban went to call after him, it was too late.

One saw two streetlights shining, and a station clerk came out of a door.

Without hesitation he walked to the engine through the rain, stood quietly with his arms folded, waiting for the engineer to bend over the railing to speak with him. A valet was called, came, and was sent back. There were passengers standing at some of the train windows, and since all they had to look at was a mundane station building, their gazes must have been dulled, their eyelids narrowed, just as during the trip. A girl, rushing from the country road onto the platform underneath a flowered parasol, stood the open parasol on the ground, sat down, and pushed her legs apart, so that her skirt could dry faster, and ran her fingertips over her stretched skirt. There were only two streetlights; her face was blurred. The valet, passing by once, complained about the puddles forming under the parasol, rounded his arms in front of him so as to demonstrate the size of those puddles, and then moved his hands one after the other through the air like fish sinking into deeper waters to indicate that traffic was also being obstructed by this parasol.

The train started, disappeared like a long sliding door, and behind the poplar trees beyond the tracks there was the bulk of the landscape, in such a way that it interfered with one's breath. Was it a dark vista through the trees, or was it a forest, was it a pond, or a house where people were already asleep, was it a church steeple or a ravine between the hills; no one must venture there, but then who could resist?

And when Raban saw the clerk once again – he was already in front of the step to his office – he walked right in front of him and held him back: "I beg your pardon, is it far to the village, because that's where I'm going."

"No, just a quarter of an hour, but by bus – it's raining, you know – you'll get there in five minutes. You're welcome."

"It's raining. It hasn't been a nice spring," Raban replied.

The station clerk had placed his right hand on his hip, and through the triangle formed by his arm and body, Raban saw the girl who had already closed her parasol, on her bench.

"Anyone who's going on a summer getaway now and has to stay there is to be pitied. I actually thought that someone was expecting me." He looked around so as to appear credible.

"You're going to miss your bus, I'm afraid. It doesn't wait very long. Don't thank me. The path is over there between the hedges."

The road in front of the train station was not illuminated, only three ground-level windows of the building exuded a misty glow – but it did not reach far. Raban tiptoed through the dirt and called out: "Driver!" and

"Hello!" and "Omnibus!" and "I'm here" many times. But when he came to scarcely interrupted puddles on the dark side of the road he had to stomp on his soles until he felt a horse muzzle [refreshingly] touch his forehead. There was the omnibus; he swiftly stepped into the empty interior, sat down by the glass behind the driver's box and bent his back into the corner, for he had done everything necessary. For if the driver was sleeping, he would wake up in the morning, if he was dead, a new driver would be coming, or the innkeeper, and if even that were not to happen, passengers would be coming on the early train, people in a hurry, making noise. At any rate, one could be quiet, could even draw the curtains in front of the windows and wait for the jolt with which the omnibus was bound to start up.

Well, after everything I've done it is certain that I'm going to get to Betty and Mama tomorrow, no one will be able to prevent that from happening. But it's true and it was foreseeable, too, that my letter wasn't going to get there until tomorrow; I might as well have stayed in the city and spent a pleasant night at Elvy's without having to be afraid of the next day's work, which usually spoils any enjoyment for me. But look, my feet are wet.

He lit the stump of a candle that he had taken from his vest pocket and put it on the bench opposite him. It was bright enough; due to the darkness outside one saw black washed bus walls missing windowpanes. One didn't have to think right away of the fact that there were wheels underneath the floor and the harnessed horse in front.

Raban rubbed his feet thoroughly on the bench, put on fresh socks, and sat upright. Then he heard someone calling from the train station: "Hey!" if there were a passenger on the bus, he could let him know.

"Yes, yes, and he would really like to go," Raban replied, leaning out the opened door, holding onto the post with his right hand, the left one close to his mouth, open. Rainwater gushed between his collar and his neck.

Wrapped in the canvas of two cut-up sacks, the driver walked over; the reflection of his stable lantern bounced through the puddles underneath him. Morosely, he set out to explain. Listen, he'd been playing cards with Lebeda, and they'd just gotten going when the train arrived. So it had actually been impossible for him to see if anyone was there, but then he wouldn't mean to insult anyone who didn't understand that. Incidentally, this place here was a rotten hole all around, and he couldn't see how a gentleman such as himself might have any business here, and he'd get there soon enough so that he wouldn't have to make any complaints. Just now Mr. Pirkershofer – I beg your pardon, that's Mr. Adjunct – had come in and said he believed a short blond man had wanted to take the omnibus. Well, and so he'd come to inquire right away, or had he not come to inquire right away.

The lantern was affixed to the tip of the shaft, the horse, commanded in a muffled voice, started moving, and the now agitated water atop the omnibus dripped slowly into the coach through a crack.

The path might have been mountainous; certainly dirt squirted into the spokes, pockets of water from the puddles formed, splashing backward at the turning wheels, the driver held the soaking wet horse with mostly loosened reins. Couldn't one use all this to reproach Raban? Many puddles were lighted unexpectedly by the lantern trembling at the shaft and were dividing under the wheel, making waves. This only happened because Raban was going to his bride, to Betty, an elderly pretty girl. And who would, come to think of it, appreciate the merits Raban had here – be it only the fact that he endured those reproaches that, to be sure, no one could make openly. Of course, he was happy to do it: Betty was his bride, he was fond of her; it would be disgusting if she thanked him for it, but anyway. Involuntarily, his head kept hitting the wall upon which he was leaning; then he looked up at the ceiling for a while. At some point, his right hand slid from his thigh, on which it had been resting. But his elbow remained at the angle between his stomach and his leg.

The bus was now passing between houses; here and there the inside of the coach partook in the light of a room, a staircase – Raban would have had to stand up to see the first few steps – led up to a church; a lantern with a great flame was shining in front of a park gate, but the statue of a saint was highlighted in black only by the light of a grocery store; now Raban noticed his burned-down candle, its molten wax hanging, immovable, from the bench.

When the coach came to a stop in front of the inn, the rain could be heard loudly as could – a window was probably open – the voices of the guests. Raban wondered whether it was better to get off immediately or to wait for the innkeeper to come to the coach. He was unaware of the custom in this town, but surely Betty had spoken of her fiancé, and according to his magnificent or unimpressive appearance, her prestige here would become greater or smaller, and hence his own, too. Now, he neither knew what her standing was at this point nor what she had said about him; all the more unpleasant and difficult. What a nice place, and what a nice way home! If it rains there, one takes the electric trolley home across wet bricks; here, the cart through the morass to an inn. –The city is far from here, and even if I were on the verge of dying from homesickness, no one could take me there today anymore. –Now, I wouldn't die either – but there the dish I expected for tonight would be placed on the table in front of me, on the right behind the plate the newspaper, to the left the lamp, here I will be served an extremely heavy meal – they don't know that I have a weak stomach, and even if they did – a different newspaper, lots of people I can already hear will be present, and a lamp will be shining for everyone. What kind of light might it give, enough for playing cards, but for reading the paper?

The innkeeper doesn't show up, he doesn't care about his guests; he's probably a rude man. Or does he know that I'm Betty's fiancé and that is a reason for him to not come for me? This goes with the fact that the driver made me wait for such a long time at the train station. Betty had sometimes talked about how much she was harassed by lecherous men and how she had to reject their advances, perhaps here, too–

As Eduard Raban came through the hallway and stepped into the open doorway, he could see that it was raining. It was not raining much.

On the sidewalk right in front of him, not higher up, not lower down, there were lots of people walking in spite of the rain. Every now and then, one of them would step forward and cross the road.

A little girl was carrying a gray dog in her outstretched arms. Two gentlemen were making announcements to each other on some matter; occasionally they would turn fully toward each other only to slowly turn away again; it was reminiscent of doors opened in the wind. The one was holding his hands out with their insides up and moving them steadily up and down as if he were balancing a load, testing its weight. Then a slim lady came into view whose face was twitching slightly just like the lights of the stars and whose flat hat was brimming with unknown items and towering; unintentionally she seemed a stranger to everyone passing by, as if by law. And a young person rushed past with a thin cane, his left hand – as though it were paralyzed – laid flat on his chest. Many passers-by had errands to run; although they were moving rapidly, one would see them longer than others; first on the sidewalk, then lower down; their coats were ill-fitting, and they did not care about their posture, they let people shove them and shoved others in turn. Three gentlemen – two holding light overcoats in the crook of their forearms – walked at regular intervals from the building to the curb, to see what was going on in the road and on the sidewalk opposite.

Through the gaps between the passers-by, one glimpsed, first fleetingly, then comfortably, the neatly joined cobbles of the road, where carriages shaking on their wheels were swiftly pulled by horses with outstretched necks. The people reclining on their padded seats silently took in the pedestrians, the shops, the balconies, and the sky. Should one carriage pass another, the horses would press against each other, their bridles dangling. The animals would pull on the shaft; the carriage would roll, swaying in haste, until the arc around the preceding carriage was completed and the horses would spread apart again, their narrow heads still tilted toward one another.

An elderly gentleman quickly approached the front door, stopped on the dry mosaic tiles, turning around slowly. And then gazed into the rain that fell in confusion, trapped into this narrow street.

He set down his valise sewn with black cloth and bent his right knee a little in doing so. At the edge of the road, the rainwater was already running in streaks that extended almost to the low-lying canals.

The elderly gentleman stood freely near Raban, who was leaning somewhat on the wooden door leaf, and looked toward Raban now and then, even though this obliged him to twist his neck. But unoccupied as he was, he did this only out of the natural desire to observe everything in his surroundings exactly. As a consequence of this purposeless looking to and fro, there were many things he did not notice. Hence, it slipped his attention that Raban's lips were very pale and were not very far behind the entirely faded red of his fat tie, which displayed a striking Moorish design. If he had noticed it, he would have started a true ruckus about this on the inside, which would not have been the right thing to do either, for Raban was always pale, even though a few things in particular might have tired him out lately.

"Now look at this weather," said the gentleman softly and shook his head consciously and yet somewhat like a very old man.

"Indeed, indeed, and if one is supposed to go on a journey," said Raban and quickly straightened up.

"And it isn't the kind of weather that'll get better," the gentleman said and, to verify everything at the last moment, leaned forward and gazed down the street, then up, then toward the sky: "This may take days, this may take weeks. As far as I remember, the forecast isn't any better for June and early July. Well, that's nothing to be pleased about. As for me, for example, I'll have to do without my walks, which are of utmost importance for my health."

Then he yawned and seemed weary, since he had now heard Raban's voice, and, engaged in the conversation, had no more interest in anything, not even in the conversation.

This made quite an impression on Raban, since, after all, the gentleman had approached him, and so he tried to boast a little bit, even though it might go unnoticed. "That's right," he said, "in the city, one can very well do without the things that aren't beneficial to one. If one doesn't renounce them, then one can only blame oneself for the consequences. One will be sorry and thereby see clearly how to behave next time. And if already in the detail..."

[1 page missing]

"I don't mean anything by it. I don't mean anything at all," Raban hastened to confirm, as ready as ever to excuse the gentleman's absentmindedness, since he intended to boast some more. "Everything is from the aforementioned book, which I've been reading, among others, in the evenings lately. I've mostly been by myself. There were some family relations. But apart from everything else, what I like most is a good book after dinner. For as long as I can remember. I read a brochure recently with a quotation from some writer: 'A good book is a man's best friend,' and that is certainly true, that's exactly it, a good book is a man's best friend."

"Sure, when one is young–" the gentleman said, not meaning anything in particular by it, but just trying to convey how it was raining, how the rain had become heavier again, and that it wasn't stopping at all now, but to Raban it sounded as if, even at sixty years old, the gentleman thought of himself as young and youthful and in turn considered Raban's thirty years as nothing, and, apart from that, intended to say, as far as permissible, that he himself at thirty had certainly been more reasonable than Raban. And he thought that even if one had nothing else to do, just like himself, an old man, for example, it would be wasting one's time to stand here in the hallway in front of the rain like that; but if one were to pass the time with chatter, it was doubly wasted.

Now Raban believed that nothing other people said about his skills or opinions had been able to touch him for some time; rather, he had virtually left the place where he had raptly listened to everything, so that now people were talking into the void whether they were against or in favor of him. Thus, he said: "We're speaking of different things, since you didn't bother to wait for what I meant to say."

"Go ahead, go ahead," the gentleman said.

"Well, it isn't that important," said Raban, "I was just saying that books are useful in every sense, and particularly where one wouldn't expect it. For if one plans to undertake an endeavor, it's precisely the books whose content has nothing at all in common with that endeavor that are the most useful. Yes, the most useful. For the reader, who in fact intends to undertake the endeavor and who is therefore somehow energized (and even if only the effect of the book can connect to that energy), the book will spark all sorts of ideas concerning his endeavor. And yet since the content of the book is of no import at all, the reader won't be hampered in those thoughts, and he goes right through the book with them, just as the Jews once went through the Red Sea, I might say."

The entire person of the elderly gentleman was taking on an unpleasant expression for Raban now. It seemed to him as if he had moved considerably closer – but that was insignificant

[1 page missing]

The newspaper as well. –But another thing I meant to say: I'm just going to the countryside, just for two weeks; I'm taking a vacation, for the first time in a long while, it's necessary for a number of reasons, and yet, for example, a book I read recently as I mentioned, has taught me more about my little journey than you could imagine."

"I'm listening," the gentleman said. Raban remained silent and, standing there so upright, pushed his hands into the pockets of his overcoat, which were somewhat too high.

Only after a while, the old gentleman said: "This journey seems to be of particular importance to you."

"Well, you see, you see," said Raban, leaning against the door once more. Only now did he notice that the hallway had filled up with people. They were even standing in front of the stairs to the building, and a civil servant who rented a room from the same woman as Raban had to ask people to make room for him as he came down the stairs. To Raban, who only pointed at the rain, he called out, "Have a good journey," over several heads that were now all turning to Raban, and renewed a promise he had apparently given earlier to absolutely come and visit Raban the following Sunday.

[1 page is missing]

has a pleasant post that he's satisfied with and that had always been waiting for him. He's so persevering and inwardly jovial that he doesn't need anyone for his entertainment, but everyone needs him. He's always been healthy. Ah, don't say that."

"I won't argue," the gentleman said.

"You won't argue but you also won't admit your error, why are you insisting like that! And however distinctly you may remember now, I bet you would forget everything if you were to talk with him. You would reproach me for not having disproven you better now. Just when he talks about a book. He gets instantly fired up about everything beautiful."

When Eduard Raban, in a bluish gray overcoat, came through the hallway and stepped into the open doorway, he saw that it was raining. It was not raining much.

Raban gazed at the clock of a rather high tower standing apparently nearby in a lower-lying street. For just a moment, a small flag attached at the top was blown in front of the clock face. A throng of small birds flew down, firmly joined together, and then spread apart. It was just past five o'clock.

Raban set down his valise, which was sewn with black cloth, propped his umbrella against a stone doorstep and set his pocket watch, a women's watch attached to a narrow black ribbon around his neck, according to the tower clock, gazing back and forth between them several times. For a while, he was completely engrossed in doing this, and his face, now bent down, now lifted, he was not thinking of anything else in the world.

Eventually, he put his watch back and licked his lips out of joy that he had enough time, and so didn't have to go back out into the rain.

On the sidewalk right in front of him, not higher up, not lower down, there were many people walking, close together along the walls of the buildings or under umbrellas at some distance. A little girl was carrying in her outstretched arms a gray dog that was gazing into the girl's face.

Two gentlemen were making announcements to each other; in their flapping overcoats they occasionally turned fully toward each other; the one was holding his hands out with insides up and moving them steadily up and down – his fingers immobile – as if he were balancing a load, to test its weight.

Then a lady came into view whose face was twitching just like the lights of the stars and whose flat hat was laden to the brim with a tower of unknown items; unintentionally she seemed a stranger to everyone passing by, as if by law.

And a young person rushed past with a thin cane, his left hand, as though paralyzed, laid flat on his chest.

Many passers-by had errands to run; although they were walking rapidly, with their backs straightened, one would see them longer than others, for one moment they were walking on the sidewalk, the next they were continuing to walk on the road as if jumping off a coach's running board; since they were pushing everywhere and not giving way to anyone, they were shoving and being shoved themselves a great deal.

Raban saw a few acquaintances and said hello a few times; at one point, he was about to talk to someone, but he did not take notice and passed him in his haste without slowing.

Three gentlemen – two holding light overcoats in the crook of their forearms, on both sides of a tall white-bearded gentleman – walked from the building to the curb to see what was going on in the road and on the sidewalk opposite.

A small child, dragged by her governess, was running with short steps, her free arm stretched out; her hat, as everyone could see, was woven from red straw and had a green wreathlet on its undulating brim.

With both hands, Raban pointed this out to an old gentleman who was standing next to him in the hallway to protect himself from the rain, which – driven by an unsteady wind – thundered down all at once, but then again hovered in desolation, falling uncertainly.

Raban laughed. Everything was fine for children, he said, he liked children a lot. Now that was no wonder, if one rarely had contact with them. He rarely had contact with children.

The elderly gentleman laughed as well. The governess had not had much pleasure. Once one was older, one did not easily feel enthusiastic either. When one was young, one was enthusiastic, and as one could see in old age, it had yielded little, that was why one is even

[5]

ACCOUNT OF A STRUGGLE

And dressed up for a stroll
folks sway on the gravel
under the great heavens
stretching from hills afar
to the faraway hills.

I

Toward midnight a few people stood up, took their bows, shook hands, said they had enjoyed themselves very much and then walked through the large doorframe into the hall to put on their coats. The lady of the house stood in the middle of the room and made supple bows as her dress fell in dainty folds.

I sat at a small table – it had three taut thin legs – sipping my third glass of Benedictine and while drinking looked over my little stock of pastries, which I had picked out and piled up myself, for they had a fine flavor.

Then my new acquaintance came up to me, and smiling somewhat distractedly at my occupation, said with a trembling voice: "Excuse me for troubling you. But up to this moment I was sitting with my girl alone in an adjoining room. Since ten-thirty: that's not long ago at all. Excuse me for telling you this. After all, we don't know each other. You know, we just met on the stairs and exchanged a few polite words, and now I'm already telling you about my girl, but you must – please – forgive me, my happiness can't be contained, I couldn't help it. And since I have no other acquaintances here I can trust–"

This is what he said. But I looked at him sadly, – for the piece of fruit cake in my mouth didn't taste very good – and said into his pleasantly reddened face: "I'm glad that I seem trustworthy to you, but I'm sad that you told me about it. And you yourself – if you weren't so confused – would feel how inappropriate it is to tell someone sitting by himself drinking liquor about a loving girl."

Once I had said that, he sat down abruptly, leaned back, and let his arms hang loose. Then he pushed them back with pointed elbows and started to talk to himself in a fairly loud voice: "We sat there all alone – in the room –

33

with Annie, and I kissed her – kissed – her – on – her mouth, her ear, her shoulders–"

Several gentlemen standing close by suspected a lively conversation and came to join us, yawning. Thus, I stood up and said loudly: "Sure, if you want, I'll go, but it is foolish to go up to Petrin Hill now; the weather is still cool, and since it has snowed a little, the paths are like skating rinks. But if you want to, I'll go."

At first, he gazed at me in astonishment and opened his mouth with wide and red wet lips. But then, noticing the gentlemen who were already quite close, he laughed, stood up, and said: "Oh yes, the cool air will do us good, our clothes are full of heat and smoke, I may even be slightly inebriated without having drunk much, yes, let us say goodbye, and then we'll go."

So we went to the lady of the house, and as he kissed her hand, she said: "Really, I'm glad to see your face so happy today, it's usually so earnest and bored." The kindness of her words touched him, and he kissed her hand again, and she smiled.

There was a housemaid in the hall; we saw her for the first time now. She helped us into our overcoats and took a small hand lamp to light us down the stairs. Oh, the girl was beautiful. Her neck was bare, bound merely by a black velvet ribbon under the chin, and her loosely clad body was nicely bent as she went down the stairs in front of us, holding the lamp low. Her cheeks were rosy for she had drunk wine, and her lips were half-open.

Down at the foot of the stairs, she stood the lamp on a step, and, lurching somewhat, walked up to my acquaintance and hugged him and kissed him, remaining in the embrace. Only when I placed a coin in her hand did she languidly loosen her arms, slowly open the small door and let us out into the night.

Above the empty, evenly lit street, there stood a large moon in a slightly cloudy and thus more spread-out sky. Delicate snow lay on the ground. Our feet slipped when walking, so we could only take small steps.

We had barely stepped outside when I apparently got into high spirits. I boisterously raised my legs and joyously cracked my joints, I called out a name across the street as if a friend had fled around the corner; I jumped and threw my hat up, and then caught it ostentatiously.

But my acquaintance kept walking next to me without a worry. He held his head tilted. He didn't talk, either.

This surprised me because I had expected him to go wild with joy, what with the party no longer around him; I became quieter. No sooner had I given him an encouraging slap on the back than I was stricken with shame so that I awkwardly withdrew my hand. Since I had no use for it anymore, I pushed it into my coat pocket.

So we walked in silence. I listened to the sound of our steps and couldn't understand why I was unable to walk in step with my acquaintance. It upset me somewhat. The moon was clear; one could see plainly. Every now and then someone leaned out the window and watched us.

When we came to Ferdinand Street I noticed that my acquaintance had started to hum a tune; it was very soft, but I could hear it. I felt insulted. Why wasn't he speaking to me? If he didn't need me, why hadn't he left me in peace? I thought of all the sweet goodies I had left on my little table because of him. I also thought of the Benedictine and became a little more cheerful, almost haughty, one might say. I put my hands on my hips and imagined I was walking by myself. I had been at an evening party, had saved an ungrateful young man from embarrassment, and was now going for a walk in the moonlight. A boundlessly natural way of life. At the office by day, at a party in the evening, in the streets at night, and nothing in excess.

But my acquaintance was still walking behind me; he even hastened his step when he realized that he had fallen behind and acted as if this were natural. But I wondered whether it might not be convenient to turn into a side street, since I wasn't obligated to go on a walk with him. I could return home alone, and no one could stop me. In my room I would light the lamp, which is in the iron crate on the table, I would sit in my easy chair on the tattered oriental carpet. –When I was ready to go, I was overcome by a weakness that always seizes me whenever I have to think of returning to my apartment and of spending hours by myself between the painted walls and on the floor, which, in the gold-rimmed mirror on the back wall, seems to be slanting down. My legs became tired, and I had already decided to return home and lie down on my bed no matter what, when I began to wonder whether I should say goodbye to my acquaintance upon leaving or not. But I was too fearful to leave without saying goodbye and too weak to call out loudly, so I stopped again, held onto the moonlit wall of a house, and waited.

My acquaintance came walking up with a merry gait and surely a trifle worried, too. He made a great fuss, winking his eyelids, stretching out his arms in the air, vigorously craning his head, with a hard black hat on it, toward me, and all this seemed to be supposed to demonstrate that he knew very well to appreciate the joke I was performing for his amusement here.

I felt helpless and softly said: "It's been a jolly evening tonight." With this, I let out an uneasy laugh. He replied: "Indeed, and did you see how the housemaid kissed me, too." I was unable to talk, for my throat was full of tears; I tried to blow like a post horn so as not to stay silent. At first he covered his ears, and then shook my hand warmly and gratefully. It must have been cold, for he let go of it at once and said: "Your hand is very cold; the housemaid's lips were warmer, oh yes." I nodded understandingly. Begging the good lord to grant me steadfastness, I said: "Yes, you're right, let's return home; it's late, and I have to be at the office tomorrow morning; mind you, one can well sleep there, but it's not good. You're right, let's go home." I shook his hand as if the matter were settled once and for all. But, with a smile, he took up my manner of speaking: "Indeed, you're right; a night like this shouldn't be slept away in bed. Just think how many happy thoughts will be smothered by the bedcovers when you sleep in your bed alone, and how many unhappy dreams are warmed by them." And out of joy over this idea, he grabbed my coat firmly above my chest – he couldn't reach any higher – and shook me cheerfully; then he screwed up his eyes and said in a confidential manner: "You know what you are, you're strange." He continued walking, and I followed him without noticing, for I was pondering his remark.

Initially I was glad about the remark, for it seemed to show that he saw something in me – which really wasn't in me, but his assumption raised his respect for me. Such rapport makes me happy. I was pleased I hadn't gone home, and my acquaintance became very precious to me as someone who appreciates me in front of people without me having to do anything to earn it! I looked at my acquaintance with loving eyes. In my mind I protected him from dangers, especially from rivals and jealous men. His life became dearer to me than my own. I found his face beautiful; I was proud of his luck with the ladies, and I shared in the kisses he had received from two girls that night. Oh, what an amusing evening this was! Tomorrow my acquaintance would talk to Miss Anna, about ordinary things at first, as is natural, but then suddenly he would say: "Last night I was with a person like you my dear Annie have certainly never met one. He looks – how to describe him – like a dangling pole upon which a yellow-skinned, black-haired skull is perched somewhat ineptly. His body is draped with lots of fairly small, garish, yellowish pieces of cloth that covered him completely, for in the calm of last night they lay flat. He was timidly walking next to me. You my dear Annie, who are such a good kisser, I know you would have laughed a little and would have been a little scared, but me whose soul is all aflutter with love for you, I enjoyed his presence. He may be unhappy and that's why he is so silent, but next to him one is in a state of happy restlessness that doesn't end. Yesterday I was stooped by my own happiness, and I all but forgot about you. I felt as if the hard dome of the starry sky were rising with the breaths from his flat chest. The horizon broke apart, and beneath ignited clouds, the landscapes became visibly endless, just the way they do when they make us happy. –Good heavens, how I love you, Annie, and I prefer your kisses to any landscape. Let's not talk about him anymore and let's love each other."

As we walked onto the quay with slow steps, I envied my acquaintance his kisses, but with joy I also sensed the embarrassment he had to be feeling inside toward me, they way I appeared to him.

That's what I thought. But then my thoughts got confused, for the Vltava and the neighborhoods on the far bank lay in the dark. There were only a few lights shining and toying with eyes gazing.

We stood by the railing. I put on my gloves for a cold breeze was blowing from the water; then I sighed for no reason, just as one might by a river at night, and was about to go on. But my acquaintance was staring into the water and didn't budge. Then he stepped even closer to the railing, propped his elbows on the iron, and placed his forehead into his hands. That seemed silly to me. I was cold and turned up the collar of my coat. My acquaintance stretched and laid his upper body, now resting on his taut arms, across the railing. Ashamed, I quickly started talking, so as to suppress a yawn: "It's peculiar, isn't it, that it's precisely the night that manages to steep us in memories. Right now I remember this, for example: One night I was sitting in a contorted position on a bench by the river. My head lying on my arm, which rested on the wooden backrest of the bench, I saw the cloudlike mountains on the other bank and heard a tender violin playing at the riverside hotel. Now and then, there were trains with gleaming smoke moving on both banks." –That's how I was talking, and behind my words I was frantically trying to make up romances with odd twists; even some crudeness and aggravated rape might work nicely.

But no sooner did I utter the first few words than my acquaintance, indifferent and merely surprised to still see me there – or so it seemed to me – turned to me and said: "You see, it always turns out that way. As I was descending the stairs today to take an evening stroll before going to the party,

I was wondering about my reddish hands swinging back and forth in their white cuffs and how they did so with rare cheerfulness. That is when I expected an adventure. It's always like that." This he said upon leaving, in passing, as a small reflection.

I, however, was very touched by this, and it started to trouble me that my tall form might bother him, next to which he may have appeared short. And although it was nighttime and we encountered almost no one, this circumstance distressed me so much that I hunched my back enough for my hands to touch my knees when walking. So my acquaintance wouldn't notice my intention, I took great caution to change my posture very gradually, and tried to divert his attention from me by making remarks about the trees on Archer Island and about the reflection of the bridge lights in the river. But with a brisk movement he turned his face to me and said patiently: "Now why are you walking like that? You are all hunched now and almost as short as me."

Since he had spoken kindly, I replied: "This may be true. But for me, this posture is comfortable. I'm quite weakly, you know, and it's too hard for me to hold my body upright. This is no small matter; I'm very tall–."

He said, somewhat suspiciously: "This is just a whim, isn't it. You were walking quite upright earlier, I believe, and even at the party you carried yourself fairly well. You even danced, or didn't you? You didn't? But you were walking upright, and so you should be able to do so now."

With a dismissive wave of my hand, I replied adamantly: "Indeed, indeed, I was walking upright. But you underestimate me. I know what good manners are, and that's why I'm walking hunched over."

But that didn't seem simple to him, rather dazed with happiness he didn't comprehend the context of my words and only said: "Sure, just as you like," and looked up at the clock of the Mill Tower, which showed almost one o'clock.

But I said to myself: "What a heartless person he is! How telling and how plain is his indifference to my humble words! Well, he's happy, and it's the way of the happy to find everything happening around them to be a matter of course. Their happiness makes for splendid coherence. And if I had jumped into the water or if seizures had started tearing me apart on the ground in front of him right here under this arch, I would still fit into his happiness. Well, if he did get in the mood – a happy person is so dangerous, there's no doubt about it – he would even kill me like a street murderer. That's for sure, and since I'm a coward, I would be too terrified to scream. –For heaven's sake!" – I looked around me in fear. In front of a distant coffeehouse with black rectangular windowpanes, a policeman was skidding over the cobbles. His saber was somewhat in his way; he took it in his hand, and now it worked much more beautifully. And when, even at this moderate distance, I heard him shriek faintly with delight, I was convinced that he wouldn't save me if my acquaintance were to murder me.

But now I knew what to do, since, especially when faced with terrible events, I'm overcome with great resolve. I had to run away. It was as simple as that. Upon turning left to the Charles Bridge, I could slip into Charles Street to the right. It was an angled street, with dark entranceways and taverns that were still open; there was no need to despair.

As we emerged from under the arch at the end of the quay, I ran into the street with raised arms; but just as I got to the small door of a church I fell, for there was a step I hadn't noticed. There was a crash. The next streetlight was far away; I lay there in the dark. A fat woman with a smoky lamp came out of a tavern opposite to see what had happened in the street. The piano stopped playing, and a man opened the half-open door completely. He spat grandly onto a step and, tickling the woman between her breasts, said that what had happened, at any rate, was of no importance. They turned back, and the door closed again.

When I tried to get up, I fell again. "It's black ice," I said, and felt a pain in my knee. And yet, I was glad that the people from the tavern couldn't see me, and so I felt that the most convenient thing to do was to remain lying there until dawn.

My acquaintance must have gone to the bridge alone, unaware of my departure, for he joined me only after some time. I didn't see him look surprised when he bent down to me and compassionately stroked me with his soft hand. He went up and down my cheekbones, and then placed two thick fingers on my low forehead: "You've hurt yourself, haven't you? It is black ice, and one has to be careful – your head is hurting? It isn't? The knee, oh well." He spoke in a singsong, as if he were telling a story and a very pleasant story at that, of some very distant pain in some knee. He moved his arms, too, but it didn't occur to him to lift me up. I supported my head with my right hand – my elbow was on a cobblestone – and said rapidly so that I wouldn't forget: "I don't really know why I went to the right. But under the arcades of this church – I don't know the name, oh please, forgive me – I saw a cat running. A small cat, and it had light fur. That's why I noticed it. –Oh no, that wasn't it, I'm sorry, but it takes enough effort to control oneself during the day. So one sleeps to strengthen oneself for such efforts, but if one doesn't sleep, then it's not uncommon that pointless things happen to us; but it would be impolite of those accompanying us to wonder out loud about it."

My acquaintance had his hands in his pockets and gazed across the empty bridge, then to the Church of the Knights of the Cross, and then up to the sky, which was clear. Since he hadn't listened to me, he said anxiously: "Now why aren't you saying anything, my dear friend; are you sick – actually, why aren't you getting up – it's cold here after all, you'll get cold, and, besides, we were headed for Petrin Hill."

"Of course," I said. "Excuse me," and I stood up by myself, but in a lot of pain. I wobbled and had to fix my eyes on the statue of Charles IV to be sure of my stance. But the moonlight was unfavorable and set Charles IV in motion as well. I was astonished about that, and my feet became much stronger out of fear that Charles IV might topple over if I didn't stay calm. Later on, my effort seemed futile to me, for Charles IV toppled nonetheless, just when I remembered that I was loved by a girl in a beautiful white dress.

I do useless things, and I miss out on a lot. What an auspicious thought that was, about the girl! –And how sweet of the moon to shine on me, too, and out of modesty I was about to go stand under the arch of the bridge tower when I realized that it was only natural for the moon to shine on everything. So I spread my arms with joy so as to fully enjoy the moon. –Which was when I remembered this verse:

> *I bounded through the streets*
> *like a drunken runner*
> *stomping through air*

and it felt easy to me when, making casual swimming strokes with my arms, I advanced without effort and pain. My head floated well in the cool air, and the love of the white-clad girl sent me into gloomy raptures, for it felt like I was swimming away from the loving girl and from the cloudy mountains of her region, too. –And I remembered that I had hated a happy acquaintance once who was perhaps still walking next to me, and I was glad that my memory was good enough to even recall such immaterial details. For the memory has a lot to bear. Thus I suddenly knew all the many stars by name, even though I had never learned them. Oh, they were odd names, hard to remember, but I knew

40

them all and very precisely. I raised my index finger and said each of their names aloud. –But I didn't get very far in naming the stars for I had to resume swimming if I didn't want to sink too much. And just so that no one could say later on that anyone could swim above the ground and it wasn't worth mentioning, I raised myself above the railing by speeding up and swam circles around each statue of a saint I encountered. –At the fifth, as I was moving above the sidewalk with masterful strokes, my acquaintance took my hand. So I stood on the sidewalk again and felt a pain in my knee. I had forgotten the names of the stars, and the only thing I remembered about the sweet girl was that she had been wearing a white dress, but I couldn't remember at all what made me believe in the girl's love. Inside me there grew a great and well-founded rage against my memory, and a fear of losing the girl. And thus I kept repeating, forcefully and incessantly: "white dress, white dress" to at least retain that one sign of her. But to no avail. My acquaintance pushed ever closer to me, talking, and the moment I began to understand his words, a white gleam delicately skipped along the bridge railing, swept through the bridge tower and leapt into the dark street.

"I've always loved," said my acquaintance, pointing toward the statue of St. Ludmila, "the hands of this angel here to the left. There are no bounds to their delicacy and their spreading fingers tremble. But as of tonight I can say that I'm indifferent to those hands, for I have kissed hands–." At that he embraced me, kissed my clothes, and butted his head against my body.

I said: "Yes, yes. I believe you. I have no doubt," and with my fingers pinched his calves, as far as they were exposed. But he didn't feel it. So I said to myself: "Why are you walking with this person? You don't love him and you don't hate him either, for his happiness is in a girl, and it isn't even sure that she's wearing a white dress. So you're indifferent to this person – repeat it – indifferent. He isn't dangerous either, as it turns out. So go up to Petrin Hill with him just as well, for you're already on your way and it's a beautiful night, but let him talk and enjoy yourself in your own fashion, this is also – say it softly – your best protection."

II
AMUSEMENTS OR
PROOF THAT IT IS IMPOSSIBLE TO LIVE

1
Ride

Then, with unusual nimbleness, I leapt onto my acquaintance's shoulders, and, by pumping my fists into his back, brought him to a light trot. When he continued to stomp somewhat reluctantly and sometimes even stopped, I kicked my boots into his stomach a few times to liven him up. It worked, and, at a good speed, we got ever farther into the interior of a large but still unfinished area where it was night.

The country road on which I was riding was stony and ascended considerably, but that is precisely what I liked about it, and I made it get even stonier and steeper. Whenever my acquaintance stumbled I pulled him up by his hair, and whenever he sighed I punched him in the head. And I felt how healthy this evening ride was for me in this good mood, and to make him even more furious I made a strong headwind blow into us in long gusts. Now I even exaggerated the bouncing motion of the ride on my acquaintance's broad shoulders, and, holding on tight to his neck with both hands, I bent my head far back and watched the varying clouds that, weaker than I, were flying heavily in the wind. I laughed and trembled with daring. My coat spread out and gave me strength. I pressed my hands together firmly and acted as if I didn't know that in doing so I was choking my acquaintance.

But to the sky, which became blocked from view by the curved branches of the trees I made grow at the sides of the road, I called out in the heated movement of the ride: "I have better things to do than listen to amorous ramblings all the time. Why did he come to me, this loquacious man in love? They're all happy, and even more so if someone else knows about it. They think they're spending a happy evening, and that in itself is reason enough to enjoy their future lives."

Then my acquaintance fell, and when I examined him I found that his knee was badly injured. Since he was no longer of use to me, I left him lying on the rocks and whistled a few vultures down from the skies, which obediently and with earnest beaks sat down on him to keep watch.

2
Walk

I walked on, carefree. But since, as a pedestrian, I dreaded the exertion of the mountainous road, I made the road become flatter and flatter and finally drop into a valley in the distance.

The rocks vanished at my will, and the wind died down and became absorbed in the night. I marched at a brisk pace, and since I was going downhill, I held my head high and stiffened my body and folded my arms behind my head. Since I love spruce forests, I went through spruce forests, and since I enjoy looking at the starry sky in silence, the stars rose slowly and calmly on me in the sprawling sky, as is their nature. I saw only a few stretched clouds pulled through the air by a wind blowing only at their height.

Rather far across from my road, most likely separated from me by a river, I made a high mountain arise whose brush-covered peak bordered on the sky. I could clearly see even the tiny entanglements and movements of the highest branches. This sight, common as it may be, delighted me so much that I, a small bird rocking on the twigs of those distant scrubby bushes, forgot to make the moon come up – it already lay behind the mountain, surely fuming at the delay.

But now the cool gleam that precedes the rise of the moon spread over the mountain, and suddenly the moon hoisted itself up behind one of the restless bushes. I, however, had meanwhile looked the other way, and when I peered in front of me now and saw it all of a sudden, shining in almost all its roundness, I stopped with dull eyes, for my sloping road seemed to lead straight into this terrifying moon.

But after a while I got used to it, and dispassionately observed its difficulty in rising, until finally, it and I having moved toward one another quite a bit of the way, I felt a pleasurable drowsiness, brought on, I thought, by the stresses of the day, of which admittedly I had no memory. I walked with my eyes closed for some time, keeping myself awake by loudly and regularly clapping my hands.

But then, as the road threatened to slip away under my feet and everything, weary like me, began to disappear, I hurried to anxiously scale the slope on the right side of the road so as to still reach the high, tangled spruce forest in time, where I was planning to sleep overnight. The haste was warranted. The stars already grew dark, and the moon sank weakly into the sky as into choppy waters. The mountain had already become part of the night;

the road ended, alarmingly, where I had turned toward the slope, and from inside the forest I heard the crashing of falling tree trunks draw closer. Now, I could have hurled myself down onto the moss to sleep right there, but since I'm afraid of ants I crawled, my legs wrapped around its trunk, up on a tree that dangled even without the wind; I lay down on a branch, with my head resting at the trunk, and hastily went to sleep as a squirrel of my fancy sat rocking on the trembling end of the branch.

The river was wide, and its small, loud waves were shone upon. There were meadows on the other bank as well, changing into shrub behind which bright avenues of fruit trees could be seen at a distance, leading to green hills.

Pleased by this view, I lay down, and, covering my ears against the crying I dreaded, I thought I might be content here. "For this place is isolated and beautiful. It doesn't take a lot of courage to live here. One will have to struggle here as much as elsewhere, but one won't have to move about gracefully in doing so. That won't be necessary. For they are only mountains and a large river, and I'm still sharp enough to consider them inanimate. So when I stumble along on the ascending meadow paths at night, I won't be any more abandoned than the mountain; it's only that I will feel it. But I believe that this, too, shall pass."

And so I toyed with my future life and adamantly tried to forget. In so doing I squinted into that sky, which was of an unusually happy hue. I hadn't seen it like this for a long time; I was touched and reminded of specific days when I also had believed I saw it this way. I removed my hands from my ears, spread my arms and let them drop into the grasses.

I heard someone sob far away and faintly. It got windy, and great amounts of dead leaves that I hadn't seen earlier flew up with a whoosh. Unripe fruit from fruit trees hit the ground madly. Ugly clouds came up behind a mountain. The river waves creaked and receded from the wind.

I stood up quickly. My heart ached, for it seemed impossible now to escape my suffering. I was about to turn back and leave this region behind and return to my former way of life, when I had this idea: "How odd it is that even nowadays distinguished people are carried across a river in this intricate manner. There is no other explanation than that it is an old custom." I shook my head, for I was surprised.

3
The Fat Man

Out of the shrubs on the other bank there stepped four massive naked men holding a wooden litter on their shoulders. On this litter sat an immensely fat man in an oriental posture. Even though he was being carried through the shrubs on an untracked path, he didn't push the thorny branches aside but rather calmly broke through them with his immobile body. His folds of fat were so carefully spread out that, while covering the entire litter and hanging over the sides like the hems of a yellowish carpet, they nonetheless didn't bother him. His hairless skull was small and gleamed yellow. His face bore the inane expression of a person who is thinking and not trying to hide it. Occasionally he closed his eyes; once he opened them again, his chin became contorted.

"This landscape inhibits my thinking," he said softly. "It makes my thoughts sway like suspension bridges in a furious current. It's beautiful and must therefore be beheld."

"I close my eyes and say: You, green mountain by the river, you that has rolling rocks against the water, you are beautiful."

"But it is not content; it wants me to open my eyes to it."

"But when I say with closed eyes: Mountain, I don't love you, for you remind me of the clouds, the red sunset, and the rising sky, and those are things that almost make me cry, for one can never reach them if one lets oneself be carried on a small litter. But showing me this, treacherous mountains, you're obscuring my view in the distance, which cheers me up, for it shows what is reachable in a nice panorama. That is why I don't love you, mountain by the water, no, I don't love you."

"But it would be as indifferent to this speech as to my previous one, if I didn't speak with open eyes. Otherwise it isn't satisfied."

"And don't we have to strive to stay in its favor so as to even keep it up, it, which has such a capricious predilection for the mush of our brains. It would cast its jagged shadows down on me, it would silently push terribly bare walls in front of me, and my litter bearers would stumble over little rocks by the wayside."

"But not only the mountain is this vain, this obtrusive, and this vindictive; everything else is, too. Thus with my circular eyes – oh how they ache – I must keep repeating:

"Yes, mountain, you are beautiful, and the forests on your western slope please me. –You, too, dear flower, you satisfy me, and your pink cheers my soul. –You, grass in the meadows, stand high already and are strong and soothing. –And you, exotic bushes, you sting so unexpectedly that our thoughts gain momentum. –But you, river, you enchant me so much that I will let myself be carried through your supple waters."

Having called out this praise ten times, with some humble shifting of his body, he lowered his head and said, his eyes closed:

"But now – I beg you – mountain flower grass, bushes and river, give me some space so that I can breathe."

There was a zealous reshuffling in the surrounding mountains that pushed behind low-hanging fogs. While the avenues stood firmly, and rather guarded the width of the road, they blurred prematurely. In the sky, in front of the sun, there hung a wet cloud with its rim softly glistening; in its shade, the country sank deeper while all things lost their beautiful boundaries.

The bearers' steps could be heard up to my side of the river, and yet I was unable to make out anything specific in the dark oblong of their faces. All I was able to see was how they were inclining their heads to the side and bending their necks, for the burden was an unusual one. I worried about them, for I noticed how tired they were. So I looked on eagerly as they stepped into the grass on the bank, continued at an even pace through the wet sand, until they eventually sank into the muddy reeds, where the two rear bearers stooped even further down to maintain the level position of the litter. I pressed my hands together. Now they had to lift their feet at every step so that their bodies glistened with sweat in the cool air of this wavering afternoon.

The fat man sat quietly, his hands on his thighs; the long tips of the reeds brushed against him when they shot up behind the front bearers.

The bearers' movements became less regular the closer they came to the water. Now and then the litter rocked as if it were already on the waves. Small puddles in the reeds had to be leapt over or bypassed, for they might be deep.

Suddenly wild ducks rose up crying and soared into the rain cloud. This is when, with a quick movement, I glimpsed the fat man's face; it looked disturbed. I stood up and, in angular leaps, rushed down the stony slope separating me from the water. I paid no heed to the fact that it was dangerous – I thought only about coming to the fat man's aid if his servants could no longer carry him. I ran so rashly that I was unable to stop but had to run into the splashing water and only came to a halt when the water was up to my knees.

On the other bank the servants had taken the litter to the water with contortions, and while they steadied themselves with one hand above the troubled waters, they pushed the litter up high with four hairy arms so that one could see their unusually raised muscles.

The water first licked up against their chins, then rose to their mouths, the bearers' heads bent backwards, and the litter handles dropped to their shoulders. The water was already lapping about the bridges of their noses, and they were still straining even though they had barely made it to the middle of the river. This is when a low wave beat down on the heads of the bearers in the front, and the four men drowned silently, pulling the litter down with them with fierce hands. Water gushed as they fell.

Then the flat shine of the evening sun broke from the rims of the great clouds and softened the hills and mountains around the edges, while the river and the landscape lay under the cloud in a hazy light.

The fat man slowly turned toward the gushing water and was carried downstream like an idol made of light-colored wood that had become superfluous and was therefore discarded into the river. He rode on the reflection of the rain cloud. Elongated clouds pulled him and small bent ones pushed him, so that there was an enormous turmoil I could feel by the water beating up against my knees and the rocks along the bank.

I quickly crawled up the embankment in order to accompany the fat man on his way, for I truly loved him. And perhaps I could learn something about the dangers of this seemingly safe country. I walked on a strip of sand, getting accustomed to its narrowness, my hands in my pockets and my face turned to the river at a right angle so that my chin almost sat on my shoulder.

There were delicate swallows perched on the rocks by the bank.

The fat man said: "Dear sir on the bank, don't try to rescue me. This is the revenge of the water and of the wind; I'm lost now. Yes, it is revenge; how often have we attacked these things, me and my friend, the praying man, our blades singing, the cymbals lighting up, the vast splendor of the trombones, and the leaping gleam of the kettledrums."

A small seagull with extended wings flew through his belly without reducing its speed. The fat man continued:

There was a time when I went to church day after day, for a girl I had fallen in love with prayed on her knees there for a half hour every evening, and during this time I could quietly contemplate her.

Once, when the girl hadn't come, and I couldn't help but gaze at the people in prayer, I noticed a young person who had thrown himself to the floor with the full length of his thin body. Now and again, with all of his body's strength he took his skull, and, with a sigh, smashed it into his palms, which were resting on the stone floor.

There were only a few old women in the church; they frequently turned their wrapped little heads sideways to check on the praying man. This attention seemed to please him, for before each of his pious outbursts he let his eyes wander to see whether there were numerous onlookers.

I thought this unseemly and decided to approach him when he left the church and query him as to why he was praying in this fashion. Indeed, I was annoyed that my girl hadn't come.

But not until an hour later did he stand up, make a very careful sign of the cross and fitfully walk to the holy-water font. I positioned myself between the font and the door and knew that I wouldn't let him pass without an explanation. I contorted my mouth, as I always do when I work myself up to speaking with resolve. I stepped forward with my right leg and leaned on it while casually balancing the other on my toes; that too gives me steadiness.

Now it is possible that this person had already eyed me when he splashed holy water on his face; he may even have noticed me before with some trepidation, since he now made an unexpected dash for the door and left. The glass door slammed shut. And when I stepped out the door just afterward, he was nowhere to be seen; there were several narrow streets and a variety of traffic.

The next few days, he stayed away, but my girl came back. She was wearing the black dress with transparent lace on the shoulders – the crescent hem of her shift showing underneath – with the silk hanging in a well-tailored collar from the lower edge. And since the girl had come, I forgot about the young man and even paid him no mind when he returned again to pray regularly as was his custom. But he always walked past me in great haste, his face averted. This may have been due to the fact that I could only conceive of him in motion, so that, even when he was standing still, it seemed to me that

48

he was creeping along.

One day, I stayed late in my room. Nonetheless, I still went to the church. The girl was no longer there, and I was about to go home. The young man was there again, lying on the floor. I remembered the previous incident, and it made me curious.

On my toes I snuck to the doorway, handed a coin to the blind beggar sitting there, and squeezed in beside him behind the open door. I sat there for an hour and perhaps made a crafty face. I felt comfortable and decided to come back once in a while. But in the second hour I found it senseless to sit there waiting for the praying man. And yet, for a third hour, already angry, I let the spiders crawl over my clothes as the last few people stepped out of the darkness of the church, breathing noisily.

Then he came as well. He was walking cautiously, his feet lightly feeling the ground before treading.

I stood up, took a long and straight stride, and seized the young man by the collar. "Good evening," I said and pushed him, my hand on his collar, down the steps onto the lighted square.

When we got downstairs, he said in a completely unfortified voice: "Good evening, my dear, dear sir, don't be angry with me, your most devoted servant."

"Well," I said, "there are a few things I would like to ask you, sir. Last time you got away; you will hardly succeed today."

"You're compassionate, sir, and you'll let me go home. I'm pitiful; it's the truth."

"No," I yelled into the racket of a passing streetcar, "I won't let you. It's exactly the kind of story I like. You're my lucky catch. I congratulate myself."

At that he said: "Oh, God, you have a lively heart, and a block for a head. You call me a lucky catch, how happy you must feel! For my unhappiness is a shaky unhappiness, an unhappiness balancing on a thin tip, and if one touches it, it falls on the questioner. Good night, sir."

"Fine," I said and held on to his right hand, "If you won't answer me, I'll start shouting right here in the street. And all the shop girls coming out of their shops and all their lovers looking forward to them will gather here, for they'll think that a carriage horse has collapsed or something of the like. Then I'll show you off to people."

He now kissed both of my hands in turn, sobbing. "I'll tell you what you want to hear, but please, let us rather go into that side street over there." I nodded, and we went over there.

But he didn't content himself with the darkness of the street, where yellow streetlights stood far apart from one another, but led me into the low hallway of an old building under a small dripping light hanging in front of the wooden stairs.

There he pompously took his handkerchief and, spreading it on a step, said: "Just have a seat, my dear sir, so you can ask better questions; I'll stand so I can give better answers. But don't torment me."

So I sat down and, looking up at him with narrowed eyes, I said: "You're an accomplished madman, that's what you are! Just the way you carry on in church! How ludicrous that is, and how disagreeable to the onlookers! How can anyone be rapt in prayer when they have to look at you."

He had pressed his body against the wall, moving just his head freely in the air. "Don't be annoyed – why should you be annoyed about matters that don't concern you? I get annoyed about my uncouth behavior; but if it's just someone else behaving badly, I'm glad. So don't be annoyed if I tell you that it's the purpose of my praying to be looked at by people. "

"What are you saying," I shouted, far too loudly for the low hallway, but then I was afraid to lower my voice. "Really, what are you saying. Oh, I have a hunch, in fact, I've had a hunch since I first saw you, about the state you are in. I have my experience, and I'm not saying this in jest when I say that it's seasickness on dry land. Its nature is such that you forget the true names of things and hastily slap accidental names on them now. Just quick, quick! But as soon as you run away from them, you'll forget their names. The poplar in the fields that you named the 'Tower of Babel' for you didn't know or didn't care to know that it was a poplar tree, is swaying again namelessly, and you would have to name it 'Noah when he was drunk.'"

I was somewhat dismayed when he said: "I'm glad I didn't understand what you were saying."

Flustered, I said quickly: "Your being glad shows me that you understood."

"I may have shown it, sir, but you spoke in an odd manner, too."

I placed my hands on a higher step, leaned back, and, in this all but invincible posture, which is the last resort of wrestlers, I said: "It's funny how you save your neck by presupposing your own state in others."

That's when he took courage. He knotted his hands so as to give his body unity and said, with some reluctance: "No, but I'm not doing this with everyone, not with you, for example, because I can't. But I'd be glad if I could, because in that case I wouldn't need people's attention in church anymore. Do you know why I need it?"

This question made me feel helpless. Of course, I didn't know, and I don't think I wanted to know. I hadn't wanted to come here, either, I told myself at the time, but that person had forced me to listen to him. And so all I needed to do now was shake my head to show him that I didn't know, but I couldn't make my head move in any way.

The person standing opposite me smiled. Then he squatted down on his knees and told me with a sleepy grimace: "There has never been a time where I myself was convinced of my life. For I grasp things around me only in such fleeting ideas that I always think that things used to live but are now fading. I always, my dear sir, have this gnawing desire to see things the way they present themselves before they reveal themselves to me. That's when they must be beautiful and calm. It has to be that way, for I often hear people talking about them that way."

Since I remained silent and only spontaneous twitches in my face revealed how uneasy I was, he asked: "You don't believe that people talk that way?"

I felt like I had to nod my head yes, but I couldn't.

"So you really don't believe this? Oh, come on: once, as a child, when I opened my eyes after an afternoon nap, still shrouded in sleep, I heard my mother call down from the balcony in a natural voice: 'What are you doing, my dear. It's so hot.' A woman replied from the garden: 'I'm having a snack out in the garden.' She said so without thinking and not too clearly, as if everyone should have expected it."

I felt that it was my turn now. So I put my hand in my back pocket and pretended to search for something there. I wasn't searching for anything, but only sought to change my appearance so as to show my involvement in the conversation. I said that this was such a curious incident and that I didn't comprehend it in the least. I also added that I didn't believe it was true and that it must have been invented for a particular purpose, which I couldn't see at the time. Then I closed my eyes, for they were hurting.

"Oh, but it's good that you share my opinion, and you were unselfish enough to stop me to tell me that.

Well, why should I be ashamed – or why should we be ashamed – that I don't walk upright and heavy, don't bang my cane on the pavement and brush against the clothes of people who noisily pass by. Rather, shouldn't I rightly and defiantly lament that I skip along the houses as a shadow with angular

51

shoulders, at times disappearing into the panes of the shop windows?

What days I am having! Why is everything built so poorly that tall buildings occasionally crumble for no apparent reason? I then clamber over the rubble piles, asking everyone I meet: 'How could this happen! In our city. –A new building – It's the fifth one today. –Just think about it.' But no one can give me an answer.

Frequently people collapse and lie dead in the street. Then all the shopkeepers open their doors laden with merchandise, approach with agility, take the body into a house, reemerge with a smile on lips and eyes and say: 'Good morning – The sky is pale – I sell many kerchiefs – Yes, the war.' I slip into the house and, having timidly raised my hand with my crooked finger a few times, I finally knock on the janitor's little window. 'My dear sir,' I say amiably, 'a dead man has just been brought in here. Do show him to me, would you please.' And when he shakes his head as if undecided, I say firmly: 'My dear sir. I'm with the secret police. Show me the dead man at once.' 'A dead person,' he now asks and is almost offended. 'No, there is no dead person here. This is a respectable house.' I say goodbye and leave.

But then when I have to cross a large square, I forget everything. The difficulty of the undertaking confuses me, and I often think to myself: 'If such large squares are built just out of exuberance, then why don't they build a stone balustrade leading across the square. A southwesterly wind is blowing today. The air in the square is agitated. The spire of the city hall is drawing small circles. Why doesn't anyone establish peace and quiet among the mob? What a racket! All the windowpanes are roaring and the lampposts are bending like bamboo. The Virgin Mary's cloak on the column is bulging, and the stormy air is tugging at it. Doesn't anyone see? The gentlemen and ladies who should be walking on the cobblestones are levitating. When the wind catches its breath, they stop, exchange a few words, and bow in salute, but as soon as the wind starts gusting again, they cannot resist and all raise their feet in unison. They do have to hold on to their hats, but their eyes twinkle as if the weather were clement. I'm the only one who is afraid.'"

Abused as I was, I said: "The story you were telling earlier of your mother and the woman in the garden, I don't find it strange at all. Not only have I heard and experienced many such stories, I've even been involved in some. The thing is quite natural. Don't you think I could have said the same thing, if I had been on the balcony, and replied the same thing from the garden? It's such an ordinary incident."

When I had said that, he seemed very pleased. He said that I was nicely dressed and that he liked my necktie very much. And what a smooth complexion I had. And that confessions became most lucid when they were retracted.

c) The Story of the Praying Man

Then he sat down next to me, for I had become timid; I had made room for him, tilting my head. Nonetheless it didn't escape me that he, too, was sitting there with some embarrassment, constantly seeking to maintain some distance from me and speaking with difficulty:

What days I am having!

Last night I was at a party. I was bowing to a young lady in the gaslight with the words: "I'm very glad indeed that we're approaching winter" – I was just bowing while saying these words when I noticed to my displeasure that my right thigh had become dislocated. My kneecap had also loosened some.

So I sat down and, as I'm always striving to keep control over my phrases, I said: "For winter takes much less of an effort; it's easier to behave oneself, one doesn't have to be as careful with one's words. Does one, dear young miss? I hope I'm right about this." All the while my right leg was giving me trouble. Initially it seemed to have completely fallen apart, and only gradually did I manage to fix it, to some degree, by squeezing and shifting it into place.

At that I heard the girl, who had sat down in sympathy, say softly: "No, you don't impress me in the least, for–"

"Hold on," I said contently and eagerly, "dear young miss, you shouldn't spend five minutes just talking with me. Eat something between your words, would you please."

I reached to take a swollen grape hanging from the bowl raised by a bronze cherub, suspended it in the air for a moment and placed it on a small blue-rimmed plate, which I passed to the girl, perhaps not undaintily.

"You don't impress me in the least," she said, "everything you say is boring and unintelligible, but not any more true for that. For I think, sir – why are you always calling me dear young miss – I think the only reason why you're not bothering with the truth is that it is too tiresome."

God, that got me going! "Sure, young miss, young miss," I almost shouted, "How right you are! Dear young miss, do you see, it is such a spirited joy to feel so well understood without having tried."

"The truth is too tiresome for you, sir, just look at you! Your entire form is cut out of silk paper, yellow silk paper, silhouette-like, and when you walk one must hear you rustle. Therefore, it's unfair to get worked up about your attitude or opinion, for you have to bend with whatever wind happens to blow in the room."

"I don't understand. There are a few people standing around in this room. They put their arms on the backs of chairs or lean on the piano or tentatively raise their glasses to their mouths or timorously go into the next room and, having hurt their right shoulder on a cupboard in the dark, they think, breathing by the open window: There is Venus, the evening star. But I'm here at this party. If there is a connection here, I don't see it. And I don't even know if there is a connection. –And you see, dear miss, of all these people behaving so irresolutely, even ludicrously in their lack of clarity, I alone seem to be worthy of hearing very blunt truths about myself. And to cushion even that with something pleasant, you say so mockingly, so that some substance remains, the way the walls of a house burnt out on the inside are substantial. There's little to obstruct the view here; through the great window holes, you can see the clouds and the sky by day and the stars by night. But often the clouds are still hewn from gray rocks, and the stars form unnatural constellations. –What would you think if I in turn admitted to you that one day all the people trying to live would look like me, cut – as you remarked – from yellow silk paper, silhouette-like, and when they walk one will hear them rustle. They won't be any different than now, but they will look that way. Even you, dear–"

Then I noticed that the girl was no longer sitting next to me. She must have left soon after her last words because she was standing far away from me by the window now, surrounded by three young people who were talking and laughing out of high white collars.

So I merrily drank a glass of wine and walked over to the pianist, who sat apart playing a sad piece, nodding. Cautiously, so as not to startle him, I bent to his ear and said quietly, in tune with the piece:

"Would you be so kind, my dear sir, to let me play now, for I'm about to be happy."

Since he paid me no heed, I stood there in embarrassment for a while, but, suppressing my timidity, I then went from one guest to the next and said in passing: "I'm playing the piano today. Indeed."

Everyone seemed to know that I didn't know how to play, but they laughed graciously because of the pleasant interruption of their conversations. But I didn't get their full attention until I very loudly said to the pianist: "Would you be so kind, my dear sir, to let me play now. I'm just about to be happy. I'm talking about a triumph."

Even though the pianist stopped playing, he didn't leave his brown bench and didn't seem to understand me either. He sighed and covered his face with his long fingers.

Suddenly I felt a little sorry and was about to encourage him to continue playing, when the hostess approached with a group of people.

"What a funny idea," they said and laughed loudly as though I was going to do something unnatural.

The girl joined them as well, looked at me with contempt, and said: "Please, dear madam, do let him play. He may want to contribute to the entertainment somehow. That's to be lauded. Please, dear madam."

Everyone rejoiced loudly, for they seemed to believe, just like myself, that it was meant ironically. Only the pianist remained silent. He kept his head lowered and stroked the wood of the bench with the index finger of his left hand as if he were drawing in the sand. I was trembling and, to conceal it, shoved my hands into my trouser pockets. I couldn't speak clearly anymore either, for my whole face felt like crying. Therefore, I had to choose my words in such a way that the idea that I felt like crying would appear ridiculous to the listeners.

"Dear madam," I said, "I have to play because–" Having forgotten the reason, I abruptly sat down at the piano. Then I became aware of my situation again. The pianist stood up and politely stepped across the bench, for I was in his way. "Turn off the light, please, I can only play in the dark." I sat up straight.

Then two gentlemen grabbed the bench, and, whistling a tune and rocking me a bit, carried me very far away from the piano toward the dinner table.

Everyone looked on approvingly, and the young lady said: "You see, dear madam, he played quite nicely. I thought so. And you were so worried."

I understood and thanked her with an accomplished bow.

I was poured some lemonade, and a young lady with red lips held my glass while I drank. The hostess offered me some meringue on a silver plate, and a girl in a completely white dress put it in my mouth. A voluptuous young lady with a shock of blond hair held a bunch of grapes above me, and all I needed to do was pluck them off the vine while she gazed into my receding eyes.

Since everyone was treating me so well, I was surprised, naturally, that they unanimously held me back when I started back for the piano.

"That will do now," said the host, whom I hadn't noticed before. He went outside and immediately returned with an enormous top hat and a flowered copper-brown overcoat. "Here are your things."

They weren't my things, but I didn't want to make him look again. The host himself put the overcoat on me, which fit me perfectly, tightly clinging to my thin body. A lady with a kind face, bending over gradually, buttoned my coat all the way up.

"Well, farewell then," said the hostess, "and come back soon. You're always welcome, you know that." At that the whole party bowed, as if that were necessary. I tried to the same, but my coat was too tight. So I took my hat and walked to the door, certainly a little too awkwardly.

But when I stepped out of the front door with small steps, I was pounced upon by the sky, with the moon and the stars and a great vault, and by the Old Town Square with the City Hall, St. Mary's column, and the church.

I calmly walked out of the shade into the moonlight, unbuttoned my overcoat, and warmed myself; then I lifted my hand to make the hum of the night fall silent, and I started to think:

"What is it, then, that you act as though you were real. Are you trying to make me believe that I'm unreal, standing strangely on the green cobblestones. But it's been a long time since you were real, you sky, and you Old Town Square have never been real."

"Well, it's true, you're still superior to me, but only when I leave you alone."

"Thank God, moon, you're no longer moon, but it may be thoughtless of me to still call you, who are named moon, moon. But why are you no longer boisterous when I call you 'forgotten paper lantern in a strange color.' And why do you almost withdraw when I call you 'St. Mary's column,' and I no longer recognize your threatening posture, St. Mary's column, when I call you 'Moon, casting a yellow light.'"

"It really seems that it doesn't do you any good when one thinks about you; you wane in courage and in health."

"God, how beneficial it must be when the thinker learns from the drunk!"

"Why has everything gone quiet? I think there's no more wind. And the little houses frequently rolling across the square as though on tiny wheels, are all pounded down – quiet – quiet – one doesn't even see the thin black line that usually separates them from the ground."

And I broke into a run. With nothing stopping me I ran around the large square three times, and since I didn't encounter any drunks, I ran toward Charles Street without disrupting my speed and unaware of the effort. My shadow, often smaller than myself, ran next to me on the wall as if in a sunken lane between the wall and the bottom of the road.

When I passed the fire station, I heard some noise coming from the Small Square, and when I turned off there, I saw a drunken man standing at the ironwork of the fountain, holding his arms out horizontally and stamping the ground with his clog-clad feet.

I stopped to let my breath calm down first; then I went up to him, raised my top hat from my head, and introduced myself:

"Good evening, gentle nobleman, I'm twenty-three years old, but I don't have a name yet. But you surely, with an astounding name, a name one could sing, hail from that great city of Paris. The entirely unnatural scent of the decadent Court of France envelops you."

"Surely with your tinted eyes you've seen those tall ladies standing on the high and bright terrace, ironically twisting their narrow waists while the ends of their trains covering the steps still lie on the sand in the garden. –Isn't it true that all over the place servants in gray, smartly cut tuxedos, and white trousers climb up on tall poles with their legs hugging them while their upper bodies frequently bend toward the back and the side, for they must lift giant gray canvas cloths off the ground on thick ropes and spread them up high, because the grand lady desires a foggy morning."

Since he belched, I said, almost startled: "Really, is it true, you come from our Paris, from stormy Paris, alas, from this effusive hailstorm?"

When he belched again, I said with embarrassment: "I know that a great honor is being bestowed on me."

And with quick fingers I buttoned up my overcoat, then spoke fervently and timidly:

"I know you don't consider me worthy of an answer, but I would have to lead a tearful life if I didn't ask you today."

"I'm asking you, festooned sir, is it true what I've been told. Are there people in Paris who consist of ornamented clothes only, and are there houses that have only portals, and is it true that the sky above the city is a fleeting blue on summer days, only embellished by pasted-on white cloudlets in the shape of hearts? And is there a much-frequented panopticon where there are only trees standing with the names of the most famous heroes, villains, and lovers on small mounted plaques?"

"And then there's this message! This obviously mendacious message!"

"Isn't it true that those streets of Paris suddenly branch off; they are noisy, aren't they? Not everything is always all right, how would it be! So there is an accident, people gather, coming out of side streets with a big city stride that barely grazes the surface; everyone is curious but also fearful of disappointment; they breathe quickly and stretch out their little heads. But when they touch one another, they take a deep bow and apologize: 'I'm very sorry – it was an accident – there is such a crush, excuse me, will you please – how clumsy of me – I admit it. My name is – my name is Jerome Faroche, I'm a spice grocer in the rue de Cabotin – allow me to invite you for lunch tomorrow – it would be such a delight for my wife as well.' Thus they talk while the street is still torpid, and smoke from the chimneys drops between the houses. That's the way it is, isn't it. And would it be possible that all of a sudden two carriages stop on a busy boulevard of an elegant neighborhood. Servants earnestly open the doors. Eight splendid Siberian huskies frolic out, and, barking, chase each other across the road in leaps. And yet people say that they're young Parisian dandies in disguise."

His eyes were almost closed. When I fell silent, he stuck both of his hands into his mouth, tugging at his lower jaw. His clothes were all soiled. Perhaps he had been kicked out of a wine bar, and he hadn't realized it yet.

It may have been in this small, completely quiet lull between day and night when our heads, unexpectedly, hang in the backs of our necks, and when, unbeknownst to us, everything stands still since we're not watching, and then disappears. While we remain alone with arched bodies, then turn around but don't see anything anymore, and feel no resistance from the air either, but inside us hold onto the memory that, at a certain distance from us, there stand houses with roofs and, luckily, square chimneys, through which darkness flows into the houses, through the garrets into the various rooms. And it is fortunate that tomorrow will be a day when, unbelievable as it is, one will be able to see it all that.

At that, the drunken man pulled up his eyebrows so that between them and his eyes a glint was to be seen, and he explained in spurts: "Well, it's like this – I'm sleepy, so I'll go to sleep – I have a brother-in-law in Wenceslas Square – that's where I'm headed since I live there, since I have my bed there – I'm off

– I just don't remember his name and where he lives – it seems that I forgot – but it doesn't matter for I'm not even sure if I have a brother-in-law – Well, but I'm off now – Do you think I'll find him?"

To that I said, without thinking: "Certainly. But you're a stranger here, and it so happens that your servants aren't with you. Allow me to guide you."

He didn't reply. So I held out my arm for him to take.

d) CONTINUED CONVERSATION BETWEEN THE FAT MAN AND THE PRAYING MAN

But I had been trying to cheer myself up for some time already. I rubbed my body and said to myself:

"It's time for you to speak. You're embarrassed already. Do you feel harried? Just wait! You're familiar with such situations, after all. Just think about it, take your time! The surroundings will wait, too."

"It's just like at the evening party last week. Someone reads from a copy of a manuscript. I even copied out a page myself at his request. But when I see my handwriting among the pages he wrote, I get frightened. It's unfounded. People pore over them from three sides of the table. I swear, crying, that it's not my handwriting."

"But why would this be similar to today's situation. It's only up to you to begin a fenced-in conversation. Everything is peaceful. Just make an effort, my dear friend! –You'll find an objection to raise after all. –You can say: 'I'm sleepy. I have a headache. Goodbye.' Rapidly, you know, rapidly. Get yourself noticed! –What is this? Hurdles and hurdles again? What do you remember? –I remember a plateau rising toward the great sky as a shield of the earth. I saw it from a mountain and got ready to hike through it. I started to sing."

My lips were dry and disobedient when I said:

"Shouldn't one be able to live differently?"

"No," he said, questioning, smiling.

"But why do you pray in church in the evening," I then asked, while everything between me and him that I had been supporting until then as if asleep collapsed.

"No, why should we talk about it. In the evening no one who lives alone bears responsibility. One fears many a thing. That physicality may vanish, that people are really the way they appear in the twilight, that one isn't allowed to walk without a cane, that it might be good to go to church and shout in prayer so as to be looked at, and thus become a body."

As he talked like that and then fell silent, I pulled my red handkerchief from my pocket and cried, stooped over.

He stood up, kissed me, and said:

"Why are you crying? You're tall, I love that, you have long hands behaving almost as you wish; why aren't you happy about it? Always wear dark cuffs on your sleeves, let me advise you. –No–I'm flattering you, and you're still crying? This difficulty of life, you're really bearing it quite reasonably."

"We construct quite useless war machines, towers, walls, curtains of silk, and we might wonder a lot about that if we had the time. And remain suspended in the air, we don't fall, we flutter, even though we're uglier than bats. And now hardly anyone can prevent us from saying on a beautiful day: 'Oh Lord, it's a beautiful day today.' For already we are settled in on this earth, and we live on the basis of our consent."

"We are just like tree trunks in the snow. They seem to lie simply flush, and one should be able to push them aside with a little prod. But no, one can't, for they're firmly attached to the ground. But look, even that is only an illusion."

Contemplation prevented me from crying: "It's night, and no one will reproach me tomorrow for what I might say now, for it could be said during sleep."

Then I said: "Yes, that's true, but what were we saying. We couldn't very well be talking about the illumination of the sky since we're standing deep inside a hallway. No – but then, we could be talking about that, for we aren't completely independent in our conversation, since we don't want to achieve either purpose or truth, but merely jest and amusement. But couldn't you tell me the story of the woman in the garden again. How admirable, how smart that woman is! We must behave according to her example. How fond I am of her! And then it's just as well that I met and intercepted you. It's been a great pleasure talking with you. I heard a few things that might have been intentionally unknown to me – I'm glad."

He looked content. Although touching a human body is always embarrassing to me, I had to embrace him.

Then we stepped out of the hallway under the sky. My friend blew away some crushed cloudlets, so that the now uninterrupted expanse of the stars offered itself to us. My friend walked with difficulty.

4

Demise of the Fat Man

Then everything was engulfed by speed and fell into the distance. The river water was sucked down a precipice, tried to hold back, teetered on the crumbling edge for a moment, but then rushed down in lumps and smoke.

The fat man couldn't talk anymore but was forced to turn around and disappear in the deafening waterfall.

I, who had experienced so much amusement, I stood on the riverbank and looked on. "What are our lungs supposed to do," I shouted, shouted, "if they breathe quickly, they'll suffocate on themselves, on their inner toxins; if they breathe slowly, they'll suffocate from unbreathable air, from outraged things. But if they want to find their right speed, they'll drown during the search."

Then the banks of this river extended beyond measure, and yet I touched the iron of a tiny, distant signpost with the palm of my hand. I couldn't quite make sense of that. For I was short, almost shorter than usual, and a bush with white rosehips shaking very quickly towered over me. I saw it, for it was nearby just a moment ago.

But nonetheless I was mistaken, for my arms were as large as the clouds of a steady rain, only they were more rushed. I don't know why they were trying to crush my poor head.

It was so small, really, like an ant egg, only it was somewhat damaged, and therefore no longer entirely round. I performed some pleading turns, for the expression of my eyes might have gone unnoticed, that's how small they were.

But my legs, but my impossible legs extended across the wooded mountains and shaded the rural valleys. They grew, they grew! They already protruded into the distance, which had no landscape anymore, their length for a long time already reached beyond my eyesight.

But no, that's not it – I'm short, too, tentatively short – I'm rolling – I'm rolling – I'm an avalanche in the mountains! Please, passers-by, be so kind as to tell me how tall I am, measure these arms, these legs.

III

"How is it then," said my acquaintance, having left the party with me and quietly walking on a path to Petrin Hill. "Stop for a moment already, will you, so that I can come to terms with it. –You know, I have a matter to settle. It's so strenuous – this cold and also irradiated night, but this dissatisfied wind, which even seems to change the position of those acacias once in a while."

The moon shadow of the gardener's cottage loomed across the somewhat vaulted path and was ornate with the little bit of snow. When I caught sight of the bench next to the door, I pointed to it with my raised hand, for I wasn't courageous and expected reproach, and placed my left hand on my chest.

He sat down, weary, without regard for his beautiful clothes, and amazed me when he pushed his elbows against his hips and rested his forehead on his overstretched fingertips.

"Now, let me say this. You know, I live a regular life, there is nothing wrong with it, everything necessary and recognized takes place. Unhappiness, which is common in the society I associate with, hasn't spared me, as those around me and I were glad to see, and this general happiness hasn't held back either, and I've been allowed to speak of it among friends. Of course, I had never really been in love before. I regretted that once in a while but I used that turn of phrase if I needed to. Well, now I have to say: Yes, I'm in love and perfectly excited about being in love. I'm an ardent lover, just the way girls like them. But shouldn't I have considered the fact that it was exactly that previous lack that gave my circumstances an exceptional and funny, particularly funny twist?"

"Just stay quiet, quiet," I said apathetically, and thinking only of myself, "but your beloved is beautiful, from what I've heard."

"Yes, she's beautiful. When I sat next to her, I kept thinking: 'What a risk – and I'm so daring – I'm undertaking a sea voyage – drinking wine by the gallon.' But when she laughs, she doesn't bare her teeth as one would expect, but one can only see the dark narrow arch of her open mouth. And that really looks sly and senile, even though she bends her head back when she laughs."

"I can't deny it," I said, sighing, "I've probably seen it as well, for it must be striking. But it's not only that. A girl's beauty in general! Often when I see dresses with multiple folds, frills, and fringes draping beautifully over beautiful bodies, I have to think that they won't be preserved for long, but will get creases that can't be ironed out anymore, dust that can't be removed from the trimmings, and no one would want to make themselves look so sad or silly to put on the same dress in the morning and take it off every night. But I see girls who are very beautiful and show multiple lovely muscles and small ankles and taut skin and masses of fine hair, and yet they appear in the same natural costume every day, always lay that same face into their palms and have it reflected in their mirror. Only sometimes late at night when they return from a party, it appears to them in the mirror, worn, bloated, dusty, already seen by everyone and hardly wearable anymore."

"Along the way I've asked you several times whether you find the girl beautiful, but you kept turning to the other side without answering me. Tell me, are you planning to do something malicious? Why aren't you comforting me?"

I dug my feet into the shadow and said attentively: "You don't need to be comforted. You're loved." And I held my handkerchief with the blue grape pattern in front of my mouth so as to not catch a cold.

Now he turned toward me and rested his fat face against the low back of the bench: "You know, all in all I still have time: I can always end this budding romance by some disgrace or infidelity or by departing to a faraway country. For I'm really in doubt whether I should even get myself into this excitement. Nothing is guaranteed; no one can indicate direction and duration with any certainty. If I go into a tavern with the intention of getting drunk, I know that I'll be drunk that night. But in this case! In a week we want to go on an outing with a family we're friends with, now if that doesn't cause a storm in the heart for two weeks. Tonight's kisses have made me sleepy so as to make space for untamed dreams. I defy that and take a nightly walk, then it happens that I'm incessantly moving, that my face is cold and warm as if after gusts of wind, that I must keep touching a pink ribbon in my pocket, have the highest misgivings for myself without being able to pursue them, and tolerate even you, sir, while I otherwise surely would never talk this long with you."

I was very cold, and the whitish sky started tilting a little. "No disgraceful act or infidelity or departing to a faraway country will help this. You'll have to murder yourself," I said and smiled.

Opposite us on the other side of the avenue there were two bushes, and behind those bushes there was the city down below. It was still somewhat illuminated.

"Well," he shouted and punched the bench with his small firm fist and let it lie there, "but you're alive. You aren't killing yourself. No one loves you. You're achieving nothing. You can't control the next moment. And yet you talk to me like that, you mean person. You can't love; nothing but fear arouses you. Just look at my chest."

He swiftly opened his coat and his vest and his shirt. His chest was really wide and handsome.

I began to talk: "True, such defiant states do overcome us occasionally. That's how I was in a village this summer. It was located on a river. I remember it exactly. I often sat on a bench by the shore in a contorted posture. There was a riverside hotel, too. One could often hear the violin playing there. Strapping young people talked of hunting and adventures at tables in the garden behind their beers. And then there were such cloudlike mountains on the other shore."

I stood up then with a vaguely twisted mouth, stepped onto the lawn behind the bench, broke some of the snowed-on switches, and then said in my acquaintance's ear: "I'm engaged, I admit it."

My acquaintance was not surprised that I'd gotten up: "You're engaged?" He sat there, really weak, supported only by the backrest. Then he took off his hat and I saw his hair, which was fragrant and nicely combed and which set off his round head on the flesh of his neck in a distinct rounded line, as was the fashion that winter.

I was glad that I had replied to him so cleverly. "Yes," said I to myself, "how he walks around the party with his supple neck and free arms. He can lead a lady right through the middle of a large room with good conversation, and it doesn't make him nervous at all that the rain is falling in front of the house or that a shy person is standing there or that otherwise something wretched is happening. No, he bends just as nicely in front of the ladies. But there he is sitting now."

My acquaintance wiped his forehead with a cambric kerchief. "Please," he said, "lay your hand on my forehead a little. I beg you." When I didn't do it right away, he folded his hands.

As though our sorrow had obscured everything, we sat on top of the hill as in a small room, although we had already noticed the light and wind of the morning. We were close together, although we weren't fond of each other, but we couldn't move apart anymore for the walls were formal and firmly set. But we were free to behave ridiculously and without human dignity, for we didn't have to be ashamed in the presence of the twigs above us and the trees opposite us.

Without much ado, my acquaintance pulled a knife from his pocket, opened it thoughtfully, rammed it into his upper left arm as if in play and didn't remove it. Blood flowed immediately. His round cheeks were pale. I pulled the knife out, cut the sleeve of his winter coat and his tailcoat, and tore open the shirtsleeve. Then I walked down the path a short distance to see whether there was anyone who could help me. All the branch work was garishly visible and immobile. Then I sucked on the deep wound a little. Then I remembered the little gardener's cottage. I walked up the stairs leading to the elevated lawn on the left side of the house, I hurriedly examined the doors and windows, I rang angrily and stomping, although I had seen right away that the house was uninhabited. Then I looked after the wound, which was bleeding in a thin stream. I wet his kerchief in the snow and clumsily bandaged his arm.

"Dear friend, dear friend," I said, "you hurt yourself because of me. You're in such a pleasant place, surrounded by friendly people, you can go walking in bright daylight when many carefully dressed people can be seen near and far at tables or on mountain paths. Just think, in the springtime we'll go to the arboretum, no, not *we* will go, that's true, unfortunately, but you'll go with little Annie in joy and at a trot. Ah yes, believe me, I beg you, and the sun will show you at your most beautiful to everyone. Oh, there will be music, you'll hear the horses from afar, no need to worry; there will be shouting and barrel organs playing in the avenues."

"Oh Lord", he said. He stood up and leaned against me as we walked, "there is no helping it. That wouldn't please me. Forgive me. Is it late already? Perhaps I should do something tomorrow morning. Oh Lord."

A streetlight up near the wall was shining and cast shadows of tree trunks across the road and the white snow, while the shadows of the manifold branches were lying twisted, as though broken, on the slope.

Toward midnight a few people stood up, took their bows, shook hands, said they had enjoyed themselves very much, and then went through the large doorframe into the hall to put on their coats. The lady of the house stood in the middle of the room and made supple bows as dainty folds were bouncing in her skirt.

I sat at a small table – it had three taut thin legs – sipping my third glass of Benedictine and while drinking I looked over my little stock of pastries, which I had picked out and piled up myself.

Then I saw my new acquaintance appear at the doorpost of an adjoining room, somewhat disheveled and disorderly, but I tried to look away, for it was none of my business. But he came up to me, and smiling distractedly at my occupation, he said:

"Excuse me for troubling you. But up to this moment I was sitting with my girl all alone in an adjoining room. Since ten-thirty. You, man, what an evening. I know, it's not right that I'm telling you this, for we barely know each other. We just met on the stairs tonight, didn't we, and exchanged a few polite words as guests at the same house. And now – but you must – please – forgive me, my happiness simply can't be contained, I couldn't help it. And since I have no other acquaintances here I can trust–"

I looked at him sadly – for the piece of fruit cake in my mouth didn't taste good – and I said up to his pleasantly reddened face:

"Of course, I'm glad that I seem trustworthy to you, but I'm disappointed that you've confided in me. And you yourself, if you weren't so confused, you should feel how inappropriate it is to tell someone sitting by himself drinking liquor about a loving girl."

Once I had said that, he sat down abruptly, leaned back, and let his arms hang loose. Then he pushed them back with pointed elbows and started to talk to himself in a fairly loud voice:

"Just a minute ago, there in the room, we were all by ourselves, Annie with me. And I kissed her, I – did – kiss – her on her mouth, her ear, her shoulders. Lord God!"

Several guests, suspecting this to be a livelier conversation, yawningly moved closer to us. Thus, I stood up and said so that everyone could hear:

"Sure, if you want, I'll go with you, but I insist that there is no point in going up to Petrin Hill, now in winter and at night. Besides, it got cold outside and since it has snowed a little, the paths are like skating rinks. Well, as you like–"

He gazed at me in astonishment at first and opened his mouth with wet lips, but then, noticing the gentlemen who were already quite close, he laughed, stood up and said:

"Oh yes, the cool air will do us good; our clothes are full of heat and smoke; and then I'm slightly inebriated without having drunk much, yes, let us say goodbye and then we'll go."

We went to the lady of the house then, and as he kissed her hand, she said:

"You know, I am glad to see you so happy today."

The kindness of her words touched him and he kissed her hand again, and she smiled. I had to pull him away.

There was a housemaid in the hall; we saw her for the first time now. She helped us into our overcoats and took a small hand lamp to light us down the stairs. Her neck was bare, bound merely by a black velvet ribbon under the chin, and her loosely clad body was bent, stretching again and again, as she went down the stairs in front of us, holding the lamp low. Her cheeks were rosy for she had drunk wine, and her lips quivered in the weak lamplight that filled the entire stairwell.

Down at the foot of the stairs, she stood the lamp on a step, took a step toward my acquaintance and hugged him and kissed him, remaining in the embrace. Only when I placed a coin in her hand did she languidly loosen her arms, slowly open the small door and let us out into the night.

Above the empty, evenly lit street, there stood a large moon in the slightly cloudy and thus more spread-out sky. On the frozen snow we could only to take small steps.

We had barely stepped outside when I apparently got into very high spirits. I raised my legs, cracked my joints, I called out a name across the street as if a friend had fled around the corner, I jumped and threw my hat up, and then caught it ostentatiously.

But my acquaintance kept walking next to me without a worry. He held his head tilted. He didn't talk, either.

This surprised me, for I had calculated that he would go wild with joy once I got him away from the party. Now I could quiet down, too. No sooner had I given him an encouraging slap on the back than I suddenly no longer understood his situation and withdrew my hand. Since I didn't need it, I pushed it into the pocket of my overcoat.

So we walked in silence. I listened to the sound of our steps and couldn't understand why I was unable to walk in step with my acquaintance. What's more, the air was clear, so I could see his legs plainly. Every now and then someone leaned out the window and watched us.

When we came to Ferdinand Street, I noticed that my acquaintance had started to hum a tune from the "Dollar Princess;" it was soft, but I could hear it quite well. What about that? Was he trying to insult me? Now I was ready to do without this music right away, and this walk as well. Well, why wasn't he speaking to me? If he didn't need me, why hadn't he left me in peace where it was warm and where there was Benedictine and sweet goodies. It certainly hadn't been me who had insisted on this walk. Besides, I could very well go for a walk on my own. I had just been at an evening party, had saved an ungrateful young man from embarrassment, and was now walking around in the moonlight. That was all right, too. At the office by day, at a party in the evening, in the streets at night, and nothing in excess. A simply boundlessly natural way of life!

But my acquaintance was still walking behind me; he even hastened his step when he realized that he had fallen behind. Nothing was said, although one couldn't say that we were running. But I wondered whether it might not be a good idea to turn into a side street, since I really wasn't obligated to go on a walk with him. I could return home alone, and no one could stop me. I would watch my acquaintance pass by the entrance to my street without knowing. Farewell, my dear acquaintance. Upon my return, I will be warm in my room; I will light the lamp in its iron crate on the table, and, when I'm finished, I will lie down in my armchair on the tattered oriental carpet. Great prospects! Why not? But then? No then. The lamp will shine in the warm room, onto my chest in my armchair. Well, then I will cool off and spend hours by myself between the painted walls on the floor, which slants off into the gold-rimmed mirror on the back wall.

My legs became tired, and I had already decided to return home and lie down on my bed no matter what, when I began to doubt whether I should say goodbye to my acquaintance upon leaving or not. But I was too fearful to leave without saying goodbye and too weak to call out loudly. So I stopped again, held onto the moonlit wall of a house, and waited.

My acquaintance came walking toward me across the sidewalk,

quickly, as if he wanted me to catch him from falling. He winked with his eyes because of some complicity which I had obviously forgotten.

"What is it, what is it?" I asked.

"It's nothing" he said, "I just wanted to ask your opinion about the housemaid who kissed me in the hallway. Who is the girl? Have you seen her before? No? Neither have I. Was she even a housemaid? I had already meant to ask you that when she was walking down the stairs in front of us."

"I could tell by her red hands that she was a housemaid and not even the first housemaid, and when I put the money in her hand, I felt her coarse skin."

"But this only proves that she has been in service for some time, which is what I believe as well."

"You may be right there. In that lighting over there, one could not see everything but her face reminded me also of the older daughter of an officer I'm acquainted with."

"Not me," he said.

"This won't prevent me from going home; it's late and I have to be at the office tomorrow morning; mind you, one may sleep there as well, but it is no good." And I extended my hand to say goodbye to him.

"Ugh, the cold hand," he shouted, "I wouldn't want to go home with a hand like that. My dear friend, you should have let her kiss you as well; you missed out there; well, you can still make up for it. But sleep? On such a night? What are you thinking? Just consider how many happy thoughts will be smothered by the bedcovers when you sleep in your bed alone, and how many unhappy dreams are warmed by them."

"I don't smother anything, and I don't warm anything," I said.

"Oh, come on, you're such a comedian," he concluded. At the same time he continued walking, and I followed him without noticing, for I was pondering his remark.

I thought I understood from his remark that my acquaintance saw something in me which wasn't in me, but which raised his respect for me because of the assumption. Good thing, then, that I hadn't gone home. Who knows, this person next to me, thinking of housemaids and such things with his mouth steaming in the cold, was perhaps able to appreciate me in front of people without me having to do anything to earn it. Just let the girls not ruin him for me! May they kiss and squeeze him, after all that's their duty and his prerogative, but they shouldn't take him away from me. When they kiss him, they also kiss me a little, in a way; with the corner of their mouths so to speak;

but if they take him away, then they steal him from me. And he should always stay with me, always; who should protect him if not me. He is so stupid. So someone says to him in February: You, come up to Petrin Hill, and he comes along. And what if he falls down, what if he catches a cold, what if a jealous man running out of Post Street assaults him? What will happen to me then; will I just be kicked out of the world? I would love to see that! No, he won't get rid of me.

Tomorrow he would talk to Miss Anna, about ordinary things first, as is natural, but then suddenly he wouldn't be able to hold back anymore: Yesterday, Annie, during the night, after our party, you know, I was with a person as you have most certainly never met one. He looks – how to describe him – he looks like a dangling pole with a black-haired skull on top. His body is draped with lots of small, dull yellow pieces of cloth that covered him completely, for in yesterday's calm they lay flat. What, Annie, you've lost your appetite? Well, in that case it's my fault, because I told the whole thing badly. If only you'd seen him, how timidly he was walking next to me, how he could tell that I was in love, which wasn't hard to do, and walked ahead alone quite a distance so as to not disturb me in my state. Annie, I think you would have laughed a little and would have been a little afraid, but I, I enjoyed his presence. And where were you, Annie? You were in your bed, and Africa was just as far away as your bed. At times I truly felt as if the starry sky was rising with the breaths of his flat chest. You think, I'm exaggerating? No, Annie, upon my soul, no. Upon my soul, which belongs to you, no.

And I did not absolve my acquaintance – we were taking our first steps on Francis Quay – of the least part of the embarrassment he had to feel when talking this way. At the time my thoughts segued into one another, for the Vltava and the neighborhoods on the other shore lay in a joint darkness. Several lights were shining over there and toying with my gazing eyes.

We crossed the road to get down to the river railing, there we stood. I found a tree to lean on. Since a cold breeze was blowing from the water, I put on my gloves, sighed for no reason, just as one might at night in front of a river, and then I wanted to walk on. But my acquaintance was staring into the water and didn't budge. Then he stepped closer to the railing, his legs were already on the iron, propped up his elbows, and placed his forehead into his hands. What else? I was freezing already and had to turn up the collar of my coat. My acquaintance stretched himself, his back, his shoulders, his neck, and held his upper body, now resting on his taut arms, bent over the railing.

"Oh, memories, I know," I said. "Yes, remembering in itself is sad, and its object even more so! Don't indulge in such things; it's not for you and not for me. It only weakens one's present position – nothing is more plain – without strengthening the former, apart from the fact that the former doesn't need strengthening. Do you think that I don't have memories? Oh, ten for each one of yours. Now, for example, I might remember sitting on a bench in L. It was in the evening, also on the riverbank. In the summer, of course. And as is my habit on such an evening, I pulled my legs up and wrapped my arms around them. I had rested my head against the wooden backrest of the bench, from where I gazed at the cloudlike mountains on the other bank. A tender violin played at the riverside hotel. Now and then, there were trains with gleaming smoke moving on both banks."

My acquaintance interrupted me, turning around suddenly; it almost looked as if he were astonished to still see me here. "Ah, I could tell you so much more," I said, nothing more.

"Just think, and it always turns out that way," he started. "As I was descending my stairs today to take a short stroll before the evening party, I had to wonder about my hands swinging back and forth in my cuffs; and it was so funny how they did that. That is when I thought to myself right away: Wait, something's going to happen today. And it did, too." This he said upon leaving already and smiled at me out of his big eyes.

So this is how far I had come. He could tell me such things, smile and make big eyes at me. And I, I had to restrain myself from putting my arm around his shoulders and kissing his eyes as a reward for having absolutely no use for me. But the worst was that even that could no longer do any harm because it wouldn't change anything, for I had to leave now, leave no matter what.

While I was still trying to find a way to stay with my acquaintance even just a little longer, it occurred to me that my tall form might bother him, next to which, in his mind, he appeared short. And this circumstance distressed me so much – true, it was late at night and we encountered almost no one – that I hunched my back enough for my hands to touch my knees when walking. So that my acquaintance wouldn't notice my intention, I changed my posture very gradually, and tried to divert his attention from me, even turning him toward the river at one time and with my outstretched hand pointing out the trees on Archer Island and the reflection of the bridge lights in the river.

But with a brisk turn he looked at me – I wasn't quite finished – and said: "Now what is that? You're all crooked! What are you doing?"

"You're absolutely right," I said, my head at the seam of his trousers, which is why I couldn't look up properly either. "What a keen eye you have!"

"Oh, come on! Stand up straight, will you! How ridiculous!"

"No," I said looking at the ground which was very close, "I'm staying just as I am."

"Now, I have to tell you this, you can be really irritating. You're holding us up for nothing! So, stop it after all!"

"The way you yell! On a quiet night like this," I said.

"Well, just as you please," he added, and after a while: "it's a quarter to one." He had apparently seen the time on the clock of the Mill Tower.

And then I stood as though pulled up by my hair. I kept my mouth open for a moment so that my agitation could escape through my mouth. I understood: he was sending me away. There was no place for me with him, and if there happened to be one, it was not to be found here at any rate. Why, by the way, was I so intent on staying with him. No, I needed to go away – and right away at that – to my relatives and friends who were waiting for me. And if I had no relatives and friends, however, I had to help myself (there was no use complaining!), only I shouldn't leave from here any less rapidly. For around him nothing would work in my favor anymore, not my height, not my appetite, not my cold hand. If however, it was my opinion that I needed to stay with him, it was a dangerous opinion.

"I didn't need your announcement," I said, which was the truth.

"Thank God, that you're finally standing up straight. All I said was that it was a quarter to one."

"Never mind," I said and put two fingernails in the gaps between my shivering teeth. "If I don't need your announcement, I need an explanation even less. I actually don't need anything but your mercy. Please, please take back what you just said!"

"That it's a quarter to one? With great pleasure, even more so since it's already long past a quarter to now."

He raised his right arm, twitched his hand and listened to the castanet sound of his cuff bracelet.

Now, it seemed, was the time for the murder. I'll stay with him, and he'll wield the knife, which he's already holding by its handle in his pocket, up along his coat and then against me. It's unlikely that he'll be surprised by how easy it all is, but then he may be, too, who knows. I won't scream, I'll only glare at him as long as my eyes can stand it.

"Well?" he said.

In front of a distant coffeehouse with black windowpanes a policeman was skidding over the cobbles like an ice skater. His saber was in his way; he took it in his hand, slid along for a long stretch and turned almost in an arc at the end. He finally let out a faint shriek, and, tunes in his head, he began to skate once again.

It was this policeman who, two hundred steps from an imminent murder only saw and heard himself, that made me feel some sort of fear. I realized that I was finished, whether I let myself be stabbed to death or whether I ran away. But wasn't it better to run away then and thereby expose myself to the more laborious, thus more painful death. I couldn't think immediately of the advantages of this way to die, but then I couldn't spend my last moment looking for reasons. There was time for that later on, once I had only made my decision, and I had made my decision.

I had to run away, it was as simple as that. Upon turning left to the Charles Bridge, I could slip into Charles Street on the right. It was angled; there were dark entranceways and taverns that were still open; there was no need to despair.

As we emerged from under the arch at the end of the quay onto the Knights of the Cross Square, I ran into the street with raised arms. But in front of a small door to the Seminar Church I fell, for there was a step I hadn't expected. It made some noise; the next streetlight was far enough; I lay in the dark.

A fat woman with a small lamp came out of a tavern opposite to see what had happened in the street. The piano continued playing, fainter, just with one hand, for the pianist had turned toward the half-open door, which was now opened completely by a man in a high-buttoned overcoat. He spat and squeezed the woman so hard that she had to lift up the small lamp to protect it. "Nothing happened," he called into the room; then they both turned back, went inside, and the door closed again.

When I tried to get up, I fell again. "It's black ice," I said and felt a pain in my knee. And yet, I was glad that the people from the tavern hadn't seen me and that I could remain lying there until dawn.

My acquaintance must have gone to the bridge, unaware of my departure, for he joined me only after some time. I didn't notice that he was surprised when he bent down to me – lowering little more than his neck, just like a hyena – and stroked me with his soft hand. He went up and down my cheekbones, and then placed his palm on my forehead: "You've hurt yourself, haven't you? Well, it's black ice, and one has to be careful – didn't you tell me so yourself? Your head is hurting? It isn't? The knee, oh well. That's some nasty business."

But it didn't occur to him to lift me up. I supported my head with my right hand – my elbow was on a cobblestone – and said: "Here we are together again." And since I felt that fear again, I pressed both of my hands against his shins so as to push him away. "Go away, go away," I said.

He had his hands in his pockets and gazed across the empty street, then to the Seminar Church and then up to the sky. Finally, when there was the loud noise of a carriage driving around in one of the surrounding streets, he remembered me: "Now why aren't you saying anything, my dear friend? Are you sick? Well, why aren't you getting up? Should I try to find a carriage? If you want, I can get you some wine from the tavern over there. But you can't just lie here in the cold. And, besides, we were headed for Petrin Hill."

"Of course," I said and stood up by myself, but in a lot of pain. I wobbled and had to sternly fix my eyes on the statue of Charles IV to be sure of my stance. But not even this would have helped, had I not remembered that I was loved by a girl with a black velvet ribbon around her neck, if not ardently, but faithfully. And how sweet of the moon to shine on me, too, and out of modesty I was about to go stand under the arch of the bridge tower when I realized that it was only natural for the moon to shine on everything. So I spread my arms with joy so as to fully enjoy the moon. –And it felt easy to me when, making casual swimming strokes with my arms, I advanced without effort and pain. Why had I never tried this before! My head floated well in the cool air, and it was my right knee that flew best; I praised it by patting it. And I remembered that I couldn't really stand an acquaintance once, who was probably still walking below me, and the only thing that made me glad about the whole thing was that my memory was good enough to even recall such immaterial details. But I shouldn't think so much, for I had to go on swimming if I didn't want to sink too much. And just so that no one could say later that anyone could swim above the ground and it wasn't worth mentioning, I raised myself above the railing by speeding up and swam circles around each statue of a saint I encountered.

At the fifth – as I was moving above the sidewalk with my unnoticeable strokes – my acquaintance took my hand. So I stood on the sidewalk again and felt a pain in my knee.

"Always," said my acquaintance holding me with one hand, pointing toward the statue of St. Ludmila with the other, "I have always loved the hands of this angel here to the left. Just look how delicate they are! True angel's hands! Have you ever seen anything like it? Not you, but I have, for I kissed hands tonight–"

For me there was a third way to perish now. I didn't have to let myself be stabbed; I didn't have to run away, I could simply fling myself into the air. Let him go up to his Petrin Hill, I won't bother him, I won't even bother him by running away.

And now I shouted: "Start the stories! I don't want to hear any snippets anymore. Tell me everything, from beginning to end. I won't listen to anything less, let me tell you. But I'm dying to hear everything."

When he looked at me, I didn't shout quite as much anymore. "And you can trust my discretion! Tell me whatever is on your mind. You've never had as discreet a listener as me."

And very softly, close to his ear, I said: "And you don't need to be afraid of me, that's absolutely unnecessary."

I heard him laugh.

I

Then – with verve as if it wasn't the first time – I leapt onto my acquaintance's shoulders, and, by pumping my fists into his back, brought him to a light trot. When he continued to stomp somewhat reluctantly and sometimes even stopped, I kicked my boots into his stomach a few times to liven him up. It worked, and, fast enough, we got ever farther into the interior of a large but still unfinished area.

The country road on which I was riding was stony and ascended considerably, but that was precisely what I liked about it, and I made it get even stonier and steeper. Whenever my acquaintance stumbled I pulled him up in the air by his collar, and whenever he sighed I punched him in the head. And I felt how healthy this evening ride was for me in this good mood, and to make him even more furious I made a strong headwind blow into us in long gusts.

Now I even exaggerated the bouncing motion of the ride on my acquaintance's broad shoulders, and, holding tight to his neck with both hands, I bent my head far back and watched the varying clouds that, weaker than I, were flying heavily in the wind. I laughed and trembled with daring. My coat spread out and gave me strength. I pressed my hands together firmly, choking my acquaintance in doing so.

Only when the sky became gradually blocked from view by the branches of the trees that I made grow by the street, did I come to my senses.

"I don't know," I shouted soundlessly, "I really don't know. If nobody comes, well then, nobody comes. I've done nobody any harm, nobody has done me any harm, but nobody wants to help me, a lot of nobody. But that's not really true. It's just that nobody helps me, otherwise a lot of nobody would be lovely; I would quite like to take an outing (what do you say to that?) in the company of a lot of nobody. To the mountains, of course, where else? The way those lots of Nobody huddle together, their many arms stretched across or linked, their many feet tiny steps apart! It's understood that they're all in tailcoats. We walk just so so, an exquisite wind runs through the gaps we and our limbs leave open. Throats open up in the mountains. It's a wonder we don't sing."

Then my acquaintance fell, and when I examined him I found that his knee was badly injured. Since he was no longer of use to me, I left him on the rocks not unwillingly and whistled a few vultures down from the skies, which obediently sat down on him with earnest beaks to keep watch.

II

I walked on, carefree. But since, as a pedestrian, I dreaded the exertion of the mountainous road, I made the road become flatter and flatter and finally drop into a valley in the distance. The rocks vanished at my will, and the wind faded away.

I marched at a brisk pace, and since I was going downhill, I held my head high and stiffened my body and folded my arms behind my head. Since I love spruce forests, I went through such forests, and since I like looking at the starry sky in silence, the stars rose slowly on me in the sky, as is their nature. I saw only a few stretched clouds pulled through the air by a wind blowing only at their height, much to the surprise of this hiker.

Rather far across from my road, most likely separated from me by a river, I made a middling mountain arise whose brush-covered plateau bordered on the sky. I could clearly see even the tiny entanglements of the highest branches and their movements. This sight, common as it may be, delighted me so much that I, a small bird rocking on the twigs of those distant scrubby bushes forgot to make the moon come up – it already lay behind the mountain, surely fuming at the delay.

But now the cool gleam that precedes the rise of the moon spread over the mountain, and suddenly the moon hoisted itself up behind one of the restless bushes. I, however, had meanwhile looked the other way, and when I then peered in front of me and saw it all of a sudden, shining in almost all its roundness, I stopped with dull eyes, for my sloping road seemed to lead straight into this terrifying moon.

After a while I got used to it and dispassionately observed its difficulty in rising, until finally, it and I having moved toward one another quite a bit of the way, I felt a heavy drowsiness, which I thought to be a consequence of the exertion of the unusual walk. I walked with my eyes closed for some time, keeping myself awake only by the loud and regular clapping of my hands.

But then, as the road threatened to slip away under my feet and everything, weary like me, began to disappear, I hurried, with all my might, to scale the slope on the right side of the road so as to reach in time the high, tangled spruce forest where I was planning to sleep the night that lay probably ahead of us.

The haste was warranted. The cloudy stars already grew dark, and I saw the moon sink weakly into the sky as into choppy waters. The mountain already belonged to the dark, the road ended, crumbling, where I had turned toward the slope, and from inside the forest I heard the crashing of falling trees draw closer. Now I could have hurled myself down onto the moss to sleep right there, but since I'm afraid of sleeping on the forest floor, I crawled – the trunk swiftly slid down between the rings made of arms and legs – up onto a tree that swayed even without the wind; I lay down on a branch, with my head resting at the trunk, and hastily went to sleep as a squirrel of my fancy with a stiff tail sat rocking on the trembling end of the branch.

III

I was sleeping and entered the first dream with my entire being. In it I tossed and turned in fear and pain so that it couldn't bear it but also wasn't allowed to wake me, since I was only sleeping because the world around me had come to an end. And so I walked through this dream that was disrupted deep down and returned as if I was spared – having escaped sleep and the dream – to the villages of my homeland.

I heard the cars go by outside the garden fence; sometimes I glimpsed them through the gently stirring gaps in the foliage. How the wood in their spokes and shafts creaked in the hot summer! Laborers were returning from the fields, laughing so that it was a disgrace.

I sat on our small swing; I was relaxing among the trees in my parents' garden.

Outside the fence, it didn't let up. Running children went past in a heartbeat; grain carts with men and women on the sheaves and all around darkened the flowerbeds; toward evening I saw a gentleman slowly strolling with a cane, and a few girls, coming toward him arm in arm, stepped aside onto the grass as they said hello.

Then birds flew up in a spray; I followed them with my gaze, saw them soar in one breath, until I no longer felt that it was them that were soaring but rather that I was falling, and holding onto the ropes I started to sway a little out of weakness. Soon I was swaying harder, as the air blew cooler and trembling stars appeared instead of the soaring birds.

I was served my dinner at candlelight. Often I had both arms on the wooden board, and, already tired, I bit into my bread and butter. The openwork curtains bulged in the warm breeze, and once in a while some passerby would stop them with his hands when he wanted to get a good look at me and talk to me. Most of the time the candle went out quickly and the gathered mosquitoes buzzed around in the dark candle smoke for a while. If anyone asked me something from the window, I looked at him as if I was peering into the mountains or into sheer air, and he also didn't much care for my reply.

When one of them hopped over the windowsill and announced that the others were already in front of the house, I, of course, stood up with a sigh.

"Now, what are you sighing about? What's wrong? Is it some particular, some irremediable misfortune? Will we never recover from it? Is everything truly lost?"

Nothing was lost. We ran to the front of the house. "Thank God, there you are, after all! –You're just always late! –Why me? –Especially you, stay at home, if you don't want to come along. –No mercy! –What, no mercy? What are you saying?"

We pierced the evening with our heads. There was no daytime and no nighttime. One moment our vest buttons were rubbing against one another like teeth, the next we walked at a steady distance between us with fire in our mouths like animals in the tropics. Like cuirassiers in old wars, stomping and high up in the air, we drove one another down the short street and with this momentum in our legs farther up the road. A few of us went into the ditch; they had barely disappeared in front of the dark embankment when they were standing up on the dirt road like strangers, looking down.

"Come on down! –First you come up! –So that you can push us down, we don't think so, we're smart enough for that. –You're cowards, you want to say. Come on, come on! –You, really? You of all people are going to push us down? What would that look like?"

We went on the attack, were shoved in our chests and lay down in the grass of the ditch, tumbling and of our free will. Everything was evenly warm; we felt neither warmth nor cold in the grass; we only got tired.

Turned to the right side, a hand under the ear, one felt like falling asleep right there. One wanted to pick oneself up once more, chin raised, to drop into an even deeper ditch. Then, one arm held across, the legs blown to the side, one wanted to hurl oneself against the air to be sure to fall into an even deeper ditch. And one didn't want to ever stop doing that.

How one would properly stretch out to the utmost, especially in the knees, to sleep in the last ditch, one hardly thought of that and lay like a sick patient on one's back in the mood for crying. And one winked, when a boy, elbows at his hips, leapt from the embankment above us onto the road with dark soles.

The moon could already be seen at some height; a postal car passed in its light. A gentle wind came up all around; one could even feel it in the ditch, and the forest nearby started to rustle. Now one wasn't so eager to be alone anymore.

"Where are you? –Come here! –All of you together! –What are you hiding for, stop that nonsense! –Don't you know that the mail has already passed? –But no! Already passed? –Of course, it passed while you were sleeping. –Sleeping? Me? –Just shut up, you still look it. –Not at all. –Come on!"

We ran closer together; some held each other's hands; one couldn't carry one's head high up enough because we were going downhill. Someone whooped an Indian war cry; our legs broke into a gallop as never before; the wind lifted our hips when we jumped. Nothing could have stopped us; we were going so strongly that even in passing others we could fold our arms and calmly look around us.

We stopped on the bridge over the wild brook; those who had gone further, turned back. The water down there beat against rocks and roots, as if it weren't late in the evening already. There was no reason why not one of us leapt onto the railing of the bridge.

Behind shrubs in the distance a train emerged, all compartments were lit up; the glass panes securely lowered. One of us began to sing a popular tune, but we all wanted to sing. We sang much faster than the train was going, we swung our arms because voices weren't enough; our voices got us into a jam where we felt at ease. When one blends one's voice with those of others, one is caught as on a fishhook.

So we sang, the forest behind us, into the ears of the distant travelers. The grownups in the village were still awake; the mothers were making the beds for the night.

It was time. I kissed the one who was standing close to me, simply shaking hands with the three next ones, started to head back, no one was calling me. At the first crossroads where they could no longer see me, I turned, went back into the forest on dirt paths, and farther on. I hurried through the large forests, now the sunlight, now the moonlight, now on my back, now in my face. I was headed to the city in the south, of which it was said in our village:

"The kind of people that live there! Just think, they don't sleep!"
"And why not?"
"Because they don't get tired."
"And why not?"
"Because they're fools."
"Don't fools get tired?"
"How could fools get tired!

81

IV

There existed a time when I went to a church day after day for a girl I had fallen in love with prayed on her knees there for a half hour every evening, and during this time I could quietly contemplate her.

Once, when the girl hadn't come, and I couldn't help but gaze at the people in prayer, I noticed a young person who had thrown himself to the floor with the full length of his thin body. Now and again, with all of his body's strength he took his skull and, with a sigh, smashed it into his palms, which were resting on the stone floor.

There were only a few old women in the church; now and then they turned their wrapped little heads sideways to check on the praying man. This attention seemed to please him, for before each of his pious outbursts he let his eyes wander to see whether there were numerous onlookers.

Now, I thought this unseemly and decided to approach him when he left the church and simply ask him why he was praying in that fashion. For since my arrival in this town clarity was everything to me, even though I was really only irritated that my girl hadn't come.

But not until an hour later did he stand up, dust off his trousers for such a long time that I was about to shout: "Enough, enough, we can all see that you have trousers," make a careful sign of the cross and walk to the holy-water font with the heavy gait of a sailor.

I positioned myself between the font and the door and knew for sure that I wouldn't let him pass without an explanation. I contorted my mouth, which is the best preparation for a resolute speech, and leaned on my stretched-out right leg while balancing the left one on my toes because that gives me steadiness, as I have often experienced.

Now it is possible that this person had already eyed me when he splashed holy water on his face; my gaze may have caused him some trepidation even before, since he now made an unexpected dash for the door and left. Instinctively, I took another leap to hold him back. The glass door slammed shut. And when I stepped out the door just afterward, he was nowhere to be found; there were several narrow streets and a variety of traffic.

The next few days he stayed away but the girl came back and prayed again in the corner of a side chapel. She was wearing a black dress with transparent lace on her shoulders and neck – the crescent hem of her shift showing underneath – with the silk hanging in a well-tailored collar from the lower edge. And since the girl had come, I was glad to forget about that person and initially even paid him no mind when he returned to pray regularly as was his custom.

But he always walked past me in sudden haste, his face averted. However, when he was praying he gazed at me a lot. It almost was as though he were angry that I had not approached him and as though he thought that my attempt to approach him obligated me to finally do so for real. And when after a sermon, still following the girl, I ran into him in the semi-darkness, I thought I saw him smile.

Naturally, there was no such obligation to approach him, and I hardly had the desire to approach him anymore. Even one day, when I came running across the church square as the clock was already sounding seven, so that the girl was long gone from the church and there was only that man exerting himself in front of the altar railing, I still hesitated.

On my toes, I finally snuck to the doorway, handed a coin to the blind beggar sitting there, and squeezed in beside him behind the open door. There I may have sat for half an hour looking forward to the surprise I had in store for the praying man. But that did not last. Soon I very morosely let the spiders crawl over my clothes, and it was tiresome to bend forward when yet someone else stepped out of the darkness of the church breathing noisily.

Then he came as well. The ringing of the large bells had started a while ago, and it did not do him well, I noticed. He had to lightly feel the ground with his toes before actually treading.

I stood up, took a long stride and suddenly grabbed him. "Good evening," I said and pushed him, my hand on his collar, down the steps onto the lighted square.

When we got downstairs, he turned toward me as I was still holding him in the back, so that we were now standing chest to chest. "If only you would let go of me in the back!" he said. "I have no idea what you are suspecting me of, but I am innocent." Then he repeated once more: "Of course, I have no idea what you are suspecting me of."

"This is not about suspicion nor innocence. I ask you to stop talking about it. We are strangers to each other; our acquaintance is no older then the church steps are high. Where would we end up if we began to talk about our innocence at once."

"I absolutely agree with you," he said. "In fact, you said 'our innocence,' did you mean to suggest that once I had proved my innocence you would likewise have to prove yours. Is that what you meant?"

"Either that or something else," I said. "But the reason I approached you is only that I wanted to ask you something, remember that!"

"I would like to go home," he said and turned weakly.

"I believe you. Would I otherwise have approached you? You must not think that I approached you for the sake of your beautiful eyes."

"Aren't you being too sincere? Aren't you?"

"Do I have to tell you again that this is not about such matters? Why are you bringing sincerity or insincerity into this? I ask, you answer, and then goodbye. Then you can go home for all I care and as fast as you like."

"Wouldn't it be better if we got together some other time? At a more convenient hour? Perhaps in a coffeehouse? Besides, your fiancée left just a few minutes ago; you could easily catch up with her; she waited for such a long time."

"No," I yelled into the racket of a passing streetcar. "You can't get away from me. I'm liking you more and more. You are my lucky catch. I congratulate myself."

"Oh, God, you have what they call a healthy heart, and a block for a head. You call me a lucky catch, how happy you must feel! For my unhappiness is a shaky unhappiness, an unhappiness balancing on its tip, and if one touches it, it falls on the questioner. And therefore: Good night."

"Fine," I said, and surprised him by grabbing his right hand. "If you won't answer voluntarily, I'll force you. I'll follow you wherever you go, right and left, even up the stairs to your room, and in your room I'll sit down wherever there is space. Sure, just look at me, I can stand it. But how will you–"

I stepped up close to him and since he was taller than me by a head, I spoke into his throat. "But how will you find the courage to stop me?"

Stepping back, he now kissed both of my hands in turn and wet them with his tears. "It is impossible to deny you anything. Just as you knew that I would like to go home, I already knew earlier that I couldn't deny you anything. All I'm asking is that we go into that side street over there." I nodded, and we went there. When a carriage separated us and I stayed behind, he signaled to me with both hands to make me hurry.

But there he didn't content himself with the darkness of the street where street lights stood far apart from one another and were mounted almost at the level of the second floor but led me into the low hallway of an old building under a small dripping light hanging in front of the wooden stairs.

Spreading his handkerchief over the hollow of a worn-out step, he invited me to sit: "You can ask better questions when sitting; I'll stand so I can give better answers. But no tormenting!"

So I sat down because he took the matter so seriously, but then I felt compelled to say: "You lead me to this hole as though we're conspirators, whereas I'm tied to you only by curiosity, you to me only by fear. All I want to ask you is why you pray like that in church. The way you carry on there! Like a complete fool! How ludicrous that is, how disagreeable for the onlookers and how unbearable to the pious!"

He had pressed his body against the wall, moving just his head freely in the air: "It's just a misunderstanding, for the pious consider my behavior natural, and the rest consider it pious."

"My annoyance is the refutation of that."

"Your annoyance – supposing it is true annoyance – only proves that you neither belong to the pious nor to the rest."

"You're right, I was exaggerating a bit when I said that your behavior annoyed me. No, it made me a little curious as I said quite correctly in the beginning. But you, to whom do you belong?"

"Oh, it is just fun to have people look at me, to cast a shadow on the altar now and then, so to speak."

"Fun?" I asked, frowning.

"No, if you really want to know. Don't be angry with me for not expressing myself properly. Not fun, it's a need I have, the need to be nailed down by these gazes for a short hour, with the whole town around me–"

"What are you saying," I shouted, far too loudly for his little remark and for the low hallway, but then I was afraid to fall silent or lower my voice. "Really, what are you saying. Now I know, by God, that I've had a hunch from the start about the state you are in. Isn't it this fever, this seasickness on dry land, a sort of leprosy. Isn't it so that for all your fervor you can't content yourself with the true names of things, that they don't satisfy you, and you hastily slap accidental names on them now. Just quick, quick! But as soon as you run away from them, you'll forget their names. The poplar in the fields that you named the 'Tower of Babel' for you didn't care to know that it was a poplar tree, is swaying again namelessly, and you would have to name it 'Noah when he was drunk.'"

He interrupted me: "I'm glad I didn't understand what you were saying."

Flustered, I said quickly: "Your being glad shows me that you understood."

"Haven't I said so before? It's impossible to deny you anything."

I placed my hand on a higher step, leaned back, and, in this all but invincible posture, which is the last resort of wrestlers, I said: "Excuse me, but it is insincerity to throw an explanation I gave you back at me."

That's when he took courage. He knotted his hands so as to give his body unity and said, with some reluctance: "You ruled out disputes over sincerity right from the start. And really, nothing matters more to me than making you completely understand my way of praying. So do you know why I pray like that?"

He was testing me. No, I didn't know and I didn't want to know. I hadn't wanted to come here, either, I told myself at the time, but that person had virtually forced me to listen to him. All I needed to do now was shake my head no, and everything would be all right, but I couldn't make myself do so at that moment.

The person opposite me smiled. Then he squatted down on his knees and told me with a sleepy grimace: "Now I can finally tell you, too, why I let you approach me. Out of curiosity, out of hope. Your gaze has been comforting me for a long time. And I hope to learn from you how things really stand which sink around me like falling snow, whereas for others, even a small shot glass in front of them on the table stands firm like a monument."

Since I remained silent and only a spontaneous twitch flashed over my face, he asked: "You don't believe that people feel that way? You really don't? Oh, come on! Once, as a young child, when opened my eyes after a short nap, yet not quite reassured of my life, I heard my mother call down from the balcony in a natural voice: 'What are you doing, my dear? How hot it is today!' A woman replied from the garden: 'I'm just having a snack out in the garden.' She said so without thinking and not very clearly as if that woman had expected the question, and my mother the reply."

I felt that it was my turn now, so I put my hand in my back pocket and pretended to search for something there. I wasn't searching for anything, but only sought to change my appearance so as to show my involvement in the conversation. I said that this was such a curious incident and that I didn't comprehend it in the least. I also added that I didn't believe it was true and that it must have been invented for a particular purpose, which I couldn't understand at that moment. Then I closed my eyes to shut out the bad lighting.

"Just look, take courage, so in this instance you agree with me and stopped me to tell me so out of unselfishness. I lose one hope, and gain another.

Well, why should I be ashamed that I don't walk upright and in strides, don't bang my cane on the pavement and brush against the clothes of people who noisily pass by. Rather, shouldn't I rightly and defiantly lament that I skip along the houses as a shadow without distinct contours, at times disappearing into the panes of the shop windows.

What days I am having! Why is everything built so poorly that tall buildings occasionally crumble for no apparent reason. I then clamber over the rubble piles and ask everyone I meet: 'How could this happen! In our city – a new building – how many does that make today! – Just think about it.' But no one can give me an answer.

Frequently people collapse and lie dead in the street. Then all the shopkeepers open their doors laden with merchandise, approach with agility, take the body into a house, reemerge, a smile around their lips and eyes, and the talk begins: 'Good morning – the sky is pale – I sell many kerchiefs – Yes, the war.' I hurry into the house and, having timidly raised my hand with my crooked finger a few times, I finally knock on the janitor's little window. 'My good man,' I say amiably, 'I understand a dead man was brought in here just now. Would you be so kind as to show him to me?' And since he shakes his head as if he couldn't decide, I add: 'Be careful! I'm with the secret police, and I demand to see the dead man at once.' Now he's no longer undecided: 'Get out!' he yells. 'Now such lowlifes make a habit of creeping around here! There is no dead man here; maybe next door.' I say goodbye and leave.

But then when I have to cross a large square, I forget everything. If such large squares are built just out of exuberance, then why don't they build a balustrade across the square? A southwesterly wind is blowing for once today. The spire of the city hall is drawing small circles. All the windowpanes are roaring and the lampposts are bending like bamboo. The Virgin Mary's cloak on the column is swirling, and the air is tugging at it. Doesn't anyone see? The gentlemen and ladies who should be walking on the cobblestones are levitating. When the wind lets up, they stop, exchange a few words and bow in salute, but as soon as it starts gusting again, they cannot resist and all raise their feet all in unison. They do have to hold on to their hats, but they make happy eyes and have no complaint whatsoever about the weather. I'm the only one who is afraid.'"

To that I could say: "The story you were telling earlier of your mother and the woman in the garden, I don't find it strange at all. Not only have I heard and experienced many such stories, I've even been involved in some. The thing is quite natural. Do you really think I couldn't have asked the same thing, had I been on that balcony in the summer, and replied the same thing from the garden? It's such an ordinary incident."

When I had said that, he finally seemed placated. He said that I was nicely dressed and that he liked my necktie very much. And what a smooth complexion I had. And that confessions became most lucid when they were retracted.

But I had been trying to cheer myself up for some time already. I just wanted to say a few quick words, if only to move my face away from his a little more. For it was already so close above me that I had to bend back; otherwise I would have bumped into his forehead. For the time being I silently laughed into his face with my mouth open, then looked away for as long as it took for the laughter to subside, turned my eyes back, but couldn't help but laugh again right away, and turned away again. And through all this, I wanted nothing so much as to be home in my bed, the wall in front of me and everything else behind my back.

It was also getting hot in the hallway, making my face glow. For a little relief, I bent my head back even further until my hat fell off my head. The ceiling of the vaulted staircase was painted with reddish cherubs and flowers. I looked at it and with my bare hand wiped off the sweat from my forehead and cheeks.

I still wanted to get up, push the man away from me with all my weight, open the door and breathe the fresh air outside, as I needed it. I did get up, hit my heels hard on the ground, while he jumped back a little behind his upheld palms, I clutched the wooden railing and climbed around to get used to standing, but he, tall as he was, lay down on the stairs, arched the small of his back, lowered himself again, pushed his legs out and stretched out his arms on a higher step so that the fingers of his left hand were sticking up on the wall, while those of his right hand were knocking against the base of the staircase.

I stood outside the railing and put my entwined hands over my mouth. He slowly turned his head on the edge of a step until he could look me straight in the face and said: "You're standing there like a loafer on the quay, and I'm lying here as if I had drowned."

"That wouldn't be so bad," I thought, lifted my head and said: "You really made yourself comfortable." My lips were so dry that I couldn't believe it and had to touch them.

He brushed off my remark and said: "It used to be the other way around, only that I wasn't standing as apathetically as you are now."

I repeated what I had said: "I said that you really made yourself comfortable here," and compelled by these words, I smiled.

"Do you regret it?" he said and suddenly closed his eyes. "If you regret it, just open the door and breathe the air outside the way you need it."

"You!" I shouted – this was a reproach – ran around the railing in small steps, blindly, as if in battle, and dropping down next to him I started to cry on his chest.

"Hush! Hush!" he said and stroked my hair. "You fool, now I can't get up! Are you trying to crush me at all cost! No, unless you're a fool! "

But in the rush of crying I couldn't think of any better place to put my face, and so I left it where it was.

"That you didn't notice!" he continued. "I've been meaning to make you cry from the start. I didn't say a word without this intention, until I had finally almost given up hope that I would succeed. Then I go and make a joke at the end, and you really do me the favor and start crying. Come on! Shame on you!"

"I'm not crying anymore," I said and gazed at him, resting my chin on him. "With a friend like you, why would I cry." But I kept crying, for I couldn't stop right then.

"That would be really silly," he said, almost contorting his neck to see me, took the handkerchief from my hand and dried my eyes. "Discontentment wouldn't be any sort of reason to cry, but where in the world would you find a reason for discontentment! It should stay just the way it is. The fear that it might change would be me my utmost concession."

"For look – I'm telling *you* this – we construct quite useless war machines, towers, walls, curtains of silk, and we might wonder a lot about that if we had the time. And we remain suspended in the air, we don't fall, we flutter, even though we're almost uglier than bats. In turn hardly anyone can prevent us from saying on a beautiful day: 'Now, what a beautiful day.' For already we are settled in on this earth, and we live on the basis of our consent."

At that he gave me such a slap on the back that I jumped, got up and preferred to stay bent over him, my hands on his shoulders. "You should pay better attention," he said, laughing and shaking me with him. "Did you know that we're like tree trunks in the snow? They seem to lie simply flush, and one should be able to push them aside with a little prod. But no, one can't, for they're firmly attached to the ground. Never mind, even that is only an illusion."

"No, you see," I said. Then he pushed my hands aside, I fell with my mouth onto his mouth and was immediately kissed.

"Well, and now let's go," he said and we both stood up.

"But your mother!" I added. "She must have been quite some woman! If only I had had such a mother!"

"What use was she to me? Forget the story!" he said dusting off my overcoat with my handkerchief.

"Sure, go ahead and forbid me even that!" I said and took a step so that he had to follow me with the handkerchief.

"What do you want?" he said. "It's just a story I made up. It's so easy to tell that it is made up."

"Oh, I know," I said.

"You don't know a thing!" he said. "And the party you were supposed to go to tonight?"

"True, the party! Imagine I would have completely forgotten about the party! Such forgetfulness! Such forgetfulness is completely new to me, by the way."

"Thanks to me!"

"That is probably so! Will you at least accompany me there? It's nor far. Will you?"

"Of course."

"And come up, too? Please!"

"No, not that."

"But why? And what if I ask you really nicely? Then you'll come along, won't you?"

"Let's just go! It's late!"

"I don't know if I'll even go to the party without you."

"Well, come on! Let's go! You're helpless since you seem to like it best here."

"Almost," I said, biting my lower lip and looking at him. He put one arm around my, opened the door and pushed me outside in front of him.

So we stepped out of the hallway, under the sky. My friend blew away some crushed cloudlets, so that the now uninterrupted expanse of stars offered itself to us. Yet he walked with difficulty, but didn't make a very elegant impression, he rather looked like a sick peasant. He placed his hand on my shoulder as if to be really close to me, but he really just wanted to support himself; I allowed it and even pulled his hand higher up on my shoulder by his fingertips.

In front of the house where I was invited we stopped.

"Well, goodbye, then," I said.

"So here it is?"

"Yes, here."

"It wasn't far."

"Just as I said."

"You," I said and gave him a quick nudge with my knee, "don't fall asleep." When he opened his eyes, my eyes slid off his face everywhere; as much as I tried to keep them up, I kept seeing only his throat. "You almost fell asleep," I said, and since I didn't want to touch my disintegrating face and yet tried to make it firm somehow, I smiled to make it seem that I thought what I had said was a joke. I noticed this right away and was cold under my coat, without losing the sense of the moderate coolness of the night and the warmth of the coat. So the other world was trying to march away or fly away over my head the very moment I recognized it, and I was made to believe that the nudge of the knee had actually awakened it.

"You are really rough," he said, holding his lower lip a little behind the upper perhaps on account of his sleeping, "and then he goes and wakes me with his knee. And in general you are rough with me."

"You're so sensitive! Was it really that bad? Now you have complained in public about me. This means that I'll have to show myself, too." I turned toward the street and lifted my hat for the public.

"But you shouldn't push me."

"Of course, I shouldn't. But you would have fallen asleep if I hadn't woken you."

"I really did sleep, don't you even see that anymore."

Among my classmates I was stupid, but not the stupidest. And even though some of my teachers still frequently asserted the latter to my parents and me, they only did so out of the delusion of many people who believe they have conquered half of the world by daring to pass such a radical judgment.

But it was a generally held belief that I was stupid, and there was good evidence that could easily be shared if, say, the need arose to enlighten a stranger whose initial impression of me hadn't been so bad and who expressed it in front of others.

This often annoyed me and made me cry, too. And at the time those were the only moments when I felt insecure about the present predicament and desperate about the future one, theoretically insecure, theoretically desperate, however, for when there was a task to be done a moment later, I was self-assured and doubtless, almost like the actor storming out of the wing, pausing for a moment far from center stage, his hands placed on his forehead if you will, as the passion which will be needed a moment later has grown so great that he cannot hide it, even though he bites his lips with narrowed eyes. The present, half-past insecurity elevates the rising passion, and the passion boosts the insecurity. Insecurity continually arises anew, enclosing both and us.

That is why meeting strangers made me miserable. I was already uneasy when some of them gazed at me along their nasal walls, just as one looks through binoculars out of a small house across the lake or even into the mountains and thin air. Ridiculous claims were presented, statistical lies, geographical errors, false doctrines, as illicit as they were absurd, or passable political views, respectable opinions on current events, laudable ideas, surprising the speaker almost as much as the audience, and everything was proved again by a gaze of the eyes, a grasp at the edge of a table or a leap from a chair. As soon as they started this, they stopped gazing at one constantly and strictly, for their upper bodies curved forward or backward from their usual postures of their own accord. Some virtually forgot about their clothing (buckled their legs sharply at the knee to stand merely on their toes or pressed their coat hard against their chests in creases), others didn't, many held onto a pince-nez, a fan, a pencil, a lorgnette, a cigarette with their fingers, and even if they had a firm skin the faces of most were heating up. Their gaze slid off us just as a raised arm drops.

I was admitted to my natural state; I was free to wait and then listen, or to leave and lie down on my bed, which I always looked forward to, for I was often sleepy, since I was shy. It was like a long break at a dance where only a few people decide to leave; most of them just stand or sit here or there, waiting, as the musicians, about whom no one loses a thought, have a snack somewhere before playing on. Only it wasn't as quiet, and not everyone was aware of the break; rather there were several balls going on in the hall at the same time.

Through all this I still felt my fear, this fear of a man to whom, entirely numb, I had extended my hand, whose name I didn't know, if not one of his friends had called out his first name, and opposite whom I ended up sitting for hours, completely calm, merely a little exhausted – the way young people are – even by the rare gazes this adult directed at me.

Let us suppose I had let my eyes meet his several times, and, unoccupied as I was, and, since I knew that no one was counting on me, I had tried to peer into his good blue eyes for a little longer, even if this meant that one basically left the party. And if it didn't succeed, this proved as little as the attempt did. Well, I didn't succeed; I proved this inability right from the beginning and couldn't conceal it even for a minute later on either, but the feet of inept ice skaters also each want to go in another direction and both away from the ice. If there were an otherwise able

(gap in the text)

and a smart one, but who was neither before nor next to nor behind this hundred so as to be noticed immediately and easily, but who was amid the others, so that one could only glimpse him from a very much elevated place, and even then one only saw him disappear. This is how my father judged me, who had been a very respected and successful man within the political world in my fatherland. I overheard this remark when I was about seventeen years old, reading an American Indian book with the door ajar in a room next to my father's room. I took note of his words at the time, I remembered them, but they didn't make the least impression on me. Just as it happens most of the time that general judgments about them do not have any effect on young people. For whether they are still entirely at peace with themselves, or constantly reflecting back on themselves, they sense their own nature loud and strong, like a military march.

But the general judgment is based on, to them, unknown premises, unknown intentions, which makes it inaccessible from all sides; it pretends to be a person strolling on the island in the pond where there are neither boats nor bridges, he hears the music, but is not heard in turn.

By this I don't mean to attack the logic of young people

7

This choice should be thoroughly welcomed. Herewith a man enters into a position for which he is, indeed, philosophically suited, and the position receives the man it needs.

Dr. Marschner's unremitting capacity for work has qualified him for such far-reaching and in itself diversified activity that no one individual can easily do him justice, for one can only grasp part of this activity at a time. As the Institute's long-time Secretary Dr. Marschner knows the entire apparatus, all the better since he himself has been involved in its improvement as far as his influence has permitted up to this point; he has employed his extensive advocatory knowledge and skills for the Institute. Experts know and appreciate him as a meticulous writer; his influence on drafts of social legislation of recent years (liability laws in particular) is not to be underestimated. As a speaker he has appeared at the great international insurance conventions, and in Prague's lecture halls we have heard his always welcome, highly instructive interventions dealing with insurance issues of general importance and timeliness; as a lecturer at the Technical University he puts his mutually complementary knowledge and experiences to use so as to prepare the studying youth for the more and more urgent issues of the social insurance business. He established the insurance curriculum at the Technical University and proved particularly suitable for this, since he is also an expert in actuarial theory; his pedagogical gift became evident to a larger public in his course on insurance at the Prague Commercial College and was publicly acknowledged when he was appointed member of the State Board of Examiners. Let us summarize: He is a man who has worked and continues to work very effectively, very persistently in all areas of his discipline and who engages in an active professional exchange with all generations of our times.

All of this, of course, is of utmost importance and casts Dr. Marschner as an expert in such a light that, in his field, no one in Bohemia can claim to measure up to him, without a certain audacity, we might add.

However, in view of this very responsible, greatly visible position at the head of such a complex operation that Dr. Marschner has now received, the human aspect of his scientific and social activity is actually of even greater importance.

There is not a step he has taken that was not informed by honest objectivity; open action is natural to him; sure of himself – in this he may be particularly unique – he has sought no distinction other than the one he has found in his work; it has been his sole ambition to aspire to the sphere of activity where he was needed; his impartiality, his sense of justice are unwavering, and the Institute's employees will probably appreciate their good fortune to receive precisely him as their superior. Those familiar with his writings, his professional work, his personality are moved by his strong and vivid empathy with the situation of the workers, who have an avid friend in him who will, however, always respect the limitations the law and the current economic circumstances impose on his efforts. He has never made promises, leaving that up to others (whose nature it is, who need it, and finally who have the time for it), but he has always done the actual work himself, quietly, without intentionally drawing public attention and relentless only toward himself. Therefore he probably has, apart perhaps from the realm of scholarship, no opponents; if he had any, it would be a sad opposition.

Among diverse influences the Institute's board followed only practical reasons and thereby made this fortunate choice. For this it deserves our joint gratitude: the government, the employers, the workers, and the civil servants.

Complaints against the Institute, justified and unjustified, have accumulated in the past few years, but one thing is certain now: good work will be done, and the required and useful reforms possible within the current laws will be implemented.

Little soul
you leap in dance
lay your head in balmy air
you lift your feet from glistening grass
blowing in the breeze in gentle stirs

We didn't really know if we had the desire to see an occult draftsman. And just as it happens that a slight and unnoticed, always existent desire almost wishes to escape with increasing attention and feels held in its due place by a soon-to-emerge reality, we had been discreetly curious for a long time to see draw before us one of those ladies who with inner but unfamiliar force draw one a flower from high up in the moon, then deep-sea plants, then heads with great coiffures and helmets distorted by ornamentation, and other things, just as they have to.

One does not immediately know whether one has the desire to see an occult draftsman.

[10]

Samuel knows at least all of Richard's superficial intentions and skills through and through, but since he is used to thinking precisely and comprehensively, he is even surprised by small, not entirely expected irregularities in Richard's statements, and they make him wonder. For Richard the embarrassing aspect of his friendship is the fact that Samuel never needs any support that is not publicly announced; therefore, simply out of a sense of fairness, he never wants any support on his part to be felt and consequently does not tolerate any subordination in their friendship. It is his unconscious principle that that which one admires in a friend, for example, one does not so much admire in the friend but in the fellow human, and that friendship then must begin deep there, underneath all differences. This, however, hurts Richard's feelings, who would often like to surrender to Samuel, who would often love to make him understand what an excellent person he is, but who could only begin to do so if he foresaw the permission to never have to stop. At any rate, from this relationship imposed by Samuel he gains the questionable advantage of elevating himself above Samuel, well aware of the independence he has so far outwardly maintained, of seeing him become small, and of making, if only inwardly, demands on him, whereas otherwise he would have liked to ask Samuel to make them against him. Hence, Samuel's need for Richard's money, for example, at least in his mind, has nothing to do with their friendship, whereas Richard already regards this view as something admirable since this, Samuel's, need for money on the one hand embarrasses him and makes him valuable on the other, both at the core of his friendship. That is why Richard, despite being a slower thinker embedded in the wealth of his insecurities, actually judges Samuel more accurately than Samuel him, since the latter, albeit with good reasoning power, thinks the safest way to encapsulate Richard in judgment is the shortest, and so he does not wait for him to settle into his true shape. Therefore it is actually Samuel who is the aside speaker and the withdrawer in their relationship. It seems that he takes away ever more from the friendship, whereas Richard contributes ever more on his end, so that, strangely and yet naturally enough, the friendship keeps shifting toward Samuel until it stops in Stresa where Richard is tired for all their well-being, Samuel,

100

however, is so strong that he can do anything and even encircles Richard until – foreseen by Samuel, no longer expected by Richard, and hence endured with death wishes – the final stab occurs in Paris, which brings the friendship to rest at last. Despite this situation, which might rule this out outwardly, Richard is the more conscientious one in the friendship, at least up to Stresa, for he set out on the journey with a finished but false friendship, Samuel, however, with a friendship that took a long time to begin but is true. For this reason, Richard reaches ever deeper inside himself on the journey, perceives more casually, with half glances, but with a stronger sense of connection, whereas Samuel – his character demands this as much as his friendship – thus doubly impelled, can and must perceive quickly and truly out of his true inner self and virtually sustained Richard a lot of the time. As conscientious as Richard, obliged anew by every little incident, is in his friendship until Stresa, and always ready to give explanations in this regard that no one demands and at least of all he, for he struggles enough to bear the mere manifestations of their changing friendship, whereas he is numb toward everything else that comes with the journey, finds it difficult to deal with the changing hotels, does not comprehend simple correlations that might not give him any trouble at home, is often very serious, but by no means out of boredom, why, not even out of the desire to be patted on the cheek by Samuel, has a great desire for music and women. Samuel only knows French, Richard French and Italian, which in Italy, without either one of them having aimed at it and even though Richard knows that the opposite would be more likely, puts him in a sort of subservient position to Samuel whenever it comes to enquiries. Also, Samuel knows French very well, while Richard is not perfect in either of his languages.

What a sight it is when great works, even if arbitrarily divided up, come to life again from their indivisible core, and thus may appear particularly striking to our dulled eyes. Therefore each edition, which focuses its attention once and for all within specific boundaries, has actual merit even when, as with this collection of Kleist's anecdotes, it respects a new unity and thereby, in fact, expands the scope of Kleist's oeuvre. It expands it even if we are familiar with all of the anecdotes, which to the delight of many readers does by no means have to be the case. The expert will, of course, be able to explain why some of these anecdotes are missing from the various complete editions, even from the Tempel edition; the non-expert will not understand this, but will stick all the more to this new text, which the Rohwohlt publishing house offers in clear print and serious design (especially the slightly tinted paper appears fitting to us) for a mere 2 marks.

Before you hear the first few verses by Jewish poets from Eastern Europe, I would like to tell you, dear ladies and gentlemen, how much more Jargon you understand than you realize.

I am not really worried about the effects tonight's event holds in store for each of you, but I would like for these effects to occur at the time they deserve. This, however, will not be the case as long as some of you fear the Jargon so much that it may almost be seen in your faces. I am not even speaking of those who are arrogant toward Jargon. But fear of Jargon, fear combined with a certain fundamental reluctance, is ultimately understandable, if you will.

Our Western European circumstances, viewed with a cautious, fleeting gaze, are well ordered: everything takes its quiet course. We live in nearly joyful harmony; we get along when necessary, can do without one another if we so desire and get along even then; against the context of such an order of things, who could understand this jumbled Jargon or who would even care to?

Jargon is the youngest European language, just four hundred years old and actually even younger. It has not yet developed linguistic structures of the clarity we require. Its expression is curt and rash.

It does not have grammar books. Amateurs have attempted to write grammar books, but Jargon is continuously spoken; it does not settle down. The populace just will not leave it to the grammarians.

It consists entirely of foreign words. These do not come to rest within it, but preserve the speed and vivacity with which they were borrowed. Mass migrations run through Jargon from one end to the other. All this German, Hebrew, French, English, Slavic, Dutch, Romanian, and even Latin contained within the Jargon is imbued with curiosity and levity; it does need a certain force to keep all these languages together in this state. Therefore no reasonable person even thinks of making Jargon a world language, as much as this actually might suggest itself. Only thieves' cant has happily borrowed from it because it uses not so much linguistic coherence but individual words. This is also due to the fact that Jargon was a disparaged language after all.

But then again, the use of the vernacular is governed by fragments of known linguistic principles. The beginnings of Jargon, for example, originate from the time when Middle High German evolved into Modern High German. There were elective forms, of which the Middle High German adopted the one, Jargon the other. Or, Jargon developed Middle High German forms more consistently than even Modern High German did: for example, the Jargon-y "mir seien" evolved more naturally from the Middle High German "sîn" than the Modern High German form "wir sind" ("we are"). Or, Jargon stuck with Middle High German forms despite the Modern High German. Once something entered the ghetto, it did not leave it any time soon. Thus forms such as "kerzlach" (candles), "blümlach" (flowers), "liedlach" (songs) have remained.

And then the dialects of Jargon enter into this linguistic fabric of arbitrariness and principle. Yes, the entire Jargon consists of dialects only, even the written form, although, for the most part, agreement has been reached concerning the spelling.

With all of this I believe I have convinced most of you, dear ladies and gentlemen, that you won't understand a word of Jargon.

Do not expect any assistance from the poems' interpretations. If you simply cannot understand Jargon, no momentary explanation can help you. At best you will understand the explanation and know that something complex will come up. That will be all. I could tell you this, for example:

Mr. Löwy will, as is actually true, recite three poems for you. Firstly "Die Grine" by Rosenfeld. Grine are the green ones, the greenhorns, the new immigrants to America. In the poem, a small group of such Jewish immigrants walk through a New York street with their dirty travel bags. Of course, a crowd gathers, marveling at them, then follows them, laughing. The poet, utterly upset by this spectacle, speaks to Jewry and to humanity beyond this street scene. One has the impression that the group of immigrants stalls as the poet speaks, although they are far away and cannot hear him.

The second poem, entitled "Sand und Sterne," is by Frug.

It is a bitter reading of a biblical prophecy. There it says that we will be like the sand by the seashore and the stars of the heaven. Well, we are already being walked upon like the sand, so when will the promise about the stars come true?

The third poem is by Frischmann and is entitled: "Die Nacht ist still" (The night is still).

One night a loving couple encounters a pious scholar on his way to the temple. They are frightened, fear they have been betrayed, but calm one another later on.

As you can see, such explanations are not sufficient.

Informed by these explanations you will look for that which you already know during the recitation, and you will not see that which will actually be there. But, fortunately, anyone familiar with the German language is also able to understand Jargon. For seen from a rather great distance, the superficial comprehensibility of Jargon is owed to the German language; this is an advantage it has over all languages on earth. In turn, it is only fair that it also has a disadvantage above all. For one cannot translate Jargon to the German. The ties between Jargon and German are too meaningful and fragile that they would not break immediately when Jargon is transferred back into the German, which means that it is no longer Jargon that is being transferred back but something without substance. When translated to French, for example, Jargon can be rendered to the French reader; if translated to German it will be annihilated. "Toit," for example, just is not "tot" (dead), and "blüt" is under no circumstances "Blut" (blood).

But not only from this distance to the German language can you, dear ladies and gentlemen, understand Jargon; you may step a little closer. Until quite recently the colloquial lingua franca of German Jews, depending on whether they lived in the city or in the country, more in the East or in the West, appears to have been like a distant or closer stage of Jargon, and many remnants persist. Therefore the historic development of Jargon could be traced in the sphere of the present as much as in the depths of history.

You will come quite close to Jargon if you remember that, apart from knowledge and skills, there are also forces and ties to forces at work within yourself, which enable you to intuit Jargon. Only then can the interpreter help, comforting you so that you no longer feel excluded and realize that you can no longer complain of not understanding Jargon. This is most important because understanding dissipates when you complain. But if you keep quiet, you will suddenly find yourself within the Jargon. And once Jargon has seized you – and everything is Jargon: words, Hassidic melody, and the reality of the Eastern Jewish actor himself – you will no longer find your former serenity. Then you will experience the true unity of Jargon, with such violence that you will be fearful, though no longer of Jargon but of yourselves. You would be unable to bear this fear alone if Jargon did not also give you the confidence to withstand this fear and that is more powerful than it. Enjoy it as much as you can! When it finally fades away, tomorrow and later on, –how could it last just from the memory of one single evening of recitation! –I do wish you that you may forget the fear as well. For it isn't our intention to punish you.

13

Those, I am one of them, who find even a small ordinary mole repugnant, would likely have died from repugnance if they had seen the giant mole a few years ago, observed near a small village which gained a certain fleeting fame from it. It has long fallen back into oblivion and thus shares the lack of fame of the entire phenomenon, which has remained completely unexplained, but which no one has made much of an effort to explain either, and, which due to an unfathomable neglect of the circles that should have seen to it and that do make every effort to see to much more trifling matters, has been forgotten without further exploration. The fact that the village is located remote from the railroad is by no means an excuse for it, because many people came from far away out of curiosity, even from abroad; only those who should have displayed more than curiosity, those did not come. Well, if not a few very simple people, people whose ordinary day's work hardly allowed them a quiet reprieve, if those people had not selflessly taken matters into their own hands, rumor of this phenomenon would hardly have spread beyond their immediate environment. It must be admitted that even rumor, which otherwise can hardly be stopped, was downright sluggish in this case, and would not have spread if it had not actually been given a push. But that, too, was certainly no reason not to deal with the matter; on the contrary, this very phenomenon should have been examined as well. Instead, it was left to the old village schoolmaster to compose the only written treatise, an excellent man in his profession, but whose abilities and prior experience hardly enabled him to provide a profound and useful account of the phenomenon, let alone an explanation. The small treatise was printed and sold to many visitors to the village; it did find some recognition, but the schoolmaster was wise enough to realize that his isolated, unsupported efforts were practically worthless. If, however, he did not give up and made the matter his lifework, even though it was, naturally, getting more desperate year after year, this goes to show, on the one hand, how great an effect the phenomenon exerted, and on the other hand, what endurance and conviction an old, unnoticed village schoolmaster can muster. That he was badly hurt by the cold attitude of the authoritative figures is evident in a brief supplement that followed his first treatise, though not until a few years later, at a time when hardly anyone remembered what it was all about. In this supplement, he complains convincingly, if perhaps not by skillfulness but by honesty, about the lack of understanding he encountered in people where one should least expect it. He aptly says about these people: "Not I, but they talk like old village schoolmasters." And, among other things, he cites the remark of a scholar whom he specifically went to see regarding this matter. The name of the scholar is not given, but from several indicators one can conclude who it was. After the schoolmaster had overcome great difficulties to receive audience with the scholar at all, to whom he had announced his coming weeks in advance, he noticed already when the scholar greeted him that he was caught up in insurmountable prejudice concerning the matter. The absentmindedness with which he listened to the schoolmaster's long report, given on the basis of the treatise, became obvious in the remark he made after some apparent reflection. "Surely, there are different moles, small and large. And the soil in the area is particularly black and heavy. Now for that reason it also provides especially rich nutrition to the moles, and they become extraordinarily large." "But not that large," the schoolmaster cried out and measured, slightly exaggerating in his rage, two meters on the wall. "Oh yes," replied the scholar, to whom the whole matter seemed to appear very droll, "Why wouldn't they." With this opinion, the schoolmaster returned home. He recounts how his wife and six children had waited for him in the falling snow on the country road at night and how he had to admit to them his ultimate failure of his hopes.

When I learned of the scholar's behavior toward the schoolmaster, I hadn't read the schoolmaster's main treatise. But I decided right away to find out everything about this case, to collect and compile information. Since I couldn't well shake my fist in the scholar's face, my paper should at least defend the schoolmaster, or, to be more accurate, not so much the schoolmaster as the good intentions of this honest but uninfluential man. I admit I regretted this decision later on, for I sensed that its execution was to put me in a peculiar situation. On the one hand, my influence was by far not sufficient to sway the scholar or even public opinion in the schoolmaster's favor, but on the other hand, the schoolmaster was bound to realize that I was not so much concerned with his main objective, proving the existence of the large mole, as the defense of his honor, which to himself, however, was self-evident and in no need of defense. So it had to come to a point where, intending to support the schoolmaster, I was not being understood by him, and rather than being of assistance, would probably need support instead, which was very unlikely to appear. Moreover, my decision burdened me with a great deal of work. If I intended to be persuasive, I couldn't very well invoke the schoolmaster who had been unable to persuade. Reading his treatise would only have been a distraction, and I therefore avoided reading it before completing my own paper. Why, I did not even get in touch with the schoolmaster. He learned of my investigations through intermediaries, but he didn't know whether I was working in his favor or against him. He probably suspected the latter, although he denied it later on, for I have proof that he put various obstacles in my way. It was easy enough for him to do, for I was forced to undertake all the investigations he had already made all over again, and he could therefore always beat me to it. But that was the only objection one might rightly make against my method, an unavoidable reproach at that, which was very much refuted by the caution, even self-denial, of my conclusions. Otherwise my treatise was free of influence from the schoolmaster; I may even have been far too meticulous in this respect. It was as if no one had investigated the case before, as if I were the first person to question eye and ear witnesses, the first to string together the data, the first to draw conclusions. When I read the schoolmaster's essay later on – it bore the rather cumbersome title: A mole as large as no one has seen before – I actually found that we disagreed on some substantial aspects, although we both thought we had proved the main point, the existence of the mole. All the same, these few differences of opinion stood in the way of a friendly rapport with the schoolmaster, which I had actually expected in spite of everything. There almost arose some hostility on his part. He remained modest and humble toward me at all times, but that made it all the easier to discern his true mood. To wit, he was of the opinion that I had done quite some harm to him and the matter, and that my belief that I had been or could be of use to him was simplicity at best but more likely presumption or cunning. Most of all he kept pointing out that all of his previous opponents had expressed their opposition not at all, or merely in private, or at least only verbally, whereas I had felt I needed to put all of my criticisms to print at once. Furthermore, the few opponents who had really dealt with the matter, if only superficially, had at least listened to his, the schoolmaster's opinion, hence the definitive opinion in this matter, before voicing their own; however, I had culled results from unsystematically collected and in parts misinterpreted data that, while being correct with regard to the main point, must appear dubious both to the general public and to the educated. But the slightest hint of implausibility was the worst that could happen here. I could easily have responded to those, however veiled, accusations – his treatise for example was precisely the pinnacle of implausibility – but it was much less easy to defend myself against his overall suspicion, and this was the reason why I avoided him pretty much in general. For he secretly believed that I had intended to rob him of the fame of having been the first to publicly advocate the mole. Now he really did not enjoy any fame whatsoever, only ridicule that was dwindling to an ever-smaller circle, and I certainly was not competing for that. Moreover, in the foreword to my treatise I had explicitly stated that the schoolmaster should be considered the discoverer of the mole for all times to come – even though he wasn't even the discoverer – and that it was only my sympathy for the schoolmaster's fate that had pushed me to compose the treatise. "It is the purpose of this treatise," – I concluded all too emotionally but in keeping with the excitement I felt at the time – "to encourage the well-deserved distribution of the schoolmaster's treatise. If it succeeds, my name which is temporarily and only externally connected to this affair should immediately be erased from it." In this way, I practically disclaimed any major involvement with the matter; it was almost as if I had somehow anticipated the schoolmaster's incredible accusations. Nonetheless, it was precisely this passage that he turned against me, and I will not deny that there seemed to be a hint of justification in what he said, or rather implied, just as I noticed in general on several occasions that in some respects he demonstrated almost more cleverness with regard to me than he did in his treatise. Thus he claimed that my foreword was duplicitous. If I really intended to propagate his treatise, why then did I not exclusively deal with him and his treatise, why did I not discuss its merits, its irrefutability, why did I not simply emphasize and explain the significance of the discovery, why did I instead venture into the discovery itself while completely ignoring his treatise? Had not the discovery been made? Was there anything left to be done in this respect? If I really thought I had to make the discovery all over again, why then did I so solemnly distance myself from it in my foreword? This might have been feigned modesty, but it was something worse. I devalued the discovery, I called attention to it with the sole purpose of devaluing it, I had researched and discarded it, it may have become a little quieter around the matter, and there I was making noise again, while at the same time making the schoolmaster's situation more difficult than it had ever been. What did the schoolmaster care about the defense of his honor? The matter, the only thing that counted for him was the matter. It was the matter, however, that I betrayed, because I did not understand it, because my appraisal of it was incorrect, because I had no sense

110

of it. It was far beyond my intellect. He sat in front of me and looked at me calmly with his wrinkled old face, and yet that was what he thought. It was certainly not true that he only cared about the matter; he was actually quite ambitious and wanted some financial gain as well, which with regard to his numerous family was very understandable. Nonetheless, by comparison my investment in the matter seemed so small to him that he thought he could make himself out to be completely disinterested without telling too much of an untruth. And in fact, it did not even placate my own inner self when I told myself that the man's accusations are basically owed to the fact that, in a sense, he holds onto his mole with both hands and calls anyone a traitor who tries to lay a finger on it. This was not so, his behavior could not be explained by avarice, at least not avarice alone, but rather by the edginess his enormous efforts and their complete lack of success had caused in him. But his edginess does not explain everything either. Perhaps it was indeed my interest in the matter that was not great enough; the schoolmaster was accustomed to indifference in strangers. He suffered from it on a general, but not on an individual level; but then here there was finally someone who took on the matter in an extraordinary way, and yet even he did not understand the matter. Once exposed in that sense I could not deny it at all. I am no zoologist; perhaps if I had discovered it myself, I would have dedicated myself to his case wholeheartedly, but I had not discovered it. Such a giant mole is surely a curiosity but one cannot expect that the whole world should pay enduring attention to it, especially if the existence of the mole has not been proved beyond doubt, and, in any event, it cannot be produced. And I also admitted that, even if I had been the discoverer, I would never have stood up as readily and voluntarily for the mole as I did for the schoolmaster.

Now the disagreement between me and the schoolmaster would certainly have dissolved quickly, had my treatise been successful. But, as it were, this success did not materialize. Perhaps it was not well written, not persuasive enough, I'm a salesman; the composition of such a treatise may well exceed my scope even more than that of the schoolmaster, although I certainly by far surpassed the schoolmaster by far in all the skills this required. Also, there may be a different explanation for the lack of success: that the timing of the publication was unfavorable. On the one hand, the discovery of the mole that had not caught on at the time had not been so long ago that it had been completely forgotten and that my treatise would have been a surprise, on the other hand, enough time had elapsed to exhaust the little interest that had originally existed. Those who gave my treatise any thought at all told themselves with the sort of despondency that had informed the discussion years ago already that now the useless efforts in this lost case would start all over again, and some even confused my treatise with that of the schoolmaster. A leading agricultural journal ran the following comment, fortunately all the way at the end and in fine print: "We have once more been sent the pamphlet about the giant mole. We remember our heartfelt laughter about it years ago. Since then, it has not become any sharper nor have we become any more dim-witted. It is just that we cannot laugh about it a second time. However, we are asking our teacher's associations if village schoolmasters cannot find anything more useful to do than chasing after giant moles." An unpardonable mistake! They had neither read the first nor the second treatise, and the two words giant mole and village schoolmaster, skimmed from the text, were enough for these gentlemen to pose as representatives of reputable interests. A few things could have been undertaken to fight this, even with success, but my disagreement with the schoolmaster precluded any steps on my part. Instead, I tried to keep the journal secret from him as long as possible. But he very soon found out about it, as I already recognized from a remark in a letter announcing his visit for the Christmas holidays. In it he wrote: "The world is evil and it gets away with it easily," trying to imply that I was part of the evil world but did not content myself with my inherent evil but rather made it easy on the world, i.e. actively lured out the general evil and helped it to victory. Now I had already made the necessary decisions, and so I calmly awaited him and I calmly watched him arrive, greeting me even less politely than usual, silently sitting down opposite me as he carefully pulled the journal from the breast pocket of his strangely quilted overcoat and pushed it toward me opened at the page in question. "I'm familiar with it," I said and pushed the journal back unread. "You're familiar with it," he said with a sigh; he had the old teacher's habit of repeating the other person's replies. "Of course I will not take this uncontested," he continued, nervously tapping his finger on the journal as he sharply glanced at me as if I had the opposite opinion. He most likely had an idea of what I was about to say, for, in general, I gathered not so much from his words but from other indicators that he frequently had a very true sense of my intentions but did not give in to it and let himself be distracted. I can repeat almost literally what I said to him at the time because I took notes shortly after our meeting. "Do as you please," I said, "we will part ways as of today. I believe that this neither unexpected nor unwelcome to you. The remark in this journal is not the reason for my decision; it has only consolidated it. The actual reason lies in the fact that I originally believed that my intervention could be of use to you while I now have to realize that I have harmed you in every respect. Why everything turned out this way, I don't know; the reasons for success and failure are always manifold; don't just single out those that speak against me. Think of yourself, you only had the best intentions yourself and yet failed, judged as a whole. I don't mean this as a joke; after all, it is directed against me when I say that the alliance with me is another one of your failures. It is neither for cowardice nor betrayal that I withdraw from the matter. It is even with some reluctance; it is quite obvious from my treatise how much I respect you as a person: in a way you have even become my teacher, and even the mole almost became dear to me. Still, I am stepping aside; you are the discoverer, and whatever way I were to go about it, I would always be in the way of potential fame that might come your way, while I attract failure and pass it on to you. At least that is your opinion. Enough of that. The only atonement I can make is to ask your forgiveness and, if you so require, to repeat the confession I have made here in public, e.g. in this journal." Those were my words at the time; they were not entirely sincere, but the sincere part could easily be inferred. It affected him in the way I had expected. Most old people have something deceitful, something untruthful in their comportment toward younger people; one quietly goes on living on next to them, believes the rapport to be settled, knows the prevalent opinions, continually receives affirmations of peace, takes everything for granted, and, suddenly, when something important happens and the peace one had prepared for such a long time should come into effect, these old people rise up like strangers, have more entrenched, stronger opinions, and only then proceed to virtually unfurl their flag on which one reads the new slogan with horror. This horror stems above all from the fact that what the old people say then is really much more justified, meaningful and, if there were a comparative form of matter of course, even more matter of course. But the ultimate deceit of it is that they have basically always said what they say now and that in general, however, it could never really be foreseen. I must have really penetrated deep into this village schoolmaster, for he did not surprise me now. "Child," he said, placing his hand on mine and patting it amicably, "what gave you the idea to get involved in the matter. The very first time I heard about it, I talked to my wife about it." He moved away from the table, spread his arms and gazed down onto the floor as if his wife were standing there all tiny and he were talking to her. "'For so many years,' I said to her, 'we have struggled here alone, but now there seems to be this great benefactor from the city who stands up for us, a businessman by the name of such and such. Now we should be very happy, shouldn't we? A businessman in the city that is quite something; if a mere peasant believes us and says so that cannot be of help to us, for what the peasant does, is always improper, whether he says: The old village schoolmaster is right, or whether he spits out quite inappropriately, either has the same effect. And if instead of the one peasant ten thousand peasants stand up for us, the effect might be even worse. A businessman in the city, however, is a completely different matter, such a man has connections, even what he just says in passing is repeated and spread; new benefactors make the matter their own; one says for example: There is something to learn even from village schoolmasters, and the next day a crowd of people whisper such things to one another, who, concluding from their outward appearance, one would never assume to do so. Now funds will be found for the matter, the one collects them and the others count the money into his hand, some say the village schoolmaster must be brought from the village, they arrive, not minding what he looks like, take him into their midst, and since his wife and children are attached to him, they take them along. Have you ever watched people from the city? They twitter incessantly. When they sit or walk together in a row, they twitter from the right to the left and back again and up and down. And thus, twittering, they lift us into the carriage, one barely has time to take a nap. The gentleman on the coachbox adjusts his pince-nez, brandishes his whip, and off we go. Everyone waves goodbye to the village, as if we were still there, rather than sitting among them. A few carriages with some particularly impatient people come to meet us from the city. When we draw closer, they get off their seats and stretch to see us. The one who collected the money straightens out everything and tells everyone to be quiet. By the time we enter the city, it has become a long caravan of carriages. We thought the welcomes were over, but now they are only starting in front of the inn. In the city a lot of people immediately gather on the first announcement. What one person cares about, the other cares about right away as well. Their breaths snatch their opinions from one another and make them their own. Not all of those people can go in carriages, so some wait in front of the inn. Others could well go by carriage, but don't, out of self-confidence. Those are waiting as well. It is unconceivable how the person who collected the money keeps his eyes on everyone.'"

I had listened to him calmly; in fact, I had grown calmer and calmer as he was speaking. On the table I had piled up all the copies of my treatise still in my possession. Only very few were missing, for in a recent circular letter I had demanded that all copies that had been sent out be returned, and I had received most of them back. Quite a few parties had replied very politely that they did not even remember having received such a treatise and that, if it had nonetheless arrived, they must have regrettably lost it. That was just as well; I really did not want anything else in the end. Only one person asked whether he might keep the treatise as a curiosity, obligating himself, in keeping with the circular, to show it to no one for the next twenty years. The village schoolmaster had not seen this circular before; I was glad that his words made it so easy for me to show it to him. I was able to show it to him without worry because I had been very careful in composing it, at all times mindful of the village schoolmaster's interests and his matter. The letter's main phrases were the following: "The reason I request the return of the treatise is not that I might have revised any of the opinions argued in the essay, or that I regard any of its parts erroneous or simply unprovable. I have merely personal, yet very compelling reasons for my request; however, this does not in the least allow conclusions about my stance on the matter: I am asking you to take particular note of this and divulge it at your leisure."

For the time being I covered the circular with my hands and said: "Are you blaming me that it didn't turn out that way? Why would you do that? Let us not make this a bitter parting. And try to see that, while you did make a discovery, this discovery by no means exceeds all others and that therefore the injustice inflicted on you does not exceed all others either. I'm not familiar with the statutes of learned societies, but I don't think that even in the most favorable of circumstances you would have been given a reception anywhere close to the one you described to your poor wife. If I had hopes for the impact the treatise might make, I thought that perhaps some professor would learn about your case so that he would order some young student to look into the matter, that this student would come to see you and verify your and my investigations one more time in his own way and that eventually, if the result appeared noteworthy to him – it should be mentioned at this point that all young students are full of doubt – that he would then publish his own treatise, in which your findings would be scientifically founded. But even if this hope had been fulfilled, not much would have been achieved. The student's treatise, which defended such a peculiar case, may have been ridiculed. The example of the agricultural journal shows you how easily this can happen, and scientific journals are even more ruthless in this respect. This is understandable; after all, professors bear a lot of responsibility toward themselves, toward science, toward posterity; they cannot embrace every new discovery offhand. We, the others, have an advantage over them. But let us disregard this for a moment and assume that the student's treatise had caught on. What would have happened next? Your name would have been honorably mentioned a few times; this would have benefited your standing, people would have said: 'Our village schoolmasters have their eyes peeled,' and, if journals had a memory and a conscience, this journal would have owed you a public apology, and some well-intentioned professor would have been found to secure a scholarship for you, it is also very well possible that one would have tried to move you to the city, find you a post at a municipal school and thus give you the opportunity to use the scientific tools available in the city for your further education. But to be frank, I must tell you that I think one would have tried, nothing more. You would have been summoned here, you would have turned up, an ordinary petitioner among hundreds without any splendid reception, you would have been talked to, commended for your honest aspirations, but at the same time, it would have been noted that you are an old man, that taking up scientific studies at such an age is futile and most of all that you came to your discovery more by accident rather than systematic research and that, apart from this individual case, you were not intending to continue your work. On these grounds, one would probably have left you in your village. Your discovery would surely have been taken further, for it is not inconsequential enough that, once having received recognition, it could ever be forgotten again. But you would not have heard much more about it, and what you would have heard you would barely have been able to understand. Any discovery is immediately introduced into the realm of science, and thereby ceases to be a discovery in a way, it is merged into the whole and disappears, and one must have a scientifically trained eye to still discern it. It is immediately connected to guiding principles of whose existence we have never heard, and in the scientific dispute it will be raised up to the sky by those guiding principles. How could we understand this? If we listen to such a discussion, we might think for example that it is about the discovery, but meanwhile it is about something completely different."

"All right," said the village schoolmaster, taking out his pipe and beginning to fill it with tobacco he carried loose in all his pockets. "You took on this unrewarding matter at your free will, and now you are pulling out at your free will as well. Everything is quite all right." "I am not stubborn," I said, "do you find anything wrong with my proposition?" "No, not at all," said the village schoolmaster, and his pipe was already smoking. I couldn't stand the odor of tobacco and therefore got up and walked around the room. From previous encounters I was already accustomed to the village schoolmaster taciturnity toward me and knew that once he had come he did not want to budge from my room. I had sometimes been quite taken aback by this; there is something else he wants, I then thought and offered him money, which he accepted as a rule. But he didn't leave until he was ready to. Usually this happened when the pipe was smoked; he then swung around the chair, which he carefully and respectfully pushed to the table, grabbed the gnarled stick in the corner, ardently squeezed my hand and left. Today, however, it was downright annoying me to have him sit there in silence. Once someone has offered a final farewell the way I did and the other person calls this quite all right, then the little that is left to be done together should be dealt with as quickly as possible, and one does not pointlessly burden the other with one's silent presence. If one studied the tough little old man from behind as he was sitting there at my table, one could be made to believe that it would be entirely impossible to coax him out of the room.

tired of hunting down miscreants; in that case the district judge would certainly be the first target. But there is no point resenting him. Therefore the assistant district attorney does not resent him; he only resents the stupidity that placed such a person in the seat of the district judge. So it is stupidity that wants to practice justice.

It is actually very unfortunate for the assistant district attorney's personal circumstances that he holds such a low rank but as for his true aspirations, it might not even suffice to be the district prosecutor. He would have to become a much higher prosecutor to be able to effectively arraign all the stupidity he sees before his eyes. He absolutely would not deign to arraign the district judge; he would not even recognize him from the height of his prosecutor's seat. But he would surely establish such magnificent order all around that the district judge would not last in it, that, even though no one laid a finger on him, his knees would start shaking, and he would eventually perish. At that point it might also be time to bring the case of the assistant district attorney himself from the closed disciplinary courts to the open courtroom. At which point, the assistant district attorney would no longer be personally involved; by virtue of force majeure he would have broken the chains put upon him and could himself sit in judgment on them. He envisages some powerful personality whispering in his ear before the trial: "Now you will obtain satisfaction." And then there is the trial. The accused disciplinary counsels lie, of course, they lie through clenched teeth, they lie the way people lie in court when, for once, they are indicted. But everything is set up in such a way that the facts themselves shake off all the lies and can unfold freely and truly in front of the courtroom audience. It is a large audience, sitting on three sides of the room, only the bench is empty, no judges have been found; the judges crowd into the dock were the defendant usually stands and try to stand trial before the empty bench. Only the public prosecutor, the former assistant district attorney, is present, of course, and in his usual place. He is much calmer than usual, just nodding now and then; everything is taking its due course, clocklike. Only now that the case is stripped of any written statements, depositions, minutes of the proceedings, verdict deliberations and reasons for the decision does one appreciate its instantaneously overwhelming simplicity! The matter itself goes back about fifteen years. The assistant district attorney was in the royal capital at the time; he was renowned as a capable lawyer, well liked by his superiors and even had hopes of soon becoming the tenth district attorney before many competitors. The second district attorney was particularly fond of him and let him substitute for himself even in not entirely trivial matters. That is what happened in a small lese-majesty case. A business employee, not uneducated, politically very active, had committed a lese-majesty in a wine tavern, glass in hand, half-intoxicated. Another guest at the next table, probably even more inebriated than the first, had filed the charge; in his daze he had probably thought that he was doing an excellent deed, had immediately gone for a police officer and had returned with him, smiling blissfully, so as to turn in the man. Later he upheld his testimony at least in its most important part; besides, the lese-majesty must have been very clear, for no witness completely denied it. It proved impossible to ascertain the exact wording beyond doubt; the most justified assumption was that the defendant had pointed at the king's wall portrait with his wine glass, saying: "You scoundrel up there!" The gravity of the insult was only mitigated by the defendant's partial insanity at the time as well as by the fact that the insult was uttered in some connection with the song line "As long as our little lamp still glows" and had thereby obscured the meaning of the exclamation. As for the relation between the exclamation and the song, almost every witness had a different opinion, and the complainant even claimed that not the defendant but someone else had sung it. What aggravated the case against the defendant immensely was his political activity, which made it seem very plausible, indeed, that he was capable of uttering the exclamation in complete sobriety and with the fullest conviction. The assistant district attorney remembers very precisely – after all he has so often thought about those things – how he took on this arraignment almost with enthusiasm, not only because conducting a lese-majesty trial was honorable but because he sincerely hated the defendant and his cause. There he stood, a political careerist for whom his honest trade as a business employee was not enough, most likely because it did not procure the means necessary for his wine binges, a man with giant jowls moved by giant, sturdy muscles, a natural stump orator who even yelled at the prosecutor, in this case unfortunately an agitated, anxious creature. The investigation, which the assistant district attorney had frequented out of interest, was a continuous bickering. At one point the prosecutor leapt up, another time it was the person being questioned, one yelling at the other.

This, of course, had an adverse effect on the results of the investigation, and when it was to the assistant district attorney to build his indictment on these results, he had to apply a lot of effort and acumen to make it sound enough. He worked through the nights, but with joy. Those were lovely spring nights; the building, of which the assistant district attorney inhabited the ground floor, had a two-foot wide front yard. When the assistant district attorney was tired of working, or when his pressing thoughts required calm and composure, he climbed out the window into the front yard and walked to and fro or leaned on the garden grille with closed eyes. He drove himself hard, he revised the entire indictment several times, some parts ten or twenty times. Moreover, he accumulated an inscrutable abundance of prepared materials for the main hearing. "God grant that I can grasp and make use of all this," was his constant entreaty in those nights. With the indictment itself he regarded only the least part of his work as finished; he therefore deemed the praise with which the second district attorney returned the bill of indictment after thorough scrutiny not as a reward but just as encouragement, and it was grand and came from a strict, taciturn man. The praise went, as the assistant district attorney frequently repeated in his later petitions, without being able to make the second district attorney remember it: "This file, my dear colleague, not only contains the indictment; in all human probability it also contains your appointment as the tenth district attorney." And when the assistant district attorney modestly kept silent, the second district attorney added: "Trust me." At the main hearing, the assistant district attorney was firm and composed. No one in the courtroom knew all the subtleties and interrelations of the lawsuit as well as he did. The defense attorney posed no danger to him, a small man the assistant district attorney knew well, always shouting but not very sharp. That day he certainly was not even very belligerent; he defended because he was obligated because this was about a member of his political party, because there might be an opportunity for tirades, because the party press was paying some attention to the case, but he had no hopes of pulling his client through. The assistant district attorney remembers how, just before the beginning of the trial, he observed this defense attorney with a barely suppressed smile; unable to control himself as this defense attorney was overall, he messed up everything on his table, tore sheets from his files, and, as in a breath of wind, they were immediately covered with notes; meanwhile he was tapping his little feet under the table and, unconsciously, he stroked across his bald head in an anxious movement every few moments as though checking for injuries. To the assistant district attorney he seemed to be an unworthy opponent. When he leapt up right at the beginning of the hearing, and, with an ugly whooping voice, filed a motion that the hearing be in open session, the assistant district attorney almost clumsily rose from his seat. Everything was so clear-cut and thought-out, it was as if everyone around meddled with a matter that belonged only to him, a matter that, due to its nature he could bring to an end in itself without judges and defense attorneys and without defendants. And he joined the petition of the defense attorney; his behavior was as unexpected as that of the defense lawyer had been obvious. But he explained his behavior, and during his explanation the courtroom was so quiet that, had not all those eyes from all sides been directed at him as if wishing to pull him toward them, he might have thought he was speaking to himself in an empty room. He immediately noticed that he was convincing. The judges craned their necks and looked at one another in astonishment, the defense attorney stiffly leaned in his chair, as if the form of the assistant district attorney had just emerged from the ground; the defendant gnashed his giant teeth in suspense, people in the crowd held each other's hands. They realized that here was someone who wrested this entire case, in which they had some or other feeble investment, away from them to make it his indisputable property. Everyone had thought to be attending a minor lese-majesty trial, and here, in his first petition already, they heard the assistant district attorney in few words graze the insult itself like some minor detail

The hussars rode through the dark narrow street

[15]

A young ambitious student who was fascinated by the case of the Elberfeld horses and had thoroughly read and pondered everything published on the matter, decided to carry out his own experiments on the subject and right from the start to go about it in an entirely different and to his mind incomparably more correct manner than his predecessors. His financial means as such, however, were insufficient to allow experiments on a large scale, and if the first horse he intended to buy for his experiments turned out to be stubborn, which, even with the most vigorous work can only be determined after weeks, he would not have any chance to undertake any new experiments for a while. But he was not too worried about it because his method could most likely overcome any stubbornness. At any rate, in keeping with his cautious nature, he proceeded quite systematically even when calculating the expenditure that would incur and the means he could raise. Thus far his parents, poor merchants in the countryside, had sent him the amount he needed for his measly sustenance as a student each month, and he was not planning to do without it either, even though, of course, he was forced to give up his studies, which his parents were following with great hopes from afar, if he wanted to achieve the anticipated great success in the new territory he was about to enter. It was out of the question that his parents would appreciate his efforts or even support him, so he had to conceal his intentions to them, as painful as that was, and lead them to believe that he was making continuous progress in his current studies. Deceiving his parents was only one of the sacrifices he wanted to impose on himself for the benefit of the cause. His parents' allowance would not be enough to cover the expected large costs he needed to expend for his project. Therefore, the student planned to spend the majority of the day, thus far devoted to his studies, to private tutoring. The majority of the night, however, was to be used for the actual work. It was not only forced by his unfavorable external circumstances that the student chose the nighttime for training the horse, the new principles he planned to introduce for the horse's training also suggested the nighttime for several reasons. He believed that even the slightest distraction of the horse's attention caused irredeemable harm to its training, from which they were relatively safe during the night. The irritability that overcomes humans and animals alike when they stay awake and work at night was an explicit requirement of his plan. Unlike other experts he did not fear the wildness of a horse, rather he demanded it, even sought to generate it, if not with the whip but by the irritant of his unremitting presence and of his unremitting training. He claimed that when the horse was taught correctly there could not be any partial progress; partial progress that some horse lovers have taken excessive pride in lately, is nothing but either the product of the trainer's imagination or, even worse, the surest sign that there will never be any overall progress. He himself wanted to be on his guard, especially of achieving partial progress; the contentment of his predecessors who believed that the success of minor calculations was an achievement already seemed unfathomable to him, it was as if one were to begin a child's education by drumming nothing but the multiplication tables into the child, regardless of whether it was blind, deaf, or numb toward all of humankind. That was all so foolish, and sometimes the mistakes of the other horse trainers seemed so grossly glaring that he then even became suspicious of himself, for it was almost impossible that one individual, what is more an inexperienced individual, only propelled by an untested but nonetheless profound and downright fierce conviction, would be proved right against all the experts.

16

One evening Blumfeld, an elderly bachelor, was climbing the stairs to his apartment, which was an arduous task, for he lived on the sixth floor. While climbing up, he thought, as he had so often lately, how tiresome this utterly lonely life was: that he had to climb these six floors virtually in secrecy, only to reach his empty room upstairs, put on his dressing gown there, again virtually in secrecy, light his pipe, read a little in the French magazine he had been subscribing to for years, sip on his homemade kirsch, and eventually go to bed a half hour later, not without completely rearranging his bedding, which the charwoman, who was absolutely unteachable, had tossed on the bed at her whim. Any companion, any spectator of these chores would have been most welcome to Blumfeld. He had already considered acquiring a small dog. Such an animal is amusing, and most of all grateful and loyal; a colleague of Blumfeld's has such a dog; it never follows anyone but his master and when it hasn't seen him for a few moments, it immediately greets him by barking loudly, surely expressing its joy at having found its master once again, this extraordinary benefactor. To be sure, such a dog has its disadvantages, too. Even if kept in the cleanliest manner, it is bound to make the room unclean. This simply can't be avoided, for one cannot give it a hot bath before taking it into the room every single time; also, its health wouldn't stand it. But then Blumfeld cannot stand uncleanliness in his room – the cleanliness of his room is indispensable for him; several times a week, he argues about this with his charwoman, who is not very meticulous in this respect. Since she is hard of hearing, he usually pulls her by the arm to point out where in the room he finds cleanliness to be lacking. Due to his strictness, he has achieved a degree of tidiness in his room more or less to his wishes. By acquiring a dog, however, he would voluntarily introduce into his room the dirt he had warded off so carefully. Fleas, the steady companions of dogs, would arrive. Once the fleas were there, it wouldn't be long until Blumfeld would have to cede his cozy room to the dog and find another room for himself. But uncleanliness was only one of the disadvantages of dogs. Also, dogs become sick, and no one really understands dogs' diseases. Then the animal crouches in a corner or limps around, whimpering, coughing, choking on some kind of pain; one wraps it in a blanket, whistles for it, pushes some milk in front of it, in short, takes care of it in hopes that, which is very well possible, it might be a temporary ailment, whereas it could be a serious, nasty, and infectious disease. And even if the dog stays healthy, it will eventually become old; one had been unable to resolve to give away the faithful pet in time, and there comes the time where one's own age gazes at one out of the dog's teary eyes. Then one has to deal with the half-blind, weak-lunged animal, almost immobile with fat, and thus pay dearly for all the joy the dog had brought earlier on. As much as Blumfeld would love to have a dog at this moment, he would rather keep climbing these stairs by himself for another thirty years than be bothered by such an old dog later on, dragging itself from step to step next to him and moaning louder than he himself.

So Blumfeld will remain alone after all; he does not have the spinster's desire, wishing for the company of some subordinate living being that she can protect, that she can be tender with, that she continuously wishes to serve, so that a cat, a canary bird, or even goldfishes would fit the purpose well enough. And if she cannot have that, she will even be contented with a few flowers outside her window. But Blumfeld just wants a companion, an animal that does not need a lot of care, that is not bothered by the occasional kick in the side, that can spend the night in the street if need be, but which, if Blumfeld so desires, is immediately at hand to bark, jump, lick hands. Blumfeld wants something of the kind, but since, as he admits, it cannot be had without serious disadvantages, he forgoes it, even though, due to his thorough nature, he revisits the same idea from time to time, such as this evening.

Upstairs in front of the door to his room, as he takes the key out of his pocket, he hears a sound coming from the room. A curious clattering sound, very vivid, very regular. Since Blumfeld has just been thinking of dogs, it reminds him of the sound made by paws alternately hitting the floor. But paws don't clatter, so those aren't paws. He quickly unlocks the door and turns on the electric light. He was not prepared for what he sees. Why, this is magic, two small white blue-striped celluloid balls are jumping up and down next to each other on the wood floor; when one of them hits the floor, the other is in the air, and they tirelessly continue their game. Once, in grammar school, Blumfeld had seen small balls jumping like this in a well-known electrical experiment, but these balls are relatively large, jump freely in the room, and no electrical experiment is being conducted. Blumfeld bends down to have a closer look at them. They are, no doubt, ordinary balls; they probably contain several smaller balls, and it is those that make the clattering sound. Blumfeld reaches in the air to see whether they are hanging on any threads, but no, they are moving entirely of their own accord. It is too bad that Blumfeld is not a little child; two such balls would have been a joyous surprise, whereas now the whole thing strikes him as rather unpleasant. It really is not entirely without virtue to live in secrecy as an unnoticed bachelor; now someone, regardless who, has uncovered his secret and sent him these two strange balls.

He tries to grab one, but they evade him and lure him farther into the room behind them. "This is really too silly," he thinks, "running after the balls like this," stops and watches them, as they, with the pursuit seemingly abandoned, also remain in the same spot. "But I'll still try to catch them," he thinks and rushes toward them. Right away they flee, but, his legs apart, Blumfeld pushes them into a corner of the room, and in front of the trunk standing there, he manages to catch one of the balls. It is a small cool ball, turning in his hand, obviously eager to escape. And the other ball, too, as if aware of its comrade's distress, jumps higher than before, lengthening its jumps until it touches Blumfeld's hand. It beats against the hand, beats in ever faster jumps, changes the points of attack, then, not getting anywhere against the hand enclosing the other ball, jumps even higher, probably trying to touch Blumfeld's face. Blumfeld could catch that ball as well and lock both of them away, but at that moment taking such measures against two small balls appears too undignified to him. Besides, it is fun, too, to own such balls, they will also grow tired soon enough, roll under a wardrobe and keep quiet. In spite of this consideration, Blumfeld flings the ball to the ground in a sort of rage; it's a miracle that the fragile, almost transparent celluloid shell doesn't break. Immediately, the two balls resume their previous low and mutually coordinated jumps.

Blumfeld undresses calmly, organizes his clothes in the wardrobe; he always makes sure that the charwoman has left everything in order. Once or twice, he glances over his shoulder at the balls, which, unpursued, seem to pursue him in turn now; they have followed him and are jumping just behind him. Blumfeld puts on his dressing gown and is about to go to the opposite wall to get one of his pipes hanging there in a rack. Before turning around, he instinctively kicks back one foot, but the balls know how to dodge him and are not hit. As he goes for his pipe, the balls join him right away; he shuffles in his slippers, takes irregular steps – but without a pause each footstep is followed by the impact of the balls; they keep up with him. Blumfeld suddenly turns back to see how the balls manage to handle that. But as soon as he has turned, the balls delineate a semicircle and are already behind him; this is repeated as often as he turns around. Just like subordinated companions, they try to avoid lingering in front of Blumfeld. For now, it seems, they only dared to do so to introduce themselves; but by now they have entered into his service.

So far, in emergencies where he didn't have enough strength to master the situation, Blumfeld has always resorted to the ploy of pretending that he hadn't noticed anything. This has often worked and at least improved the situation most of the time. So this is what he does now as well: he stands in front of the pipe rack, his lips pursed, picks a pipe, takes his time filling the pipe from the tobacco pouch and leaves the balls behind him to their jumps without a care. He only hesitates to walk to the table, for it almost physically hurts him to hear their jumps synchronize with his own steps. So he stands there, filling his pipe longer than necessary, and appreciates the distance separating him from the table. Finally, he overcomes his weakness and travels the distance stomping his feet so loudly that he does not hear the balls at all. But as soon as he is seated, they jump behind his armchair as audibly as before.

Above the table, a board is mounted within easy reach on the wall where the bottle of kirsch stands surrounded by small glasses. Next to it, there lies a stack of issues of the French magazine. But instead of taking down everything he needs, Blumfeld just sits there, glaring into the bowl of his still unlit pipe. He is lying in wait. Suddenly, unexpectedly, his daze goes away, and he turns his armchair with a jerk. But the balls are just as vigilant, or thoughtlessly follow the law that governs them; simultaneously with Blumfeld they also change their position and hide behind his back. Blumfeld now sits with his back to the table, his cold pipe in his hand. The balls are jumping under the table now and are barely audible, as there is a rug there. This is a great advantage; there are only very faint, muffled noises, and one has to be very attentive to hear them. Blumfeld, however, is very attentive and can hear them clearly. But that is only for now; in a little while, he will most likely not hear them at all. The fact that they can barely make themselves heard on the rugs, it seems to Blumfeld, is an enormous weakness of the balls. All one has to do is shove one, or, even better, two rugs underneath them, and they are almost powerless. Only for a time, of course, and just their very presence bespeaks a certain power.

Blumfeld could really use a dog now; such a young wild animal would quickly take care of the balls: he pictures the dog striking at them with its paws, throwing them from their positions, chasing them all over the room and finally getting them between his teeth. It is easily possible that Blumfeld will acquire a dog in the near future.

For the time being, however, the balls only need to fear Blumfeld, and he does not feel like destroying them now; he just may well lack the determination to do so. He comes home from work, tired, and now that he needs to rest, he is met with this surprise. Only now does he feel how tired he really is. For sure, he will destroy the balls and in the very near future at that, but not for the time being and probably not until the next day. If one looks at the whole matter impartially, the balls act modestly enough. For example, they could jump out from time to time, show themselves and then return to their place, or they could jump higher to hit the tabletop and compensate for the damping effect of the rug. But they don't do that; they do not want to irritate Blumfeld without cause; they apparently limit themselves to the absolutely necessary.

But even the necessary is enough to spoil sitting at the table for Blumfeld. He has been sitting there for just a few minutes and is already thinking of going to bed. One reason is that he cannot smoke here, for he left his matches on the nightstand. So he would have to go get the matches, but once by the nightstand, it might well be better to stay there and lie down. He has an ulterior motive here, for he believes that, in their blind obsession to keep behind him, the balls will jump up on the bed so that, lying down, he will – wittingly or unwittingly – crush them. He dismisses the objection that the remnants of the balls might go on jumping as well. Even the unusual must have limits. Whole balls jump as a rule, even if not ceaselessly; fragments of balls, however, never jump, and so they won't jump here either.

"Get up!" he shouts, rendered almost mischievous by this thought, and stomps off to the bed with the balls behind him once more. His hope, it seems, comes true: as he makes a point of standing very close to the bed, a ball immediately jumps up on it. But then the unexpected happens: the other ball moves under the bed. The possibility that the balls could jump underneath the bed as well had not occurred to Blumfeld. He is indignant at this one ball, even though he feels how unfair this is, for, by jumping under the bed, the ball may fulfill its task even better than the ball on the bed. Now everything depends on which place the balls opt for, since Blumfeld does not believe that they can operate separately for very long. And indeed, in the next moment, the lower ball also leaps up on the bed. "Now I got them," Blumfeld thinks hot with joy and tears his dressing gown from his body to throw himself on the bed. But just then the same ball leaps under the bed again. In excessive disappointment, Blumfeld literally slumps into the bed. The ball has probably just looked around on top and did not like it. And now the other one follows and stays underneath, of course, for it is better underneath. "I will have those drummers here all night now," Blumfeld thinks, biting his lips and nodding his head.

He is sad without actually knowing how the balls could harm him during the night. His sleeps soundly; he will easily deal with this small noise. To be really sure, and in view of his recent experience, he pushes two rugs under them. It is as if he had a little dog he was trying to put on a soft bed. And as though the balls were tired and sleepy as well, their jumps have also become lower and slower than before. As Blumfeld kneels in front of the bed and shines his night lamp underneath, he has the fleeting thought that the balls will stay lying on the rugs for good, as weakly as they are falling now, as slowly as they are rolling for a bit. But then they rise again dutifully. It might very well be that, when Blumfeld checks under his bed in the morning, he will find two quiet, harmless children's balls there.

But it seems that they may not even be able to keep up their jumps until the morning, for as soon as he lies in bed, Blumfeld no longer hears them. He strains to hear something, leans out of bed, listening – not a sound. The rugs cannot be that effective; the only explanation is that the balls are no longer jumping, either because they cannot sufficiently push off the soft carpets and have therefore temporarily given up their jumps, or, which is more likely, because they will never jump again. Blumfeld could get up and see how things stand, but content that it is finally quiet, he prefers to stay prone, does not even want to touch upon the resting balls with his gaze. He is even glad to renounce his smoking, turns to the side, and falls asleep right away.

He does not remain undisturbed; his sleep is dreamless as always but very troubled. Countless times in the night he wakes up with a start, with the delusion that someone is knocking on the door. He knows for certain that no one is knocking: who would knock at night, and at his, the door of a lonesome bachelor. Even though he knows this for certain, he starts upright again, and again, and keenly gazes at the door for a while, his mouth open, his eyes wide, and strands of hair shaking on his sweaty forehead. He tries to count how many times he is woken up, but stunned by the enormous numbers he comes up with, he falls back to sleep. He thinks he knows where the knocking originates; it is not produced at the door, but in an entirely different place, but wrapped in sleep he cannot remember what he is basing his conjectures on. He only knows that many tiny nasty beats build up before they come out as a great big knock. But he would be ready to endure all the nastiness of the little beats to avoid the knocking, but for some reason it is too late, he cannot intervene, he missed it, he does not even have words, his mouth just opens in a silent yawn, and, angry about this, he thrusts his face into the pillows. Thus the night goes by.

In the morning his charwoman's knocking wakes him; with a sigh of relief he welcomes this gentle knock, even though he has always complained about it being inaudible. And he is about to call "Come in!" when he hears another lively, if feeble, but almost belligerent knocking. It is the balls under the bed. Have they woken up, have they – unlike him – gathered new strength during the night? "One moment," Blumfeld calls to the charwoman, jumps out of bed, cautiously, and in such a way so as to keep the balls behind his back. With his back turned toward them, he throws himself to the floor, glances at the balls with his twisted head and – almost feels like swearing. Just like children pushing away their annoying blankets in the night, the balls – probably by twitching constantly but almost unnoticeably throughout the night – have pushed the rugs so far from under the bed that they themselves have the bare wood floor underneath them and can make noise. "Back onto the rugs," Blumfeld says with an angry expression. Only when, due to the rugs, the balls have become silent again does he call the charwoman inside. While she, a fat, obtuse, always stiffly upright woman, is placing the breakfast on the table and doing the few necessary chores, Blumfeld stands motionless by the bed in his dressing gown so as to keep the balls down there. He follows the charwoman with his eyes to see if she notices anything. Since she is hard of hearing, this is very unlikely, and Blumfeld attributes it to his irritation brought on by his poor sleep that he imagines seeing the charwoman pause now and then, holding onto a piece of furniture and listening with arched eyebrows. He would be glad if he could make the charwoman hurry up her work, but she is almost slower than usual. She tediously burdens herself with Blumfeld's clothes and boots and trudges into the hallway with them, staying away for a long time: The monotonous and scattered beats with which she cleans his clothes outside sound over to him. And during all this time, Blumfeld has to sit tight on the bed and cannot stir if he does not want to drag the balls behind him; he has to let the coffee, which he loves to drink as hot as possible, get cold and cannot do anything but stare at the drawn window curtains, behind which the day is dimly dawning. Finally the charwoman is finished, wishes a good morning and is about to leave. But before she finally leaves, she stands by the door for a while, moves her lips, and gives Blumfeld a long look. Blumfeld is about to take her to task when she finally leaves. More than anything Blumfeld wants to tear the door open and yell after her what a dumb, old, obtuse woman she is. But when he thinks about what exactly he has against her, he only finds the paradox that she undoubtedly had not noticed anything and yet tried to give the impression that she had noticed something after all. How confused his thoughts are! And just because of one poorly slept night! He finds some explanation for his poor sleep in the fact that he deviated from his habits last night, not smoking and not drinking liquor. "When for once," that is the conclusion of his pondering, "I don't smoke and drink, I sleep poorly."

From now on he will pay more attention to his own well-being and, for a start, takes some cotton from the medicine cabinet above the nightstand and stuffs two small cotton balls into his ears. Then he stands up and takes a trial step. While the balls follow him, he almost cannot hear them, and an extra wad of cotton makes them completely inaudible. Blumfeld takes a few more steps; it works without any particular inconvenience. Everyone is for themselves, Blumfeld as much as the balls; even though they are bound together, they don't interfere with one another either. Only once, when Blumfeld turns around more quickly and one ball is not quick enough to do the countermovement, does Blumfeld touch it with his knee. This is the only incident; other than that, Blumfeld quietly drinks his coffee; he is hungry as if he had not slept that night and walked a long distance instead; he washes in cold, immensely refreshing water and puts on his clothes. So far he has not pulled up the curtains but rather stayed in the semidarkness as a precaution; he has no use for someone else's eyes on the balls. But as he is ready to leave, he has to somehow provide for the balls in case that they would dare – even though he does not think so – to follow him into the street. He has a good idea for that: he opens the large wardrobe and stands against it with his back. The balls, as if sensing what was intended, stay clear of the wardrobe's inside, they use every bit of space between Blumfeld and the wardrobe, when there is no other way, they even bounce inside the wardrobe for a moment but then flee the dark right away. It is impossible to take them across the edge into the wardrobe; they would rather violate their duty and almost stay by Blumfeld's side. But their little ruses are of no avail, for now Blumfeld himself steps backward into the wardrobe, and so they must follow along. That is the end of them, for on the wardrobe floor there are various smaller objects such as boots, boxes, small valises that – Blumfeld regrets this now – are well organized, yet still obstruct the balls very much. And when Blumfeld, who in the meantime has almost completely closed the door of the wardrobe, gets out of the wardrobe with a great leap as he has not made one in years, pushes the door closed, and turns the key, the balls are trapped. "Now that worked out all right," Blumfeld thinks and wipes the sweat off his face. How the balls are rioting inside the wardrobe! One would think that they are desperate. Blumfeld, however, is very contented. He leaves the room, and even the dreary hallway has a soothing effect on him. He frees his ears of the cotton, and the various noises of the waking house delight him. There are only few people to be seen; it is still quite early.

Down in the hallway, in front of the low door leading to the charwoman's basement apartment, there stands her little ten-year-old boy. A spitting image of his mother, none of the old woman's ugliness has been omitted in that child's face. Bow-legged, his hands in his pockets, he stands there, wheezing, because he already has a goiter and has difficulty breathing. While Blumfeld usually hastens his step to spare himself the spectacle when the boy crosses his path, he almost feels like stopping next to him today. Even though the boy was brought into the world by that woman and bears all the signs of his origin, for the time being, he is still a child, and there are children's thoughts in that unshapely head; if one talks to him sensibly and asks him something, he will probably reply with innocence and deference, and, overcoming some reluctance, one will even be able to stroke those cheeks. Such are Blumfeld's thoughts, but he still walks past him. In the street he notices that the weather is nicer than he had thought in his room. The morning mists divide, and patches of blue sky emerge, swept by a sturdy wind. Thanks to the balls Blumfeld has left his room much earlier than usual, he even left his newspaper on the table unread; no matter, he has gained a lot of time that way and can walk slowly now. It is strange how little he has worried about the balls, since he left them behind. For as long as they were pursuing him, one might have regarded them as something belonging to him, something that should somehow be brought into play to judge him as a person, whereas now they were just toys in his wardrobe at home. And suddenly it occurs to Blumfeld that the best way to render the balls harmless is by putting them to their intended use. The boy is still standing there in the hallway; Blumfeld will to give him the balls, and not just lend them to him but make a point of giving them to him, which is surely synonymous with ordering their annihilation. And even if they did remain intact, they would mean even less in the boy's hands than in the wardrobe; the entire building will see the boy playing with them, other children will join in, the general opinion that those are balls for playing and by no means Blumfeld's life companions will become entrenched and irresistible. Blumfeld runs back into the building. Just now the boy has descended the stairs to the basement and is about to open the door. So Blumfeld has to call the boy and utter his name, which is preposterous like everything related to this boy. He does so. "Alfred, Alfred," he calls out. The boy hesitates for a long time. "Just come here, will you," Blumfeld calls, "I'll give you something." The janitor's two little girls have come out the opposite door and curiously stand to Blumfeld's left and right. They have a much better grasp of things than the boy and do not understand why he doesn't come at once. They wave to him, keeping their eyes on Blumfeld, but cannot figure out what kind of gift is awaiting Alfred. Plagued by curiosity, they shift from one foot to the other. Blumfeld laughs about them as much as about the boy. The latter seems to finally have figured out everything and comes up the stairs stiffly and awkwardly. Not even in his gait can he belie his mother, who incidentally appears in the basement door. Blumfeld shouts excessively loud so that the charwoman can hear him as well and, if need be, supervise the execution of his assignment. "Upstairs in my room," Blumfeld says, "I have two beautiful balls. Do you want them?" The boy only twists his mouth; he doesn't know how to act, thus turns around and inquiringly looks at his mother. But right away the girls start leaping around Blumfeld and asking him for the balls. "You will be allowed to play with them as well," Blumfeld tells them, still waiting for the boy's reply. He might as well give the balls to the girls right off, but they seem too reckless, and so he trusts the boy more now. Without exchanging a word, the boy has meanwhile consulted his mother and nods in the affirmative to Blumfeld's repeated question. "Then listen carefully," says Blumfeld, who gladly overlooks the fact that he won't get any thanks for his present here, "Your mother has the key to my room, you must borrow it from her; here I am giving you the key to my wardrobe, and, inside the wardrobe, there are the balls. Carefully lock the wardrobe and the room afterward. You can do with the balls whatever you like, and you don't have to return them. Do you understand me?" But unfortunately, the boy does not understand. Blumfeld has tried to make everything especially clear to this immensely dim-witted individual, but for this purpose has repeated everything too often, has talked too much about keys, rooms, and wardrobes, and consequently the boy eyes him not like a benefactor but like a tempter. The girls, however, got everything right away, push against Blumfeld and hold out their hands for the key. "Just wait, will you?" Blumfeld says and is already upset about everyone. Time is passing as well; he cannot stay much longer. If only the charwoman would finally say that she understood and would take care of it for the boy. Instead she is still standing downstairs in the door, forcing a coy smile like a deaf person, thinking perhaps that Blumfeld upstairs has suddenly gone into raptures about her boy and was checking the boy's multiplication tables. Then again, Blumfeld cannot well go down the stairs to the basement again and yell his request into the charwoman's ear that her boy should for the love of God free him of the balls. He has already overcome himself enough, entrusting this family with the key to his wardrobe for an entire day. It is not to spare himself that he hands the key to the boy now rather than leading him up the stairs himself and handing the balls to him there. But he cannot very well first give away the balls upstairs and then, as it was bound to happen, take them from the boy right away by having them trail behind him in his wake. "So you don't understand me?" Blumfeld asks almost wistfully, having started another attempt at explanation that he immediately broke off at the vacant gaze of the boy. A vacant gaze like that makes one vulnerable. It might lead one to say more than one wants to, only to fill this vacancy with reason.

"We'll get the balls for him," the girls shout. They are clever; they have understood that they can get the balls only through some kind of intermediary of the boy, that they even have to provide this intermediary themselves. The clock sounds out of the janitor's room and urges Blumfeld to hurry. "You take the key then," Blumfeld says, and the key is pulled from his hand more than it is given. Had he given the key to the boy, he would have felt incomparably more secure. "You'll get the key to the room from the woman downstairs," Blumfeld adds. "And when you return with the balls, you must give both keys to the woman." "Yes, sure," the girls shout running down the stairs. They know everything, absolutely everything, and as if Blumfeld were infected by the boy's dull wit, he himself does not understand now how they had been able to gather everything so quickly from his explanations.

Now they are already tugging at the charwoman's skirt downstairs but Blumfeld, as tempting as it is, can no longer watch how they will go about their task, not only because it is late already, but also because he does not want to be present when the balls get out into the open. In fact, he would like to be several streets away when the girls first open the door to his room upstairs. He doesn't know what next to expect from those balls! And so he steps out onto the street a second time this morning. The last thing he saw was how the charwoman was basically fighting off the girls and how the boy was moving his bowed legs to come to his mother's aid. Blumfeld does not comprehend why people like the charwoman can thrive in this world and procreate.

On the way to the linen factory where Blumfeld is employed, thoughts about work gradually gain the upper hand over everything else. He accelerates his steps and despite the delay caused by the boy, he's the first one in his office. This office is a small room enclosed by glass; it contains a desk for Blumfeld and two high desks for the apprentices answering to Blumfeld. Even though these high desks are so small and narrow as if made for schoolchildren, it is still very cramped in the office, and the apprentices are not allowed to sit down because then there would be no more space for Blumfeld's chair. Thus they stand pressed against their high desks all day long. It is certainly very uncomfortable for them, but it also makes it harder for Blumfeld to observe them. They often push up against their desks eagerly, not so much to work but to whisper together or even nod off. Blumfeld has a lot of trouble with them; they don't support him enough with the gigantic responsibility he is assigned. This responsibility consists in overseeing the entire flow of merchandise and money with the home workers, whom the factory employs for the manufacture of certain more delicate wares. To appreciate the scope of this task, one would need a closer insight into all circumstances. However, since Blumfeld's immediate superior died a few years ago, no one has had this insight anymore; therefore Blumfeld cannot concede the right to judge his work to anyone either. The manufacturer Mr. Ottomar, for example, obviously underestimates Blumfeld's work; of course he recognizes the merits Blumfeld has gained in the factory over the course of twenty years, and he not only recognizes them because he has to, but because he respects Blumfeld as a loyal, trustworthy person; and yet he underestimates his work, namely because he thinks that the office could be run in a more simple, and hence more profitable, fashion than Blumfeld's. People say, and it is not implausible, that Ottomar so rarely visits Blumfeld's department to spare himself the frustration the sight of Blumfeld's work methods causes in him. Now it is certainly sad for Blumfeld to be misjudged like this, but there is no remedy, for he cannot very well force Ottomar to, say, spend one continuous month in Blumfeld's department, study the multiple work routines to be handled there, apply his own, supposedly better, methods and let himself be convinced of Blumfeld by the collapse of the department this would inevitably entail. Therefore Blumfeld performs his work as unperturbed as before, is a little startled when Ottomar appears after a long time; out of a sense of duty as his subordinate he makes a feeble effort to explain this or that to Ottomar, whereupon the latter walks on with lowered eyes silently nodding, and as it so happens Blumfeld suffers less from this misjudgment than under the idea that at one point, when he will have to resign his position, the immediate consequence would be a great muddle that no one could dissolve, for he doesn't know anyone in the factory who could replace him and fill his position in such a way that even just the most severe failures of the smooth operation of the factory could be prevented over months. If the boss underestimates someone, the employees, naturally, try to even outdo him if possible. So everyone underestimates Blumfeld's work; no one deems it necessary to train in Blumfeld's department for a while, and when new employees are hired, no one is assigned to Blumfeld of their own accord. As a result there's a lack of new talent in Blumfeld's department. Those were weeks of severe struggle when Blumfeld, who had thus far run the department all by himself only with the assistance of a servant, demanded to be assigned an apprentice. Blumfeld appeared in Ottomar's office almost every day and, in a calm and detailed manner, explained to him why an apprentice in the department was needed. An apprentice was not needed because Blumfeld wanted to take it easy on himself; Blumfeld did not want to take it easy on himself, he worked more than his share and was not thinking of stopping, but Mr. Ottomar may want to consider how business had grown over the course of time; all departments had been expanded correspondingly, only Blumfeld's department had always been forgotten. And yet it was precisely there that the workload had increased! When Blumfeld started out, Mr. Ottomar surely could not remember those days, there were about ten seamstresses to deal with; nowadays the number varied between fifty and sixty. This kind of work requires strength, and while Blumfeld could vouch for the fact that he completely wore himself out on the job, he could, from now on, no longer vouch for being able to handle it all. Now Mr. Ottomar never outright refused Blumfeld's requests; he couldn't well do that to an old employee, but the way he barely listened, talked to other people over Blumfeld's pleading head, made half-hearted promises, forgot everything after a few days – that kind of behavior was quite insulting. Not so much for Blumfeld, Blumfeld is no fantasist: as pleasant as honor and appreciation may be, Blumfeld can do without them. He will nonetheless hold out on his job as long as is possible; at any rate he is in the right, and even though it may take a long time, what is right must eventually prevail. Hence, in fact, Blumfeld even ended up getting even two apprentices, but what kind of apprentices, indeed. One might have thought that Ottomar had realized that he could show his disregard of Blumfeld's department even more plainly, rather than by refusing him apprentices, by granting him these apprentices. It was even possible that Ottomar had only put off Blumfeld for such a long time because he had searched for two apprentices like these, and, as is well understandable, not been able to find them for a long time. And Blumfeld could not very well complain now, for the reply was foreseeable: he had even been assigned two apprentices, whereas he had only demanded for one; this is how cleverly Ottomar had set up everything. Even so, Blumfeld still complained, of course, but only because an emergency virtually pushed him to, not because he still hoped for an improvement. Also he didn't complain vigorously, only once in a while when a suitable occasion happened to arise. Nevertheless the rumor soon spread among his ill-wishing colleagues that someone had asked Ottomar whether it was possible that Blumfeld, who had now received this extraordinary support, was still complaining. To which Ottomar supposedly replied that this was correct, Blumfeld was still complaining but rightly so. He, Ottomar, had finally recognized the situation and intended to assign Blumfeld little by little one apprentice for each seamstress, so about sixty in total. If those still were not enough, he would send even more and he would not stop until it was the perfect madhouse, which had been in the making at Blumfeld's department for years already. Admittedly this remark was a good imitation of Ottomar's manner of speaking, but he himself, Blumfeld had no doubt here, was far from saying anything similar about Blumfeld. The whole thing was a fabrication of those slackers in the offices on the second floor; Blumfeld disregarded it; if only he had been able to disregard the presence of the apprentices just as calmly. But they just stood there and nothing could drive them away. Pale, weak children. According to their documents they had already passed school age, but in reality one could not believe that. Indeed, one would not even want to entrust a teacher with them, that is how clear it was that they should still be in their mother's care. They could not even move properly, long periods of standing tired them tremendously, especially in the beginning. When left unobserved, they immediately doubled up in their weakness, standing crooked and bent over in a corner. Blumfeld tried to make them understand that they would cripple themselves for life if they continued to indulge their indolence. Assigning a small errand to the apprentices was risky; once one of them had been asked to carry something just a few steps, he had run there overeagerly and injured his knee on a desk. The room had been full of seamstresses, the desks full of merchandise, but Blumfeld had been forced to abandon everything, lead the crying apprentice into the office, and put a small bandage on him. But even this eagerness on the part of the apprentices was only outward; like real children they tried to set themselves apart once in a while, but far more frequently, or, rather almost always, they simply tried to misdirect their superior's attention and deceive him. Once, at a time of most intense workload, Blumfeld had raced past them dripping with sweat and had caught them hidden among bales of merchandise swapping stamps. He had felt like pounding them on the head with his fists, which would have been the only suitable punishment for such conduct, but they were children, Blumfeld could not very well kill children. And so he continued to agonize over them. Originally he had imagined that the apprentices would support him with the actual chores, which required so much effort and vigilance during the distribution of the merchandise. He had imagined himself standing somewhere in the center behind his desk, continually overseeing everything and keeping the records, while the apprentices ran back and forth according to his orders and distributed everything. He had imagined that his supervision which, as rigid as it was, could not be sufficient for such a commotion, would be complemented by the apprentices' attention, and that those apprentices would gradually gather experiences, no longer depend on his orders for every detail and ultimately learn to distinguish between the seamstresses in terms of product requirements and trustworthiness. With regard to these apprentices those had been perfectly vain hopes; Blumfeld very quickly realized that he could not let them talk to the seamstresses at all. From the beginning on they had not even dealt with some of the seamstresses, out of dislike or fear, whereas they had often gone to meet others, whom they favored, at the door. To them they gave whatever they desired, pressed it into their hands with a kind of secrecy even if the seamstresses were perfectly entitled to receive it; on an empty shelf, they collected various scraps, worthless remnants but nevertheless usable bits, blissfully waved them at the favorite ones from far behind Blumfeld's back, and, in return, had candy popped into their mouths. Blumfeld, however, soon put an end to this mischief and rushed them behind the partition whenever the seamstresses came. But for a long time they thought of this as a grave injustice, sulked, willfully broke their pens and sometimes, not even daring to raise their heads, loudly knocked on the glass panes to alert the seamstresses to the abuse they felt they were suffering from Blumfeld.

But they do not even see their own wrongdoing. Thus, for example, they are almost always late at the office. Blumfeld, their superior, who has from his early youth considered it natural to turn up at least a half hour before the office opens – it is not zeal, no exaggerated sense of duty, just a certain feeling of propriety that leads him to do so – Blumfeld usually has to wait for his apprentices for more than an hour. Munching his breakfast roll he usually stands behind his desk in the hall balancing the accounts in the seamstresses' small books. Soon he becomes engrossed in his work thinking of nothing else. Then he is suddenly so startled that the pen in his hand still trembles for a while. One apprentice has stormed in; he looks like he is about to collapse, holding onto something with one hand, pressing the other against his heaving chest – but all this does not mean much because his apology for being late is so ridiculous that Blumfeld deliberately ignores it because, if he did not, he would have to give the boy his well-deserved beating. But he only gazes at him for a while, then points to the partition with his outstretched hand and returns to his work. Now one would expect the apprentice to acknowledge his superior's kindness and rush to his workplace. But no, he does not rush, he sashays, he walks on his toes, puts one foot in front of the other. Is he trying to mock his superior? Not even that. Once again it is this mix of fear and complacency against which one is defenseless. How else could it be explained that today, when Blumfeld himself got to the office unusually late, after a long wait – he does not feel like checking the small books – through the dust clouds stirred up by the stupid servant with his broom, he sees the two apprentices peacefully walking along the street. Their arms wrapped around each other they seem to talk about important things that, if at all, surely relate to the business in an impermissible way. The closer they get to the glass door, the slower they walk. Finally one of them grabs the door handle, but he does not push it down, they are still talking to one another, listening and laughing. "Just open the door for our gentlemen, will you," Blumfeld yells at the servant with raised hands. But when the apprentices enter, Blumfeld does not feel like quarreling anymore, does not answer their greetings, and goes to his desk. He starts doing his calculations, looking up once in a while to see what the apprentices are up to. One of them appears to be very tired, yawning and rubbing his eyes; when he has hung up his overcoat, he uses the occasion to lean on the wall for a bit; he was lively in the street but the proximity to work makes him tired. The other apprentice, however, feels like working but only certain kinds of chores. Thus it has always been his wish to have permission to sweep up. Now that of course is the kind of work that is not befitting for him, sweeping up is only for the servant. Blumfeld is not actually opposed to the apprentice sweeping up, let the apprentice sweep up, one cannot do it any worse than the servant, but if the apprentice wants to sweep up, he should come early before the servant starts sweeping and not use the time during which he must exclusively do office work. If the boy is impervious to any reasonable argument, at least the servant, this half-blind old man, whom the boss certainly would not tolerate anywhere other than at Blumfeld's department and who only lives by the grace of God and the boss, at least this servant might be accommodating and, for just a moment, leave the broom to the boy, who is clumsy, and will lose his enthusiasm for sweeping right away and run after the servant with the broom to make him sweep again. But it seems that the servant feels particularly responsible for the sweeping, one can see how he, as soon as the boy approaches him, tries to clasp the broom more tightly with his trembling hands; he stands still and stops sweeping so as to focus all his attention on possession of the broom. Now the apprentice pleads without words, for he is afraid of Blumfeld who pretends to be calculating; also ordinary words would be of no use, since the servant can only be reached through excessive shouting. So the apprentice tugs the servant on his sleeve at first. The servant, of course, knows what this is about, looks grimly at the apprentice, shakes his head, and pulls the broom closer to his chest. Now the apprentice folds his hands to plead. He does not have much hope of achieving anything by his pleading, it is only that the pleading amuses him, and that is why he pleads. The other apprentice observes the scene with soft laughter and seems to think, quite inexplicably, that Blumfeld cannot hear him. The servant is not in the least impressed by the pleading; he turns around and thinks that it is safe to use the broom again. But the apprentice has followed him, jumping on his toes and rubbing his hands to plead to him from the other side. The servant's turns and the apprentice's jumps are repeated several times. Eventually the servant feels cut off from all sides and realizes something he might have realized right at the beginning, had he been just a little less gullible: that he will grow tired more quickly than the apprentice. Consequently he seeks outside help, wags his finger at the apprentice and points to Blumfeld, with whom he will lodge complaint if the apprentice does not desist. The apprentice understands that he has to act very fast now if he wants to get the broom at all. So he impudently reaches for the broom. The involuntary shriek the other apprentice lets out forebodes the imminent decision. The servant saves the broom once more by taking a step back and pulling it toward him. But now the apprentice no longer caves in, his mouth open and eyes flashing, he leaps forward, the servant tries to escape, but his old legs quiver instead of walking, the apprentice tugs at the broom, and, even though he does not manage to grasp it, he makes the broom drop, and it is thereby lost by the servant. Lost to the apprentice as well, it seems, for at the drop of the broom all three, the apprentices and the servant, freeze, for now Blumfeld must become aware of everything. In fact, Blumfeld looks up behind his spy window as if he had noticed just now, sternly and probingly he scrutinizes each one of them, not even the broom on the floor escapes his notice. Whether the silence lasts too long or the culpable apprentice cannot suppress his desire to sweep up, at any rate, he bends down, albeit very cautiously, as if he were grabbing an animal rather than the broom, takes the broom, drags it across the floor, but immediately throws it down, startled, when Blumfeld jumps up and steps out from behind the partition. "Both of you back to work and not a sound," Blumfeld screams and with his outstretched hand directs the two apprentices toward their high desks. They obey immediately, but not abashed with hanging heads, no, rather they slink past him stiffly and stare into his eyes, as though trying to keep him from hitting them. And yet experience might have amply taught them that Blumfeld never beats anyone on principle. But they are overly anxious and always try to protect their true or imaginary rights without any sensitivity.

17

<u>Steadfast dream.</u>

She walked down the country road, I did not see her; I sat by the edge of the field and gazed into the water in the small brook. She walked through the villages; children were standing in the doors, watching her come and watching her go.

<u>Disrupted Dream.</u>

A previous prince's whim had decreed that the mausoleum needed a guard right next to the sarcophagi. Reasonable men had spoken out against it; ultimately the Prince, restricted in multiple other respects, was allowed to do as he pleased in this minor matter. An invalid from a war of the previous century, a widower and father of three sons who had fallen in the last war, applied for the position. He was accepted and accompanied to the mausoleum by an elderly court official. A laundress followed them, loaded down with miscellaneous things intended for the guard. Until reaching the avenue leading straight to the mausoleum the invalid, despite his crutch, kept pace with the court official. But then he started to fail a bit, coughing slightly and rubbing his left leg. "Well, Friedrich," the court official said who had gone ahead a bit with the laundress and was now turning back. "I have this ache in my leg," the invalid said and grimaced, "just a moment, this usually stops right away."

<u>narrowest stage free to the top</u>
Small study, a high window, a bare treetop in front of it.

<u>Prince</u> (leaning back in an armchair at his desk, looking out the window)
<u>Adjutant</u> (white beard, youthfully squeezed into a tight jacket, standing at the wall next to the middle door)
Small pause.
<u>Prince</u> (turning from the window toward the Adjutant) Well?
<u>Adjutant</u> I cannot recommend it, your Highness.

Prince Why not?

Adjutant I cannot quite put my misgivings into words at the moment; it is by far not all I mean to say when I cite the universal adage: Let the dead rest in peace.

Prince That is my intention as well.

Adjutant Then I did not understand you correctly.

Prince So it seems.

Pause

Prince The only reason you are puzzled about this might be the peculiarity that I did not give the order immediately but announced it to you beforehand.

Adjutant But then the announcement imposes a greater responsibility on me, which I must attempt to live up to.

Prince (annoyed) No responsibility.

Pause

Prince Well, let me tell you again. So far the mausoleum in Friedrichspark has been watched over by a guard, who has a cabin by the park entrance where he lives with his family. Was there anything wrong with this arrangement?

Chamberlain Certainly not. The mausoleum is more than four hundred years old and has been guarded in this manner for just as long.

Prince It could be an old abuse. But it is no abuse?

Chamberlain It is a necessary institution.

Prince A necessary institution, then. But now I have concluded that the guard up in the park is not enough, rather another guard must keep watch down in the tomb as well. This may not be a pleasant post, especially since the tomb must always be locked from the outside. But experience has shown that suitable and willing people can be found for any post.

Taking a rest near you is the greatest thing a servant can aspire to.

In order to pay a visit to the Prince

THE GRANDFATHER'S TALE

During the days of the late Prince Leo V I was the mausoleum guard in Friedrichspark. Of course, I didn't become the mausoleum guard at once. I remember exactly the first time I was asked, as an errand boy for the princely dairy, to take the milk to the mausoleum guard for the first time one evening. "Oh," I thought, "to the mausoleum guard." Does anyone really know what a mausoleum is? I was the mausoleum guard and so should know but in fact I don't. And you who hear my story will see in the end that you have to admit that even if you thought you knew what a mausoleum was, you don't know any longer. At the time I didn't really worry about this, but was just proud in general to have been sent to the mausoleum guard. And so with my milk pail I galloped through the mists on the meadow paths leading to Friedrichspark right away. Outside the gilded wrought iron gate I dusted off my jacket, cleaned my boots, wiped the moisture off my pail, then rang the bell and with my forehead on the bars waited to see what happened next. The guardhouse seemed to be between the shrubs on a knoll; a light shone from an opening door, and a very old woman came to open the gate after I had announced my purpose and shown my pail as proof of truth. She then had me go ahead but only as slowly as the woman; I was very uneasy for she held onto me from behind and stopped twice on the short stretch to catch her breath. At the top, on a stone bench next to the door, there sat a giant of a man, his legs crossed, his hands folded over his chest, his head leaning back, his gaze fixed on the shrubs just in front of him that obstructed any further view. Instinctively I gave the woman an inquiring look. "This is the Mameluke," she said, "don't you know?" I shook my head, marveled at the man once more, especially his tall Crimean lamb fur hat, but was then pulled into the house by the old woman. In a small room, at a table neatly covered with books, there sat an old bearded man in his dressing gown gazing toward me from under the lampshade of the floor lamp. Of course, I thought I had not gone the right way and turned around, to leave the room, but the old woman blocked my path and said to the man: "The new milkboy." "Come here, you little crab," the gentleman said laughing. I sat down on a small bench by his table and he brought his face very close to mine. Unfortunately the warm welcome had made me a little insolent and I said:

IN THE ATTIC

The children had a secret. Among the junk of an entire century stored in the attic, in a deep nook to which no adult could any longer grope the way, Hans, the lawyer's son, had discovered a stranger. He was sitting on a crate leaning upright against the wall. When he laid eyes on Hans his face showed neither shock nor surprise, just apathy; his clear eyes answered Hans' gaze. A large round krimmer fur hat sat low on his head. A thick mustache spread stiffly across his face. He was clad in a loose brown coat, held together by massive straps reminiscent of a horse's harness. On his lap, he had a short curved saber in a dimly glowing sheath. His feet were shod in spurred high boots; one foot was propped on an overturned wine bottle, the other one was somewhat upturned on the floor and rammed into the wood with the heel and spur. "Go away," yelled Hans when the man slowly reached for him; he ran deep into the newer reaches of the attic and did not stop until the wet laundry hung up to dry smacked him in the face. But then he returned right away nonetheless. His lower lip jutting out with some contempt, the stranger sat there and did not budge. Cautiously sneaking up on him, Hans tested whether this immobility was not a trap. But the stranger really did not seem to be up to anything bad; he sat there completely limp, and all this limpness made his head nod ever so slightly. Thus Hans plucked up the courage to push aside the old perforated fire screen, go right up to him and finally even touch him. "You're so dusty!" he said in astonishment and pulled back his blackened hand. "Dusty indeed," the stranger said, nothing else. His was an unusual pronunciation; only from the lingering sound did Hans understand the words. "I'm Hans," he said, "the lawyer's son and who are you." "Well," said the stranger, "I'm another Hans; my name is Hans Schlag, I'm a hunter from Baden hailing from Kossgarten on Neckar. Old stories."

After his mother's death, the perpetual discord between Hans and his father had erupted in such a way that Hans resigned from his father's business, traveled abroad, in a sort of absent-minded state instantly accepted a small post that had opened up, and avoided all contact with his father – be it through letters, be it through acquaintances – with such success that he learned about his father's death, which occurred from a heart attack about two years after his departure, only through the letter from the lawyer informing him about the inheritance. Hans had been designated the sole heir, but the inheritance was so burdened with debts and bequests that, as his first quick calculations indicated, little more remained for him than the parental house. That was not much: a simple old one-story building, but Hans was very attached to the house; also, there was nothing to keep him abroad after his father's death; however, his presence was indispensable for handling all the inheritance-related business, so he canceled all his obligations, which was not difficult, and went home. It was a late December evening; everything was covered with snow when Hans drove up to his parental home. The awaiting janitor came out through the gate, supported by his daughter; he was a frail old man who had already served under Hans' grandfather. Greetings were exchanged, if not very warm ones, for Hans had always viewed the janitor as a simple-minded tyrant of his childhood years and was embarrassed to find the old man approaching him with such humility. He said to the daughter, who was carrying his bags behind him up the steep, narrow stairs, that nothing in her father's situation and income would change in the least, regardless of the bequest he had received. The daughter thanked him tearfully, admitting that his words put an end to the anxiety that had scarcely allowed her father any sleep since the late master's demise. Her gratitude made it clear to Hans for the first time what inconveniences arose for him from the inheritance and might yet arise. All the more he looked forward to the solitude of his old room and, in anticipation, gently stroked the cat rushing past in all his magnitude as the first untainted memory of times past. But now Hans was not led into his room, which according to the orders he had sent in a letter should have been prepared for him, but rather into his father's former bedroom. He asked why this was so. The girl, still breathing heavily from carrying the luggage, stood opposite him; she had grown tall and strong in the past two years, and her gaze was remarkably clear. She apologized. For his Uncle Theodor had settled into Hans' room, and one had been reluctant to disturb the old man, especially since this room was larger and cozier, too. The fact that Uncle Theodor was living in the house was news to Hans.

Chamberlain Of course, every one of your Highness's orders will be executed, even if the necessity of the order is not understood.
Prince (indignant) Necessity! Is the guard at the park gate necessary? Friedrichspark is part of the manor grounds, completely contained in it; the manor grounds itself is amply guarded, even by the military. Why do we need

a special guard in Friedrichspark then? Isn't this a mere formality? A friendly deathbed for the miserable old man in charge there?

Chamberlain It is a formality but a necessary one, a homage to the late greats.

Prince And what about a guard in the tomb itself?

Chamberlain In my opinion this would have a secondary purpose as a form of policing. This would be a real guard for things unreal and far removed from anything human.

Prince (stands up) For my family this tomb marks the boundary between the Human and the other, and I would like to place a guard at this boundary. As far as the – as you put it – policing necessity is concerned, we can question the guard himself. I've sent for him. (Rings bell.)

Chamberlain He is, if your Highness will permit me this comment, a confused old man, out of control.

Prince If that is so, it would be all the more proof for the necessity of reinforcing the guard as I suggested.

Servant

Prince The tomb guard!

The servant leads the guard inside, supporting him under the arm lest he collapse. Old red, loosely hanging festive livery, shining silver buttons, various decorations. Cap in hand. He shivers under the two gentlemen's gazes.

Prince Onto the daybed!

The servant lays him down and leaves.

Pause, just guard's softly rattling breath.

Prince (again in his armchair) Can you hear me?

Guard tries to reply, can't, is too exhausted, sinks back onto the bed.

Prince Try to compose yourself, we'll wait.

Chamberlain (bending down to the Prince) What is it that this man could give us information about, and plausible or important information at that. The servant should have left him in bed.

Prince He wasn't in bed.

Guard Not in bed, not in bed – still strong – considering – still hold my own.

Prince That's the way it should be. You're only sixty years old. You look very frail, though.

Guard Will recover in a moment, your Highness, recover in a moment.

Prince It wasn't a reproach. I'm just very sorry that you're not well. Do you have any complaints?

Guard Hard service – your Highness – hard service – not complaining but exhausted very – wrestling-matches every night.

Prince What did you say?

Guard Hard service.

Prince You said something after that.

Guard Wrestling matches.

Prince Wrestling matches? What kind of wrestling matches?

Guard With the late ancestors.

Prince I don't understand. Do you have heavy dreams?

Guard No dreams, your Highness; I don't even sleep at night.

Prince Well, then tell me about these – these wrestling matches.

Guard remains silent.

Prince (to the Chamberlain) Why doesn't he speak?

Chamberlain (hastening to the Guard) It might be over with him any moment.

Prince (stands up, but remains at the table)

Guard (when the Chamberlain touches him) Go away, go away, go away (wrestles with Chamberlain's fingers, flings himself down, crying).

Prince We are tormenting him.

Chamberlain How?

Prince I don't know.

Chamberlain Walking to the manor, appearing here, the sight of your Highness, the questioning – he no longer has enough sense to handle all this anymore.

Prince (contemplating the Guard) That's not it. (Goes to the daybed, bends down to the Guard, takes his little skull between his hands) No need to cry. Why are you crying? We wish you well. I myself believe that your post is not easy. You've surely rendered great services to my House. So don't cry and tell me.

Guard screams: But I am so of the gentleman over there (gazes not timorously but threateningly at the Chamberlain).

Prince He's afraid of you, you will have to leave so that he can talk. I'll send for you later.

Chamberlain But you see, your Highness, he is frothing at the mouth, he is gravely ill. Prince (absentmindedly) Why, just go, it won't take long.

Chamberlain exits.

Prince (sits down on the edge of the daybed)

Pause

Prince Why were you afraid of him?

Guard (strikingly composed) I wasn't afraid. Me afraid of a servant?

Prince He's not a servant; he's a Count, free and wealthy.

Guard And yet just a servant; you are the master.

Prince (smiles) If you please. But you said yourself that you were afraid.

Guard Saying things in front of him that only you should know. Haven't I already said enough in front of him?

Prince So we are confidants, and yet I've seen you for the first time today.

Guard Seen for the first time. But you've always known that I (raised index finger) hold the most important office at the court. You even acknowledged it publicly by awarding me the medal "Flaming Red." Here it is. (Lifts the medal from his coat.)

Prince (smiles) No, that is a medal for twenty-five years of service to the court; my grandfather gave it to you, but I will decorate you as well.

Guard (unflustered) Do as you like and as corresponds to the significance of my service. I've been serving as your tomb guard for thirty years.

Prince Not mine, my reign has barely lasted a year.

Guard (pensive) Thirty years.

Pause

Guard (half referring to the Prince's remark) Nights last years there.

Prince I haven't received a report from your office. What is the job like?

Guard The same every night. Every night my jugular veins almost burst.

Prince Is it only the night duty then? Night duty for an old man like you?

Guard That's exactly it, your Highness. It's day duty. A slacker's job. Sitting by the front door, my mouth gaping in the sunshine. Once in a while the guard dog pats your knee with its front paws and then lies down again. That's the only change of pace.

Prince Well.

Guard (nodding) But it has been converted to night duty.

Prince But by whom?

Guard By the lords of the tomb.

Prince You know them?

Guard I do.

Prince They come to see you?

Guard They do.

Prince Last night, too?

Guard Too.

Prince What was it like?

Guard As always. (Sits up)

149

Prince stands up.

Guard As always. All is quiet until midnight. I'm lying – forgive me – in my bed smoking my pipe. My granddaughter is asleep in the bed next to mine. At midnight there is the first knock on the window. I glance at the clock; it's always on time. Then two more knocks mingling with the clock strokes from the tower and just as loud. Those are no human knuckles. I, however, know all this, and so I don't budge. Then there is throat clearing outside, as if someone is surprised that I don't open the window. Every night he's surprised. May his princely Highness be surprised! The old guard is still there. (Shakes his fist)

Prince You're threatening me?

Guard (doesn't understand right away) Not you, the one outside the window.

Prince Who is it?

Guard He shows himself promptly. Both windows and the shutter open all at once. I barely have time to throw a blanket over my granddaughter's face. The storm blows inside, puts out the light in no time. Duke Friedrich! His face covered with hair and beard completely fills my poor window. How he has evolved over the centuries. When he opens his mouth to talk, the wind blows his old beard between his teeth, and he bites on it.

Prince Wait. You said Duke Friedrich. Which Friedrich?

Guard Duke Friedrich, just Duke Friedrich.

Prince That is how he says his name?

Guard (anxious) No, he doesn't say it–

Prince How do you know (breaking off), just go on.

Guard Do you want me to go on?

Prince Of course, do go on, all this concerns me; there's a problem with the distribution of labor; you were overburdened.

Guard (kneeling down) Don't take away my post, your Highness! Now that I've lived for you for such a long time, let me die for you as well. Don't wall up the tomb in front of me to which I strive. I enjoy serving, and I'm still able to serve. An audience like the one today gives me strength for another ten years. Then, like today, just grant me once more this greatest joy for a servant, to rest a little bit in the presence of his master.

Prince (sits him down on the daybed again) No one is taking away your post. How could I do without your experience? But I will appoint another guard and you will be made head guard.

Guard Am I not enough? Have I ever let anyone through?

Prince Into Friedrichspark?

Guard No, out of the park. Who wants to go inside? If anyone stops in front of the fence, I wave my hand out the window and he runs away. But out, everyone wants out. After midnight you can see all those voices from the tomb gathered around my house. I think it's only because they huddle together that they don't all crowd inside through the narrow window hole with everything they are. However, if it gets all too bad, I take my lantern from under the bed, swing it up, and they, incomprehensible creatures, tear away laughing and whining, I can hear them murmuring even in the last shrub at the end of the park. But they soon gather themselves again.

Prince And they tell you their request.

Guard At first they give orders. Most of all Duke Friedrich. No living beings are this confident. Every night for thirty years he has been expecting to find me worn down this time.

Prince If he has been coming for thirty years, he can't be Duke Friedrich who just died fifteen years ago. But he's the only one in the tomb by that name.

Guard (already too caught up in the tale) I don't know, your Highness, I'm not learned. I just know how he starts off. "You old dog," he starts by the window, "the masters are knocking and you stay in your dirty bed." You see, they're always furious about beds. And then we say almost the same thing every night. He outside, I opposite him with my back against the door. I say: "I'm only on day duty." The Duke turns around and shouts into the park: "He's only on day duty." There's general laughter of the assembled nobility. Then the Duke says to me again: "But it is day." I say curtly: "You're wrong." The Duke: "Day or night, open the gate." Me: "It's against my orders." And with the stem of my pipe I point to a sheet of paper on the wall. The Duke: "But you're our guard after all." I: "Your guard, but employed by the reigning Prince." He: "Our guard, that's what counts. So open up, and do it now." I: "No." He: "You fool, you're losing your post; Duke Leo has invited us for today."

Prince (quickly) I?

Guard You.

Pause

When I hear your name, I lose my firmness. That's why I've leaned against the door from the start as a precaution. Outside they all sing your name. "Where's the invitation?" I ask weakly. "You bed beast," he screams and rouses me unintentionally, "You doubt my ducal word?" I say: "I don't have orders, and that is why I'm not opening, I'm not opening, I'm not opening." "He's not opening," the Duke shouts outside, "well then forward, everyone, the whole dynasty, to the gate, we are opening ourselves." And then there's no one in front of my window.

Pause

Prince That is everything?

Guard How would it be? Now, this is where my actual duty begins. Out of the door, around the house, and already I collide with the Duke, and there we are swaying in combat. He so tall, I so short, he so wide, I so thin, I wrestle only with his feet but sometimes he lifts me up and then I wrestle from above, too. All his companions are around us in a circle, ridiculing me. One, for example, cuts open my trousers in the back and then they all play with my shirttails while I'm wrestling. I don't understand why they laugh since I've always won so far.

Prince But how can it be that you win. Do you have weapons?

Guard Only in the first few years did I take weapons with me. What good could they be against him; they only weighed me down. We only fight with our fists or actually only with the strength of our breaths. And you are in my thoughts all the time.

Pause

Guard But I never doubt my victory. Only sometimes I'm afraid that he could drop me between his fingers and would not know anymore that he's fighting.

Prince And when have you won?

Guard When the day breaks. Then he throws me down and spits at me; that's his admission of defeat. But I have to lie prone for another hour until I fully recover my breath.

Pause

Prince (stands up) But tell me, don't you know what they actually want?

Guard Out of the park.

Prince But why?

Guard I don't know.

Prince Haven't you asked them?

Guard I haven't.

Prince Why not?

Guard I am afraid to, but I'll ask them today if you want.

Prince (frightened, loudly) Today!

Guard (expertly) Yes, today.

Prince And you don't have an inkling of what they want?

Guard (pensive) No.

Pause

152

Guard Perhaps I should add this: sometimes early in the morning while I lie there breathless, too weak to open my eyes as well, there comes a tender creature to me, moist and hairy to the touch, a latecomer, Countess Isabella. She touches me in many places, reaches into my beard, in all her length brushes along my neck under my chin and says: "Not the others, but me, let me out." I shake my head as much as can. "To Prince Leo, to take his hand." I don't stop shaking my head. "But me, me" I hear her say again, then she's gone. And my granddaughter comes with blankets, wraps me up and waits by my side until I can walk by myself. Such an extraordinarily good girl.

Prince An unfamiliar name, Isabella.

Pause

Prince To take my hand. (Stands by the window, looks outside)

Pause

Prince (back to the table, rings bell)

Servant

Prince The Chamberlain.

Chamberlain enters, at the same time Guard falls from the daybed with a little cry.

Prince (jumps to his side) Eternal imprudence! I should have thought of it! The doctor! The servants!

Chamberlain exits, returns right away with the servants, stays by the open door.

Prince (kneeling by the Guard) Water! Make a bed for him! Wherever you want. Next to my bedroom. Get a stretcher. Is a doctor on the way? How long it is taking him! His pulse is so weak. I can't feel his heart! This poor ribcage! How worn out it all is. And yet, the breath is better already. A healthy stock, even in the greatest misery it doesn't fail. But the doctor! Will he ever arrive. (Gazes toward the door, Guard raises his hand, strokes the Prince's cheek once)

Lord Steward enters slowly, remains standing by the door (youngish man, officer's uniform, calm observing gaze, says loudly) The doctor will be a quarter of an hour. He went out. A horseman has been sent for him.

Prince (more self-controlled, with an eye on the Guard) We can wait a little bit. He's calmer now.

Servant with stretcher

Prince (stands up, to the Lord Steward) Even you have come.

Lord Steward I saw the commotion in the hallways. I had reason to think that an accident had happened.

Prince (without replying, with the stretcher bearers, helps them load) Take him

153

gently. Oh, with your paws. Lift the head a bit. The stretcher closer. The pillow lower in the back. The arm! The arm! You're poor, poor orderlies. Will you ever be as exhausted as this one on the stretcher. –Well. –And now with the slowest step possible. And most of all evenly. I'll stay behind you.

[18]

Small study, a high window, a bare treetop in front of it.

Prince (leaning back in an armchair at his desk, looking out the window)
Chamberlain (white beard, youthfully squeezed into a tight jacket, at the wall, next to the middle door)

Pause

Prince (turning away from the window): Well?

Chamberlain: I cannot recommend it, your Highness.

Prince: Why not?

Chamberlain: I cannot quite put my misgivings into words at the moment. It's by far not the only thing I want to say, when I am only referring to the general human adage: Let the dead rest in peace.

Prince: That is my intention as well.

Chamberlain: Then I did not understand it correctly.

Prince: So it seems.

Pause

Prince: The only reason you are puzzled about this might be the peculiarity that I did not give the order immediately but announced it to you beforehand.

Chamberlain: But then the announcement imposes a greater responsibility on me, which I must attempt to live up to.

Prince: No responsibility!

Pause

Prince: Well, let me tell you again. So far the tomb in Friedrichspark has been watched over by a guard, who has a cabin at the entrance of the park where he lives. Was there anything wrong with this arrangement?

Chamberlain: Certainly not. The tomb is more than four hundred years old and has been guarded in this manner for just as long.

Prince: It could be an abuse. But it is no abuse?

Chamberlain: It is a necessary institution.

Prince: A necessary institution, then. Now I've been here in this country manor for such a long time, gained insight into details that, until then, strangers had been entrusted with – who proved worthy in a fashion – and I have concluded: the guard up in the park is not enough, rather another guard must keep watch down in the tomb as well. This may not be a pleasant post. But experience shows that willing and suitable people can be found for any post.

Chamberlain: Of course, every one of your Highness's orders will be executed, even if the necessity of the order is not understood.

Prince: Necessity! Is the guard at the park entrance necessary then? Friedrichspark is part of the manor grounds, is entirely surrounded by it, the manor grounds itself is amply guarded, even by the military. Why do we need the special guard in Friedrichspark? Isn't this a mere formality? A friendly deathbed for the miserable old man in charge there?

Chamberlain: It is a formality but a necessary one. A homage to the late greats.

Prince: And a guard in the tomb itself?

Chamberlain: In my opinion, it would have an additional, policing significance; it would be a real guard for things unreal and far removed from anything

156

human.

Prince: In my family this tomb is the boundary to the Human, and I would like to place a guard at this boundary. (Stands up) About the policing necessity, as you put it, we can question the guard himself. I've sent for him. (Rings bell.)

Chamberlain: He is, if I may be permitted this comment, a confused old man, out of control.

Prince: If that is so, it would be all the more proof for the necessity of reinforcing the guard as I suggested.

Servant

Prince: The tomb guard!

The servant leads the guard inside, supporting him under his arm lest he collapse. Old red, loosely hanging ceremonial livery, silver buttons, various decorations. Cap in hand. He is shivering under the gazes of the gentlemen.

Prince: Onto the daybed!

The servant lays him down and leaves. Pause, only soft groaning of the guard.

Prince (again in his armchair): Can you hear me?

Guard (tries to reply, can't, is too exhausted, sinks back onto the bed)

Prince: Try to compose yourself. We'll wait.

Chamberlain (bending to the Prince): What is it that this man can give us information about, and plausible or significant information at that. He should be taken to bed quickly.

Guard: Not to bed – am still strong – considering – still hold my own.

Prince: That is the way it should be. You are only sixty years old. You look very frail, though.

Guard: Will recover right away – recover right away.

Prince: It wasn't a reproach. I just feel very sorry that you're not well. Do you have any complaints?

Guard: Hard service – hard service – not complaining – but very worn out – wrestling-matches every night.

Prince: What did you say?

Guard: Hard service.

Prince: You said something after that.

Guard: Wrestling-matches.

Prince: Wrestling-matches? What kind of wrestling-matches?

Guard: With the late ancestors.

Prince: I don't understand. Do you have heavy dreams?

Guard: No dreams – I don't sleep at night.

Prince: Well, then tell me about these – these wrestling-matches.

Guard: (stays silent)

Prince: Why doesn't he speak?

Chamberlain (hastens to the Guard): It might be over with him any moment.

Prince (standing by the table)

Guard (when the Chamberlain touches him): Go away, go away, go away!

(wrestles with Chamberlain's fingers, flings himself down, crying).

Prince: We're tormenting him.

Chamberlain: How?

Prince: I don't know.

Chamberlain: Walking to the manor, appearing here, the sight of your Highness, the questioning – he does not have enough sense to handle all this anymore.

Prince (constantly looking toward the Guard): That's not it. (Walks to the daybed, bends down to the Guard, takes his little skull between his hands) No need to cry. Why are you crying? We wish you well. I myself believe that your post is not easy. You've surely rendered great services to my House. So don't cry and tell me.

Guard: But I'm so afraid of that gentleman there– (looks at the Chamberlain threateningly, not timorously).

Prince (to the Chamberlain): You will have to leave, if he's supposed to talk.

Chamberlain: But you see, your Highness, he is frothing at the mouth, he is gravely ill.

Prince (absentmindedly): Why, just go, it won't take long.

Chamberlain exits.

Prince (sits down on the edge of the daybed)

Pause

Prince: Why were you afraid of him?

Guard (strikingly composed): I wasn't afraid. Me afraid of a servant?

159

Prince: He isn't a servant; he's a Count, free and wealthy.

Guard: And yet only a servant; you're the master.

Prince: As you like. But you said yourself that you're afraid.

Guard: Saying things in front of him that only you should know. Haven't I already said enough in front of him?

Prince: So we are confidants, and yet I've seen you for the first time today.

Guard: Seen for the first time. But you've always known that I hold (raised index finger) the most important office at the court. You even acknowledged it publicly by awarding me the medal "Flaming Red." Here. (Lifts the medal from his coat.)

Prince: No, that is a medal for twenty-five years of service to the court. My grandfather gave it to you. But I will decorate you as well.

Guard: Do as you like and as corresponds to the significance of my services. I've been serving as your tomb guard for thirty years.

Prince: Not me, my reign has barely lasted a year.

Guard (pensive): Thirty years.

Pause

Guard (half referring to the Prince's remark): Nights last years there.

Prince: I haven't received a report from your office. What is the job like?

Guard: The same thing every night. Every night my jugular veins almost burst.

Prince: Is it only night duty then? Night duty for you old man?

Guard: That is exactly it, Highness. It is day duty. A slacker's job. One sits outside the front door and keeps one's mouth gaping in the sunshine. Once in a while the guard dog pats your knee with its front paws and then lies down again. That's the only change of pace.

Prince: Well.

Guard: But it has been converted to night duty.

Prince: But by whom?

Guard: By the lords of the tomb.

Prince: You know them?

Guard: I do.

Prince: They come to you?

Guard: They do.

Prince: Last night as well?

Guard: As well.

Prince: What was it like?

Guard (sits up): As always.

Prince (stands up)

Guard: As always. All is quiet until midnight. I'm lying – forgive me – in my bed smoking my pipe. My granddaughter is asleep in the bed next to mine. At midnight, there is the first knock on the window. I have a look at the clock. Always on time. Then two more knocks mingling with the clock strokes from the tower and just as loud. Those are no human knuckles. But I know all this and don't budge. Then there is throat clearing, as if someone is surprised that

I don't open the window despite such knocking. Every night, he is surprised. May his princely Highness be surprised! The old guard is still there! (Shakes his fist)

Prince: You're threatening me?

Guard (doesn't understand right away): Not you. The one in front of the window.

Prince: Who is it?

Guard: He shows himself promptly. Both windows and the shutter open all at once. I barely have time to throw a blanket over my granddaughter's face. The storm blows inside, puts out the light in no time. Duke Friedrich! His face covered with hair and beard completely fills my poor window. How he has evolved over the centuries. When he opens his mouth to talk, the wind blows his old beard between his teeth, and he bites on it.

Prince: Wait. You say Duke Friedrich. Which Friedrich?

Guard: Duke Friedrich, only Duke Friedrich.

Prince: That is how he says his name?

Guard (anxious): No, he doesn't say it.

Prince: And yet you know (breaking off) Just go on!

Guard: Do you want me to go on?

Prince: Of course. This is very much of concern to me, for there is a mistake in the distribution of work. You were overburdened.

Guard (kneeling down): Don't take away my post, your Highness! Since I've lived for you for such a long time, let me die for you, too. Don't have the tomb walled up in front of me to which I strive. I enjoy serving and I'm still able to serve. An audience like today's, to rest a little bit by my master gives me

162

strength for ten years.

Prince (sits him down on the daybed again): No one is taking your post. How could I do without your experience there? But I will appoint another guard, and you will be made head guard.

Guard: Am I not enough? Have I ever let anyone through?

Prince: To Friedrichspark?

Guard: No, out of the park. Who wants to go inside? If anyone stops in front of the fence, I wave my hand out the window and he runs away. But out, everyone wants out. After midnight you can see all the voices from the tomb gathered around my house. I think it's only because they huddle together that they don't all crowd inside to me through the narrow window hole with everything they are. However, when it is all too bad, I get my lantern from under the bed, swing it up and they, incomprehensible creatures, tear away laughing and whining; I hear can them murmuring even in the last shrub at the end of the park. But soon they gather themselves again.

Prince: And they tell you their request?

Guard: At first they give orders. Most of all Duke Friedrich. No living beings are this confident. Every night for thirty years he has been expecting to find me worn down this time.

Prince: If he has been coming for thirty years, he can't be Duke Friedrich, who just died fifteen years ago. But he is the only one by–

I was stiff and cold; I was a bridge, I lay over an abyss: the tips of my toes over here, my hands dug in over there, I had clamped myself tight into crumbling loam. My coattails were streaming at my sides. In the depths roared the icy trout stream. No tourist strayed to this impassable height; the bridge was not yet marked on the maps. –So I lay waiting; I had to wait. Unless it collapses, no bridge once erected can cease to be a bridge. One day toward evening – was it the first was it the thousandth, I don't know, my thoughts were always running in a tangle and around and around in circles – toward evening in summer, the stream was rushing more somberly, I heard a man's footsteps. To me, to me. Stretch yourself bridge, fix yourself up, you unrailed beam, hold the one entrusted to you, discreetly even out the uncertainty of his step, but if he staggers, reveal who you are and hurl him into the country like a mountain god. He came, tapped me with the iron tip of his cane, then lifted my coattails with it and straightened them out on me, he ran the tip through my bushy hair and let it rest there for a long time, probably gazing far around him. But then – I was just dreaming after him across mountains and valleys – he leapt onto my midriff with both of his feet. I shuddered in wild pain, completely unaware. Who was it? A child? A gymnast? A daredevil? A suicide? A tempter? An annihilator? And I turned around to see him. Bridge turning around! I had not quite turned around yet, when I was already falling, I fell, and presently I was ripped apart and impaled by the sharpened pebbles that had always stared at me so peacefully from the raging waters.

Two boys were sitting on the jetty wall playing dice. A man was reading a newspaper on the steps of a monument in the shadow of the saber-brandishing hero. A girl by a well was filling water into her tub. A fruit vendor was lying next to his produce gazing out onto the lake. Through the empty door and window holes two men could be seen over wine deep inside an inn. The innkeeper sat on a table in front, dozing. A bark quietly floated into the small harbor as if borne above the water. A man in a blue smock stepped ashore and pulled the ropes through the rings. Two other men in dark coats with silver buttons walking behind the boatman carried a bier, on which a man appeared to be lying under a large flowered, fringed silk scarf. No one on the jetty took note of the new arrivals, even when they deposited the bier to wait for the boatman who was still working on the ropes, no one approached them, no one asked them a question, no one took a closer look at them. The boatman was somewhat held up by a woman who appeared on deck, her hair loose, a child at her breast. Then he followed, pointing to a yellowish two-story house arising on the left close to the water in straight lines; the bearers picked up their charge and carried it through the low but slim pillared doorway. A little boy opened a window just to notice the procession disappearing inside the house, and hastily shut the window again. The door was now closed as well; it was carefully fashioned from black oak. A flock of doves that had been flying around the bell tower now alighted in the square in front of the house. The doves gathered outside the door as though their food was kept in the house. One flew up to the second floor and pecked at the windowpane. They were light-colored, well-kempt, lively animals. The woman from the bark tossed them some seeds in a great flourish, which they pecked up and then flew over to the woman. A man in a top hat with a mourning band came down one of the narrow steeply descending lanes leading to the harbor. He looked around attentively, everything bothered him, the sight of refuse in a corner made him wince; there were fruit peels on the steps to the monument, he swept them down with his cane as he passed. He knocked at the pillared door, while taking his top hat into his black-gloved right hand. The door was opened at once; and about fifty little boys lined both sides of the long hallway and bowed. The boatman came down the steps, greeted the gentleman, led him upstairs, on the second floor he walked with him around the court enclosed by slight loggias and, with the boys crowding after them at a respectful distance, the two men entered a cool, large room at the back of the house, opposite which there was no other house but only a bare grayish black rock wall to be seen. The bearers were busy putting up several long candles at the head of the stretcher and lighting them, but they did not throw more light, it only made the previously still shadows downright jump and flicker across the walls. The shroud was folded back on the bier. There lay a man with wild, matted hair and beard, tanned skin, looking somewhat like a hunter. He lay there motionless, his eyes closed, seemingly without breath, and yet only the surrounding suggested that this might be a dead man.

The gentleman stepped up to the bier, placed a hand on the forehead of the man lying there, then knelt down and prayed. The boatman signaled the bearers to leave the room; they left, chased away the boys who had gathered outside, and shut the door. But even this silence did not seem enough for the gentleman; he looked at the boatman, who understood and went through a side door into the next room. At once the man on the bier opened his eyes, turned his face to the gentleman with a painful smile and said: "Who are you?" Without any visible surprise the gentleman rose from his kneeling position and replied: "The mayor of Riva." The man on the bier nodded, with his barely outstretched arm pointed to a chair and, the mayor having followed his invitation, said: "I knew that, Mr. Mayor, but at first glance I always forget everything, everything goes round and round, and it is better to ask even if I know everything. And you, too, probably know that I'm the Hunter Gracchus." "Certainly," the mayor said. "You were announced to me during the night. We were all fast asleep. That is when my wife called out around midnight: 'Salvatore,' – that's my name – 'look at the dove in the window!' It really was a dove but as large as a rooster. It flew to my ear and said: 'The dead hunter Gracchus is coming tomorrow; welcome him in the name of the city.'" The hunter nodded and pulled in the tip of his tongue between his lips: "Yes, the doves fly ahead of me. But do you think, Mr. Mayor, that I should stay in Riva?" "I cannot say, yet," the mayor replied. "Are you dead?" "Yes," said the hunter, "as you see. Many years ago, it must have been a tremendous number of years, I fell from a rock in the Black Forest, that's in Germany, as I was tracking a chamois. I've been dead since then." "But you're also alive?" said the mayor. "In a way," said the hunter, "in a way I'm alive as well. My death bark missed its course, a wrong turn of the helm, a moment of inattention on the part of the boatman, a detour through my lovely homeland, I don't know what it was, I only know that I stayed on this Earth and that my bark has been traveling earthly waters ever since. Thus, I who only wanted to live in the mountains, sail through all the lands of the Earth after my death." "And you don't have a share in the afterworld?" the mayor asked with a frown. "I always am," the hunter replied, "on the immense stairway leading up to it. On this endlessly vast flight of stairs I linger, sometimes upstairs, sometimes downstairs, sometimes on the right, sometimes on the left, always in motion. But once I give it the greatest momentum and the gate above already shines me, I awake on my old bark sadly stuck in some earthly waters. The original mistake of my earlier death grins at me all around in my cabin. Julia, the boatman's wife, knocks and serves me on the bier the morning drink of the country whose coast we're traveling. "A terrible fate," the mayor said with his hand raised dismissively.

"And you are not at all to blame for it?" "Not at all," the hunter said, "I was a hunter, am I to be blamed for that, then? I was appointed as a hunter in the Black Forest where at the time there were still wolves. I lay in wait, shot, hit the mark, removed the skin, is there any blame in that? My work was blessed. I was called the great hunter of the Black Forest. Is that to blame?" "I am not entitled to decide that," the mayor said, "but for me as well there seems to be no blame in it. But who is to blame then?" "The boatman," the hunter said.

Every man carries a room within himself. This fact can even be proved by means of the sense of hearing. When someone walks quickly and one listens closely, say at night, when everything around is quiet, one can hear for example the clatter of a wall mirror not firmly mounted or the shade

"And now you're planning to stay with us here in Riva?" the mayor asked. "I have no plans," the hunter said with a smile and placed his hand on the mayor's knee so as to make up for the jest. "I'm here, I don't know any more than that, I can't do any more than that. My bark is without a helm, it sails with the wind that blows in the deepest regions of death."

I'm the Hunter Gracchus; my home is the Black Forest in Germany.

No one will read what I write here; no one will come to help me; if there were an assignment to help me, all doors to all houses would remain closed, all windows closed, all would lie in their beds, bedcovers drawn over their heads, the entire Earth a nocturnal shelter. This makes good sense, for no one knows of me, and if he did know about me, he would not know my whereabouts, and if he knew my whereabouts, he would not know how to keep me there, and if he knew how to keep me there, he would not know how to help me. The idea of wanting to help me is an illness, and it must be cured with bed rest.

I know this, and so I am not writing to summon help, even though in certain moments, high-strung as I am, e.g. right now, I think about it intensely. But it might be enough to rid myself of such thoughts if I look around and remind myself where I am and where – I am well at liberty to say this – I've been living for centuries. As I'm writing this, I'm lying on a wooden plank bed, wearing – it is no pleasure to look at me – a dirty shroud, hair and beard, gray and black, merging into an inextricable tangle, my legs are covered with a large, silky, flowered, long-fringed woman's scarf. At my head there stands a church candle that gives me light. On the opposite wall there is a small picture, apparently a bushman aiming his spear at me and trying to take cover behind a magnificent, painted shield. On ships one finds quite some silly images but this is one of the silliest. Otherwise my wooden cage is completely empty. The balmy air of the southerly night comes in through a hatch in the sidewall, and I hear the water lapping against the old bark.

I have been lying here since the time when I, the still live hunter Gracchus, at home in the Black Forest, was tracking a chamois and fell. Everything went according to plan. I tracked, fell, bled to death in a gorge, I was dead and this bark was supposed to take me to the afterworld. I still remember how gladly I stretched out on this plank bed for the first time; never had the mountains heard such singing from me as those four then still crepuscular walls. I had been happy to live and had been happy to die, before stepping on board I gladly threw off my ragged bundle with rifle, satchel, hunting coat, which I had always worn with pride, and I slipped into the shroud like a girl into her wedding dress. I lay down and waited.

Then it happened

THE PAIL RIDER

All coal spent, the pail empty, the shovel useless, the stove breathing cold, the room blown full of frost, the trees outside the window rigid with rime, the sky a silvery shield against he who expects help from above. I must have coal; I can't freeze to death: behind me the merciless stove, before me the merciless sky; so I must ride right in between and seek help in the middle from the coal merchant. But he has already become callous to my ordinary requests; I have to give exact proof to him that I don't have a speck of coal dust left and that he thus means the sun in the firmament to me. I have to come like a beggar ready to perish at his doorstep, groaning from hunger and down whose throat the master's cook therefore decides to pour the last coffee grounds; so, too, the merchant has to hurl a shovelful of coal into my pail in anger but under the sway of the commandment "Thou shalt not kill."

The impact of my arrival must decide it, so I'll ride there on my pail.

A pail rider, my hand up on the handle, the simplest kind of bridle, I awkwardly spin down the stairs, but once downstairs my pail rises up, splendidly, splendidly, camels kneeling low on the ground do not rise more gracefully, shaking themselves under the cane of their driver. Through the solid frozen street it goes at an even trot; I'm frequently lifted up as high as the first story; I never drop to the level of the entrance door. And I hover extraordinarily high in front of the merchant's vaulted cellar, where down below he crouches at his table to write. To let out the excessive heat, he has opened the door.

"Mr. Coal Merchant!" I shout shrouded in smoky clouds of breath with a voice burned hollow by the cold, "Mr. Coal Merchant, do please give me some coal. My pail is so empty I can ride on it. Be so kind. I'll pay you just as soon as I can."

The merchant puts his hand to his ear. "Have I heard right?" he asks over his shoulder of his wife who is knitting on the fireside bench. "Have I heard right? A customer."

"I don't hear a thing," his wife says, calmly breathing in and out over her knitting needles, pleasantly warming her back.

"Oh yes," I shout, "it's me, an old, devoted customer, currently without means."

"Wife," the merchant says, "there is, there is someone, I can't be wrong after all, it must be an old, a very old customer that he knows how to speak to my heart like this."

"What is it, man?" the wife says pressing her knitwork to her chest in respite. "It's no one, the street is empty, all our customers are provided for; we could close the business for a few days and rest."

"But I'm sitting here on my pail," I shout, and numb tears of coldness blur my eyes. "Please, just have a look up here, you'll see me right away. I'm just asking for a shovelful and if you give me two, I'll be delighted. All the other customers are provided for after all. Ah, if only I could hear coal rattling in my pail already."

"I'm coming," the merchant says and, short-legged, is about to climb up the basement stairs, but his wife is already there, holds him back by the arm and says: "You stay. If you insist in your stubbornness, I'll go out there. Remember your heavy coughing last night. But for a deal and be it an imaginary one, you forget your wife and child and sacrifice your lungs. I'll go." "Do tell him all the kinds we have in stock, I'll call the prices up to you." "All right," the wife says and climbs up to the street. Of course, she sees me right away.

"Mrs. Coal Merchant," I shout, "a heartfelt hello, just a shovelful of coal, right here into my pail, I'll take it home myself, a shovel of your cheapest. Of course, I'll pay in full, just not now, not now." How the two words "not now" ring like a bell and how bewildering it is that they mingle with the evening bells pealing from the nearby church steeple.

"What does he want then?" the merchant shouts. "Nothing," his wife shouts back, "there's nothing, I don't see anything, I don't hear anything, it's sounding six o' clock is all, and we're closing up. The cold is brutal; we'll probably do a brisk business tomorrow after all."

She doesn't see anything and doesn't hear anything, and yet she undoes her apron strings and tries to flap me away with her apron. Unfortunately, it works. My pail has all the advantages of a good mount, but no power of resistance; it's too light, swept off its feet by a woman's apron.

"You evil woman!" I shout back, while she turns toward the shop, half contemptuous, half content, beating her hand into the air, "You evil woman. I asked for a shovel of your cheapest coal, and you're not giving it to me." And I soar into the regions of the ice mountains and disappear never to be seen again.

V. W.

My sincerest thanks for the Beethoven book. I am starting Schopenhauer today. With your very tenderest hand, with your very strongest eye for truthful reality, with your fantastically vast knowledge, with the controlled and mighty core fire of your poetic nature, may you continue to erect such monuments – to my unspeakable joy.

We were encamped in the oasis. The companions were asleep. An Arab, high and white, went past me; he had tended to the camels and was walking to his sleeping place. I flung myself backward into the grass, I tried to sleep, I couldn't, the wail of a jackal in the distance; I sat up again. And what had been so distant was suddenly near. Jackals milling around me, eyes gleaming fading in dull gold, slender bodies moving consequentially and deftly as if under a whip. One of them came from behind, pushed through under my arm close against me as if he needed my warmth, then stepped in front of me and said, almost eye to eye with me: "I'm the eldest jackal far and wide. I'm glad to be able to greet you here after all. I had almost given up hope, for we have been waiting for you for ages, my mother waited, and her mother, and all their mothers before, back to the mother of all jackals. Believe me!" "I'm surprised," I said, forgetting to light the pile of wood lying ready to keep the jackals at bay with its smoke, "I'm very surprised to hear that. I have come here from the Far North by chance, and just on a short trip. What is it that you jackals want?" And as if encouraged by these perhaps all too friendly words, they drew their circle tighter around me, all of them short of breath and hissing. "We know that you come from the North," the eldest started, "that is exactly what we rest our hopes upon. There lives the kind of sensibility which one cannot find here among the Arabs. From this cold arrogance, you know, no glimmer of reason may be struck. They kill animals to eat them, and they disregard carrion." "Don't speak so loudly," I said, "there are Arabs sleeping nearby." "You really are a stranger," the jackal said. "Otherwise you would know that never in the history of the world has a jackal feared an Arab. Why would we fear them? Isn't it enough of a misfortune to be cast out among such a people." "This may be, this may be," I said. "I won't presume to judge things that are foreign to my mind; this seems to be a very old dispute, so it might be in the blood, and hence will perhaps end only in the blood." "You are very smart," the old jackal said, and all were breathing even faster, with racing lungs, even though they were standing still; an acrid stench poured out of their open muzzles, which at times was bearable only with clenched teeth. "You are very smart; what you say corresponds with our old teachings. So we take their blood, and the dispute will be over." "Oh," I said more fiercely than I meant to, "they'll fight back; they'll shoot you down in packs with their muskets." "You misunderstand us," he said, "as is the nature of humans, which is not lost in the North either it seems. It's not that we want to kill them. The Nile wouldn't carry enough water to cleanse us off. The mere sight of their living bodies makes us run away, to cleaner air, to the desert that is therefore our home." And all the jackals around me, in the meantime joined by many that had come from far away, lowered their heads between their front legs to groom themselves with their paws; it was as if they were trying to conceal disgust so terrible that I just wanted to flee from their circle with a great leap. "So what do you intend to do," I asked trying to stand up, but I couldn't; two young jackals had sunk their teeth into my coat and shirt from the back; I had to stay seated. "They're holding onto your train," the old jackal said earnestly by way of explanation, "a sign of devotion." "They must let go of me," I shouted, turning now to the old one, now to the young ones. "They will, of course," the old one said, "if you demand it. It will take a while, for as is the custom they have dug in their teeth too deep and will have to slowly undo their jaws first. In the meantime, listen to our request." "Your behavior has not made me very amenable to it," I said. "Don't make us pay for our clumsiness," he said and for the first time now employed the plaintive tone of his natural voice. "We are poor creatures, we have nothing but our teeth for everything we want to do, good and bad, all we have is our teeth." "What do you want then," I asked, only slightly placated. "Sir," he called out, and all the jackals gave a howl; it faintly sounded like a melody to me. "Sir, you should put an end to the strife dividing this world. You look just like the person our ancestors described, who would do that. We must have peace from the Arabs, air to breathe, the view of the horizon cleansed of them all around, no shrieks of pain from a ram knifed to death by the Arab, let all the creatures die a peaceful death, undisturbed they shall be drunk up by us and cleansed down to the bone. Purity, nothing but purity is what we want" – and now all of them were weeping and sobbing; distractedly the two behind me pushed their heads into me–. "How can you bear being in this world, you noble heart and sweet innards. Dirt is their white, dirt is their black, their beard is a horror, one must spew at the sight of the corners of their eyes, and when they raise their arm, hell opens up in their armpit. Therefore, oh sir, therefore, oh dear sir, with your all-powerful hands, with your all-powerful hands cut their throats with these scissors." And upon a jerk of his head, a jackal came up carrying an old rusty pair of small sewing scissors on a fang.

"Ah, the scissors at last, and that will be the end of it," the Arab leader of our caravan called out, who had crept up to us upwind and was now cracking his giant whip.

Everyone dispersed in great haste, and yet they stayed at some distance, huddling together, the many animals so close and so rigid that it looked like a narrow hurdle with orbs flying about them. "Now you, sir, have seen and heard this spectacle as well," the Arab said and laughed as gaily as the reticence of his tribe permitted. "So you know what these animals want then?" I asked. "Of course, sir," he said, "it is universally known that, as long as there have been Arabs, this pair of scissors has been traveling through the desert and will be traveling with us to the end of our days. Each European is offered it for the great deed; each European is just the one who, to them, seems destined to do it. They have this silly hope, these creatures, fools, true fools is what they are. We love them for that; they are our dogs, lovelier than yours. Just have a look, a camel died in the night; I have had it brought here."

Four bearers came and threw the heavy carcass down in front of us. No sooner was it lying there than the jackals raised their voices. As if irresistibly pulled by ropes, each one of them approached haltingly, their bodies brushing against the ground. They had forgotten about the Arabs, forgotten their hatred; the all-obliterating presence of the powerful scent oozing from the carrion enthralled them. One of them was already hanging on the throat and found the artery at first bite. Like a small hectic pump relentlessly and yet futilely struggling to put out a raging fire, every muscle in his body tugged and twitched in its place. And instantly all of them were piling up on the corpse with the same goal.

That is when the leader struck them left and right with his fierce whip. They raised their heads, half dazed in rapture, saw the Arabs standing before them, now felt the whip on their muzzles, pulled back in leaps and ran backward a bit. But the camel's blood was already lying in pools, steaming upward, the corpse was torn wide open in several places. They could not resist, they were back again, once more the leader raised his whip, I grabbed his arm. "You're right, sir," he said, "let us leave them to their trade; besides, it's time to set off. You've seen them now. Magnificent creatures, aren't they? And how they hate us!"

Old, in all my plumpness, with slight heart trouble, I was lying on the daybed after lunch, one foot on the floor, reading a historical work. The maid came in, and, two fingers on her pursed lips, announced a visitor. "Who is it?" I asked, annoyed that I was to receive a visitor when I was awaiting my afternoon coffee. "A Chinese man," the maid said, desperately trying to suppress a laugh that the visitor outside the door was not supposed to hear. "A Chinese man? To see me? Is he in Chinese dress?" The maid nodded, still struggling with the urge to laugh. "Tell him my name, ask him if it is really me he came to see, me who is unknown in the house next door and all the more so in China." The maid tiptoed over to me and whispered: "He only has a visiting card where it says that he asks to be admitted. He doesn't speak German; he speaks some unintelligible language, I was afraid to take the card away from him." "Let him come," I called out, in the agitation that my heart condition often causes me, threw the book to the floor and cursed the maid's ineptness. Standing up and stretching my gigantic form, which had to scare any visitor in this low-ceilinged room, I walked to the door. Indeed, the Chinese man had barely caught sight of me, when he scurried out again. I simply reached into the hallway and cautiously pulled the man back inside on his silk belt. He looked like a scholar, short, frail, with horn-rimmed glasses, a stiff, thinning, gray and black goatee. A friendly little man, he held his head tilted and smiled with half closed eyes

---

The lawyer Dr. Bucephalus summoned his housekeeper to his bed one morning and said to her: "Today is the beginning of the great court hearing in the trial of my brother Bucephalus against the company Trollhätta. I am representing the plaintiff, and since the hearing will last at least several days, and without real interruption, I won't be coming home at all over the next few days. By the end of the hearing or as soon as there is the prospect of an end, I will telephone you. I cannot say any more at this time nor answer any question, since naturally I have to be concerned about maintaining the full power of my voice. Therefore, bring me two raw eggs and tea with honey for breakfast." And slowly leaning back into the cushions, his hand over his eyes, he fell silent. The housekeeper, a chatterbox and yet dying of fear of her master, was very alarmed. All of a sudden such an extraordinary order. Just the night before the master had spoken with her, but not given any hint about what was coming. The hearing could not have been scheduled overnight, could it? And are there hearings that last for days without interruption? And why did the master name the litigants, which he usually never did in front of her? And what monstrous trial might the master's brother, the small greengrocer Adolf Bucephalus, be involved in, with whom the master, so it seemed, had not been on good terms for quite a while? And how did the inconceivable strains the master was facing go together with the fact that he was lying in his bed so wearily now, covering, if the morning light wasn't deceiving her, his somehow emaciated face with his hand? And he had asked only for tea and eggs to be brought, rather than the usual wine and ham to completely revive his spirits? With such thoughts the housekeeper returned to the kitchen, sat in her favorite spot by the window next to the flowers and the canary for just a moment, gazing out at the opposite part of the courtyard where behind a window grille two half-naked children were wrestling in play, then turned away with a sigh, poured the tea, took two eggs from the pantry, arranged everything on a tray, could not resist taking the wine bottle as a beneficial temptation, and with all this went into the bedroom. It was empty. Why, the master could not have left already. He could not have gotten dressed in just a minute. But his undergarments and clothes weren't anywhere to be seen either. For heaven's sake, what's wrong with the master? Into the hall. Coat, hat, and cane are all gone as well. To the window. Goodness gracious, at this very moment the master is stepping out of the door, his hat pushed back, his coat open, his briefcase pressed against him, his cane hanging in a coat pocket. Letters from Paris

---

We have a new advocate, Dr. Bucephalus. His outward appearance hardly evokes the times when he was still Alexander of Macedon's warhorse. Anyone familiar with the circumstances, however, will notice a few details. Just recently on the great stairs of the court building, I even saw a very simple court clerk marvel at the lawyer with the trained eye of the small racetrack regular as he was raising his thighs high to mount from stair to stair, his steps ringing on the marble. In general, the bar approves of Bucephalos' admission. With astounding insight people tell themselves that today's social order places Bucephalos in a difficult situation and that for that reason as well as for his role in the history of the world he by all means deserves some goodwill. Today – there is no denying it – there is no Alexander the Great. To be sure there a quite a few who know how to murder, there is no lack of adroitness at hitting one's friend with a spear across the banquet table either, and Macedonia is too confining for many so that they curse Philip the father, but no one, no one can lead the way to India. Even in those days the gates of India were out of reach, but the direction was indicated by the tip of the king's sword; today the gates have been moved to somewhere else completely and farther away and higher up, no one points the way, many hold swords but only to brandish them, and the eye attempting to follow them gets confused. Therefore it might really be best thing to immerse oneself in the books of law as Bucephalos has done. Free, his sides unrepressed by the thighs of the rider, by the light of a quiet lamp, far from the din of the Battle of Alexander at Issos, he reads and turns the pages of our old books.

Yesterday a swoon came to see me. She lives in the house next door; several times have I seen her disappear into a low doorway there at night, hunched. A tall lady with a long flowing dress and a wide hat adorned with feathers. She came swishing through the door like a doctor who fears arriving too late to see the expiring patient. "Anton," she exclaimed with a hollow and yet self-aggrandizing voice, "I'm coming, I'm here." She dropped into the chair I pointed to. "You live high up, you live high up," she said groaning. Tucked deep into my armchair, I nodded. Innumerable, the steps leading to my rooms bounced before my eyes, one after the other, untiring small waves. "Why so cold?" she asked, took off her long old fencer's gloves, tossed them on the table and winked at me, her head inclined. It was as if I was a sparrow practicing my leaps on the steps and she was ruffling my soft, fluffy gray plumage. "I'm deeply sorry that you're pining for me. Often have I gazed into your haggard face with sincere sadness when you were standing in the courtyard, looking up to my window. Now, I'm not unfavorably disposed to you and even if you don't have my heart yet, you may still win it."

What great indifference people can get themselves into, how deep a conviction to have lost the right path forever

---

A mistake. It was not my door up on the long hallway that I had opened. "A mistake," I said and was about to walk out again. Then I saw the inhabitant, a thin beardless man with a tightly closed mouth sitting at a table with nothing but an oil lamp on it,

---

In our house, this enormous house in a suburb, a tenement building intermixed with indestructible medieval ruins, the following announcement was distributed today, on this foggy, icy winter morning.

To all my fellow tenants.

I own five toy guns; they are hanging in my wardrobe, one on each hook. The first one is mine, whoever wishes to may lay claim to the other ones; if more than four lay claim, then the extra ones will have to bring their own guns and deposit them in my wardrobe. For there has to be uniformity, without uniformity we will not get anywhere. Also, I only have guns that are completely unusable for any other purpose, their mechanisms are ruined; their plugs torn off, only their triggers still make cracking sounds. So it should not be hard to procure more such guns if need be. But when it comes down to it people without guns are fine with me at first; we who have guns will take the unarmed in our midst at the crucial time. A battle technique tried and tested by the first American farmers against the Indians; why should it not work here as well, where circumstances are similar. So one can even do without the guns in the long run. And even the five guns are not absolutely necessary, but since we have them they should be put to use as well. Should the other four not want to carry them, they can let it be. In that case, I alone as the leader will carry one. But we should not have a leader, and so I will break my gun as well or put it away.

That was the first announcement. In our building people have neither the time nor inclination to read announcements or even think about them. Soon the little pieces of papers were floating in the dirty stream coming from the attic, fed from all floors, rushing down the stairs where it struggled with the counter stream welling up from below. But after a week there was a second announcement.

Fellow tenants!

So far no one has come forward. I have been at home continuously, except when out earning my living, and for the time of my absence, during which the door to my room was always ajar, there lay on my table a sheet of paper to which the name of whosoever wished could be added. Nobody did so.

Sometimes I feel as if I'm atoning for all of my past and future sins with pain in my limbs, when I come home from the machine factory in the evening or even in the morning after the night shift. I'm not strong enough for the job, I've known this for a long time and yet I haven't done anything about it.

The first epiphany I've had since the move to

In our house, this enormous house in the suburb, a tenement building intermixed with indestructible medieval ruins, on the same floor as me there lives an official clerk with a worker's family. They call him a civil servant but he can only be a petty office clerk, since he spends his nights on a straw mattress amidst the nest of an unrelated married couple and their six children. And if he is a small office clerk, why should I worry about him. Even in this building where so much of the misery that this city produces converges, there

177

must be more than a hundred people,

On the same floor as me there lives a jobbing tailor. Despite meticulous care I wear out my clothes too quickly; just recently I had to take another coat for mending. It was a beautiful warm summer evening. The tailor has only one room that doubles as a kitchen for himself, his wife, and six children. Furthermore, he has a lodger staying with him, a clerk from the tax office. Such occupancy does somewhat exceed the usual, which is bad enough as it is in our building. At any rate, each to his own; the mender surely has undeniable reasons for his frugality and it would not occur to the stranger to steer the conversation toward a discussion of those reasons. But if one comes into the room, e.g. as a customer, one cannot help but notice,

---

19 II 17

Read Herman and Dorothea today, some of Richter's memoirs, looked at pictures by him and finally read a scene from Hauptmann's Griselda. Am momentarily a different person for the next hour. All prospects, nebulous as always but transformed mirages. In the heavy boots I put on for the first time today (they were originally intended for military service) there walks a different person.

I live with Mr. Krummholz; I share the room with an office clerk from the tax office. Two of Krummholz's daughters, a six and a seven-year old, also sleep in the room in their shared bed. From the day the clerk moved in – I myself have been living with the Krummholzes for years – I have felt suspicious of him, although at first the suspicion was entirely vague. A man less than medium height, feeble, apparently with not very firm lungs, gray clothes hanging loose on his body, a wrinkled face of indeterminable age, grayish blond, longish hair combed over his ears, spectacles sitting on the tip of his nose and a small, equally graying goatee.

I sat in my wooden hut on the covered verandah. In place of a wall, I had set up a mosquito net with extraordinarily fine mesh procured from one of the foremen, the chief of a tribe through whose territory our trains were to run. Hemp netting, of combined toughness and delicacy no European manufacturer could hope to match. It was my pride and joy, and a great source of envy. Without this netting it would have been impossible to sit on the verandah in peace, turn on the light the way I did now, take out an old European newspaper to study it and heartily smoke my pipe while doing so.

I have the wrist – who can still speak of his abilities so freely – of a happy old tireless angler. Say, I sit at home before I go fishing, and I turn my right hand, once to and once fro, as I watch keenly. This is enough to reveal to me, by sight and by feel, the result of my future angling, often in all its details. I see the water of my fishing spot in the particular current at the particular hour; a cross section of the river appears to me; clear in number and kind they push toward the surface in ten, twenty even a hundred different places; now, I know how to wield the fishing rod; some break through the surface with their heads with impunity; that is when I let the hook swing in front of them and soon they dangle there; the brevity of this fateful moment delights me even when I sit at my table at home; other fish advance to my stomach; now it is high time, some I still catch, but others escape this dangerous surface even with their tail and are lost to me this time, just this time; a true angler never misses a fish.

[20]

I probably should have worried about how things stood with that staircase a little earlier after all, what the context was, what was to be expected and how one should respond to it. Why, you've never heard of this staircase before, I said to myself as an excuse, and newspapers and books constantly gossip about everything possibly out there. But there was nothing about this staircase. That may well be, I replied to myself, so you probably didn't read thoroughly enough. You were often distracted, skipped paragraphs, even contented yourself with the headlines; perhaps the staircase had been mentioned there, and that is how you missed it. And now you need precisely that which you missed. And I stood for a moment and pondered this contention. Then I thought I remembered that I might have read something about a similar staircase in a children's book once. It hadn't been much, probably merely mentioned its existence, which was of no use to me.

When the little mouse, which was loved like no other in the mouse world, got into the trap one night and, with a shriek, gave up its life for the sight of bacon, all the mice around in their holes were overcome by shivering and shaking, one by one gazing at one another with eyes blinking uncontrollably, their tails scouring the floor in futile application. Then they emerged hesitantly, pushing one another; all were drawn to the scene of death. There it lay, the sweet little mouse, its neck caught in the iron, the pinkish legs pushed in, the feeble body stiffened, well deserving of some extra bacon. The parents stood by, eyeing the remains of their child.

After a few wrong turns your letter has arrived; my address is Poríc 7. At first, let me thank you for the trust expressed in your letter, which sincerely pleases me. This surely concerns a useful or even necessary matter. The list of renowned names vouches for this as much as for the future of the entire endeavor.

And yet, I have to refrain, for I am unable to envision a Greater

Austria somehow unified in spirit, and even less, however, to picture myself as an integral part of this spirit; I balk at this decision.

Now this does not constitute a loss for your association, on the contrary. I am organically not even competent; my knowledge of people is limited; I have no substantial influence in any way. So you would soon come to regret my involvement.

Should, as it might perhaps be unavoidable, the art association become a club with member fees, etc., I will be glad to join.

Please do not take offense at my refusal; it is a necessity for me.

Yours respectfully

Building the Great Wall of China

The Great Wall of China was completed at its northernmost point. Construction proceeded from the southeast and southwest and was united there. This system of partial construction was also pursued on a small scale within the two great armies of workers, the eastern and the western army. This was done by forming groups of about twenty workers, who had to erect a partial wall of about five hundred meters, whereas a neighboring group built a wall of the same length to meet them. But then once the unification of the sections was completed, construction was not continued at the ends of those thousand meters, rather the groups of workers were sent off to completely different regions to work on the wall. In this way, naturally, many large gaps occurred, which were filled in only slowly and gradually, some even only after the completion of the wall had been announced. Why, there are supposed to be gaps that have never been filled in at all; according to some people those are far larger than the completed sections, an assertion, however, that might be one of the many legends that have sprung up around the building of the wall and that, due to the extent of the structure, are unverifiable at least for the individual person with their own eyes and at their own scale. Now one would think in the first place that it would have been more advantageous in every way to build in continuity or at least continuously within the two main segments. After all, as was widely disseminated and generally known, the wall was intended as protection against the northern tribes. But how can a wall that is not continuous offer any protection. In fact, not only can such a wall not protect, its construction itself is in constant danger. Those sections of the wall left standing abandoned in deserted areas could easily be destroyed by the nomads over and over, the more so as they, alarmed by the construction of the wall, kept changing their place of residence with incredible speed like locusts, and therefore may have had a better overview of how the construction progressed than even we, the builders, did. Nevertheless the construction probably could not have been carried out any differently than it was. To understand this, one must consider the following: the wall was intended to be a protection for centuries; therefore, the most careful construction, the application of architectural wisdom of all known ages and nations, an enduring sense of personal responsibility on the part of the builders were essential prerequisites for the work. Of course, ignorant day laborers from the populace – men women children, whoever offered themselves for a good pay – could be used for the menial jobs, but, even for the supervision of four day laborers, a knowledgeable man trained in construction was needed, a man capable of feeling deep down in his heart what was at stake here. And of course, the greater the task, the greater the demands. And such men were indeed available, if not in the quantities this construction could have used, then still in great number. The project had not been undertaken lightly. Fifty years before the beginning of the construction, throughout the parts of China that were supposed to be walled in, the art of construction, in particular masonry, had been declared the most important of the sciences, and everything else was only recognized in so far as it related to it. I remember quite well, how, as small children, hardly sure of our legs, we were standing in our teacher's little garden and had to build a sort of wall out of pebbles, how the teacher gathered up his coat, charged against the wall, naturally knocking over everything, and then proceeded to scold us for the weakness of our structure so severely that, wailing, we ran off in all directions to our parents. A tiny incident, but indicative of the spirit of the times. It was my good fortune that, when I passed the highest examination of the lowest school at twenty years of age, the construction of the wall had just begun. I say my good fortune because many who had reached the utmost level of education available to them earlier on did not know what to do with their knowledge for years, idled around uselessly, the most grandiose construction plans in their head, and went downhill in droves. But those who eventually did get to work on the construction as construction managers, albeit of the lowest rank, were indeed deserving of their positions. They were men who had long reflected on the construction and never ceased to reflect on it, who, with the first stone they had sunk into the ground, had felt that they had somehow become part of the wall. But naturally such men were driven, apart from the desire to carry out the most meticulous work, by the impatience to finally see the structure rise up in its ultimate perfection. The day laborer does not know this impatience; he is only driven by his wages. The upper-level supervisors as well, and even the middle-level supervisors saw enough of the multifaceted growth of the structure to stay strong mentally, but for the lower-level workers, whose mental capacity far exceeded their seemingly small assignments, had to be provided for in other ways. They could not be made to lay stone upon stone for months or even years at a time, for example in an uninhabited mountain region, hundreds of miles from home; the hopelessness of such diligent toil, which could not be completed even in a long lifetime, would have made them despair, and, most of all, less fit for the job. This is why the system of partial construction was chosen; five hundred meters wall could be completed in roughly five years, by that time, of course, the supervisors were, as a rule, utterly exhausted, had lost all confidence in themselves, the construction, the world. But still in the elation of the festivities for the unification of their thousand meter section they were sent far far away; on their journey they saw completed sections of the wall jutting out here and there, passed the living quarters of higher supervisors who presented them with decorations, heard the cheers of new armies of workers flocking from the depths of the country, saw forests being felled to serve as scaffolding for the wall, saw mountains being hammered into building stones, in the holy places heard the pious chants praying for the wall's completion, all of which soothed their impatience; the quiet life in their homeland where they spent some time strengthened them; the esteem which all of the builders enjoyed, the trusting humility with which their reports were received, the faith the simple quiet citizen placed in the future completion of the wall, all this tugged at their heartstrings; like ever-hopeful children they bade farewell to their homeland; the desire to return to work on the people's project became unconquerable; they left their homes earlier than would have been necessary; half the village accompanied them for long stretches of the way; wherever they went there were salutations, pennants, and banners; never had they seen how vast and rich and beautiful and endearing their country was; every countryman was a brother for whom they were building the protective wall and who thanked them with everything he had, and that was his life, Unity! Unity! Chest to chest, a pageant of the nation, their blood, no longer confined in the meager circulation of the body but rolling sweetly and yet returning through the infinite expanse of

China.

Hence, this system of partial construction becomes understandable, but there were surely other reasons, too. There is nothing peculiar about the fact that I dwell on this question for so long; it is a crucial question for the entire construction of the wall, however insignificant it may initially seem. If I want to convey and elucidate the mentality and the experiences of that time, I cannot probe deeply enough into this question.

First of all, it must be said that, at the time, certain achievements were made which are just scarcely inferior to the building of the Tower of Babel, which in terms of righteousness before God, at least by human reckoning, were the exact opposite of that structure. I mention this because in the early years of construction a scholar wrote a book in which he drew these exact comparisons. He sought to demonstrate that the construction of the Tower of Babel failed by no means due to the causes generally asserted, or, at least, that the very primary causes were not among those well known causes. His evidence consisted not only of treatises and reports, but he claimed to have conducted private investigations at the site itself and to have found that the construction failed and was doomed to fail due to the weakness of the foundation. In this respect, however, our era was far superior to that one; almost every educated contemporary was a skilled mason and infallible when it came to laying foundations. This was not at all what the scholar had aimed to prove, but he claimed that only the great wall would, for the first time in human history, provide a solid foundation for a new Tower of Babel. So first the wall, and then the Tower. At the time the book was in everyone's hands, but I admit that, to this day, I do not see how he envisaged the construction of this tower. The wall, which did not even form a circle but a sort of quarter or semicircle, should function as foundation of a tower? This could only be meant in a spiritual sense. But then why the wall, which was something concrete, product of the efforts and the lives of hundreds of thousands? And why were there plans of the Tower in the book, albeit nebulous plans, and detailed proposals as to how the force of the people could be rigorously channeled toward the future new project. There was – this book is just an example – much mental confusion at the time, perhaps precisely because so many people tried to rally for a single purpose. Human nature, which is fundamentally frivolous, akin to dust swirling up, does not endure shackles; if it shackles itself, it will soon begin to rattle those shackles like mad and tear up the wall chain and itself in all senses.

It is possible that these considerations, which actually run counter to

184

the construction of the wall, may have been taken into account when the leadership decided upon partial construction. It was only by spelling out the orders of the highest leadership that we – and I'm certainly speaking on behalf of many – actually got to know ourselves and found that, without leadership, neither our book learning nor our common sense would have been sufficient even for the modest task we served within the greater whole. In the leaders' quarters – where it was and who sat there, no one I asked knows and has known – in that room, all human thoughts and desires must have circulated, and all human goals and fulfillments in the opposite sense; through the window, however, a glimmer of divine worlds fell onto the leaders' hands as they drew up the designs.

And therefore the unbiased observer cannot understand that the leadership, had it seriously intended to, should have been unable to overcome the difficulties that stood in the way of the wall's continuous construction. So this leaves only the conclusion that the leadership intended the partial construction. But the partial construction was only makeshift and inexpedient. So the conclusion remains that the leadership wanted something inexpedient. A peculiar conclusion, indeed. And yet it may also claim legitimacy from another perspective. Today perhaps we can speak about it without danger. At the time, many people, and even the best, had a secret principle: Seek to understand the orders of the leadership with all your might, but only up to a certain limit, then stop thinking about them. A very reasonable principle, which incidentally found yet another interpretation in a later oft repeated parable: Stop thinking further, not because it might harm you; it is not at all certain that it will harm you. It is not even a question of harm or no harm. It will happen to you as it happens to a river in the spring. It rises, grows mightier, provides richer nourishment to the land along its banks, retains its character far out into the sea, becomes more on a par and more welcome with the sea. This is as far as you may think about the leadership's orders. But then the river rises beyond its banks, loses contours and shape, slows its downstream flow, against its destiny tries to form small seas inland, damages the farmland, and yet cannot maintain its expansion in the long term, but runs back between its banks, in fact, it even dries up miserably in the hot season that follows. Do not think about the leadership's orders this far.

Now this comparison might have been extraordinarily pertinent during the construction of the wall; yet for my present report, at least, it is only of limited value. My investigation is purely historical; lightning no longer flashes from those storm clouds long past, and thus I can seek an explanation for the partial construction which goes further than that with which one contented oneself at the time. The limits set by my intellectual capacity are narrow enough indeed, but the area that would need to be covered is infinite.

Against whom was the great wall to be a protection? Against the northern tribes. I hail from southeastern China. No northern tribe can threaten us there. We read about them in the book of the ancients, the atrocities they commit according to their nature make us sigh in our peaceful cabins, in the faithful representations by artists we see their faces of damnation, their gaping mouths, their jaws lined with long pointed teeth, the narrowed eyes which seem to already eye the loot that their chops will crush and rip to pieces. When the children are naughty, we just show them these pictures, and at once they throw themselves at our chests. But we do not know anything else about those northerners, we haven't seen them, and if we stay in our village, we never will see them, even if they charge and chase their wild horses straight to us; the country is too vast and will not let them reach us, they will lose themselves in the empty air.

Why then, if this is how things stand, do we leave our homeland, the river and the bridges, mother and father, the weeping wife, the children in need of education, and move away to go to school in a faraway city, and our thoughts are even farther away with the wall in the north. Why? Ask the leadership. They know us. They, who mull over immense concerns, know about us, know our small business, see us all sitting together in the lowly hut, and the prayer the father of the family says among his family in the evening pleases or displeases them. And if I may be permitted such a thought about the leadership, I have to say that in my opinion the leadership already existed earlier, did not convene as, for example, high mandarins, inspired by a pleasant morning dream, hastily call a meeting, hastily make decisions and knock the populace out of their beds in the evening to implement their decisions, and be it merely to stage an illumination in honor of a god that had shown himself favorable toward the leaders the day before, only to beat them in a dark corner the next day, as soon as the lanterns have gone out. But rather the leadership seems to always have existed and the decision to build the Great Wall as well.

In part during the construction of the wall and afterwards up to today, I have devoted myself almost exclusively to comparative people's history – there are certain issues where, as it were, this is the only means to get to the heart of the matter – and I found that we Chinese possess certain popular and

186

governmental institutions of unique clarity, and then again others of unique obscurity. Exploring the causes, particularly of the latter phenomenon, has always fascinated me, still fascinates me, and the construction of the Great Wall is also fundamentally affected by these issues.

Now one of our most obscure institutions is definitely that of the emperorship. Of course in Peking, even more so at the court itself, there is some clarity about it, even though it is probably more apparent than real; even teachers of constitutional law and history at the higher schools pretend to be well-instructed about these things and able to impart this knowledge to their students; the deeper one descends to the lower schools the more, understandably, the doubts about one's own knowledge fade away, and superficial knowledge surges up as high as a mountain around a few precepts drummed into them for centuries, which have certainly not lost any of their eternal truth, but will remain eternally unrecognized in this mist and fog.

But as concerns the issue of the emperorship, it is precisely the people that should be asked first, because this is where the emperorship has its last bastions of support. Of course, I can only speak for where I am from. Apart from the nature gods and their year-round varied and nicely fulfilling service, all our thoughts focused on the emperor. But not the current one, or, rather, they would have focused on the current one if we had known him or known anything specific about him. Naturally we were also – the only curiosity that filled us – always trying to learn something of the kind. But – as odd as this may sound – it was hardly possible to learn anything, not from the pilgrim who roams through a lot of the country after all, neither in the neighboring nor in the distant villages, nor from the sailors who not only travel our small streams but also the holy rivers. We did hear a great deal, but nothing could be made out of that great deal. Our country is so vast; no fairytale matches its size; even the sky barely envelops it. And Peking is just a dot, and the emperor's palace just a tiny dot. Then again the emperor as such, however, is great across all the storeys of the world. The living emperor, a person like us, lies, just like us, on his daybed, which, though generous in size, is in comparison still quite narrow and short. Just like us, he sometimes stretches his limbs, and when he is very tired, he yawns with his delicately drawn mouth. How are we to learn about this, thousands of miles to the south, almost on the border to the Tibetan highlands. Besides, any news, even if it did reach us, would come far too late, would be obsolete. Around the emperor swarm the glittering and yet obscure throngs of the imperial courtiers, the counterweight to the emperorship, forever trying to shoot the emperor down from his balance with poisoned arrows. The emperorship is immortal, but the individual emperor falls and falls from grace; even entire dynasties eventually decline and expire in a single death rattle. Of those struggles and sufferings the people will never know, like latecomers, like strangers to the city, they stand at the end of the congested side streets, calmly feeding on the provisions they brought along, while far in the front, in the middle of the market square, the execution of their master proceeds.

There is a legend that expresses this relationship well. The emperor, so the story goes, has sent you, the individual, the pathetic subject, a tiny shadow that fled to the farthest distance from the imperial sun, to you alone the emperor has sent a message from his deathbed. He made the messenger kneel by his bedside and whispered the message into his ear; it mattered so much to him that he had him repeat it back to him into his ear. He confirmed the accuracy of what was said with a nod. And in front of all of the spectators to his death – all obstructing walls have been taken down and the dignitaries of the empire stand in a circle on the outside stairs curving far and high – in front of all those, he has attended to the messenger. The messenger set out right away, a strong, an indefatigable man, a swimmer without equal, stretching out now this, now the other arm, he forges ahead through the crowd; if he meets with resistance he points to the sign of the sun on his chest, he moves forward with unparalleled ease. But the crowd is huge, there is no end to their living quarters; if there were an open field, how he would fly and soon you would certainly hear the magnificent pounding of his fists on your door. But instead, how futile is his struggle; he is still squeezing his way through the chambers of the innermost palace; never will he get beyond them, and, if he succeeded, nothing would have been gained; he would have to struggle down the steps and if he succeeded, nothing would have been gained; he would have to traverse the courtyards, and after the courtyards the second, surrounding palace, and again stairs and courtyards and another palace and so on, through thousands of years, and if he finally did rush out the most outermost door – but never, never can this happen – it would just be the royal capital spreading in front of him, the center of the world, piled high with its dregs. No one can get through here, and much less with a message from a dead man to a nonentity. But you sit by your window and dream it up as evening falls.

Just like this, this hopelessly and this hopefully, do our people view the emperor. They do not know which emperor is reigning, and there are even doubts as to the name of the dynasty. Many things of the kind are studied one after another in school, but the general uncertainty in this regard is so great that even the best student gets pulled into it. Long deceased emperors are placed on the throne in our villages, and the one, who lives on only in song, recently released an announcement that the priest reads before the altar. Battles from our most ancient history are only now being fought, and, with a flushed face, the neighbor blurts out the news to you. The imperial wives, overfed in their silken cushions, estranged from the noble virtue by wily courtiers, inflating in their lust for power, quick-tempered with greed, sprawling in voluptuousness, committing their evil deeds over and over; the more time has passed, the more terrible all the colors glow, and, with loud wailing, the village learns one day how, thousands of years ago, an empress drank her husband's blood in long draughts.

This is how the people deal with their past rulers; the present ones, however, they mix up with the dead ones. If for once, once in a lifetime, an imperial official traveling through the province happens to come to our village, makes some demand or other in the name of the ruler, examines the tax rolls, sits in on school classes, questions the priest about our comings and goings, and, before mounting his palanquin, summarizes everything in long admonitions to the rounded up locals, then a smile passes over all the faces, everyone steals furtive glances at another, bends over his children so as to not be observed by the official. Why, people think, he speaks of a dead man as if he were alive; this emperor died long ago, the dynasty is extinct, this official is making fun of us, but we will pretend that we didn't notice so as not to offend him. But we will give serious obedience only to our current ruler, for everything else would be a sin. And behind the official's palanquin rushing off someone arbitrarily lifted from a decomposing urn will rise and stamp his foot as the ruler of the village.

If one were to conclude from such phenomena that we basically have no emperor at all, one would not be far from the truth. Again and again I have to say: there may be no people more loyal to the emperor than ours in the south, but the emperor does not benefit from our loyalty. True, there stands a sacred dragon on the small column at the end of the village, and since times immemorial, it has been blowing its fiery breath straight toward Peking in homage; but Peking itself is much stranger to the people in the village than life hereafter. Should there really be such a village where the houses stand side by side, covering fields vaster than the view reaches from our hill, and between those houses there would be people standing shoulder to shoulder day and night? Rather than imagining such a city, it would be easier to believe that Peking and its emperor were one, like a cloud, quietly moving under the sun in the course of the times.

The consequence of such views is a free, uncontrolled life of sorts. By no means immoral, rarely have I encountered such moral purity as in my homeland on my travels. And yet a life not governed by any present law and only abiding by the orders and warnings reaching to us across from ancient times.

I refrain from generalizing and do not claim that this holds true for all ten thousand villages of our province or even in all five hundred provinces of China. But I may be allowed to say, based on the many works I have read on the subject as well as on my own observations – especially during the construction of the Great Wall when the human material afforded the feeling person with the opportunity to travel through the souls of almost all provinces – because of all that I may be allowed to say that everywhere, over and over, the prevailing view regarding the emperor shows a certain general tenor common to the view in my homeland. I am not attempting to posit this view as a virtue at all, on the contrary. While it is mainly caused by the government itself, which in the oldest empire on earth to this day has been unable and has neglected, for the sake of other things, to shape the institution of the emperorship with such clarity that it would be immediately and persistently effective, even at the most distant borders of the empire. On the other hand, however, this is also informed by a weakness of imagination or faith on the part of the people, for they do not manage to draw out the emperorship from its seclusion in Peking and pull it with all their vitality and presence to their humble chests, desiring nothing more than to feel its touch for once and to perish in it.

So this view is really not a virtue. It is all the more striking that it is precisely this weakness that seems to be one of the most important means of unifying our people, indeed, if I may say so, it is the very ground on which we live. Giving detailed reasons for a flaw here does not mean shaking our conscience, but, which is much worse, rattling the legs on which we stand. And this is why I do not wish to investigate this question any further at this point.

This was the world into which the news of the construction of the wall penetrated. It, too, with a delay of some thirty years after its announcement. It was a summer evening. I, ten years old, was standing on the riverbank with my father. Owing to the significance of this much-discussed hour, I can remember the smallest circumstance. He was holding my hand, which he loved to do well into his old age, running his other hand along his long very thin pipe as though it were a flute. His large thin stiff beard jutted into the air, for while enjoying his pipe, he was gazing across the river into the air. His braid, the object of the children's reverence, came lower, faintly swishing on the gold brocade of his festive robe. At that moment, a bark drew up in front of us, the boatman signaled to my father to come down the embankment; he himself got off the bark to meet him. They met halfway, the boatman whispered something into my father's ear; he embraced him to get really close to him. I could not understand what they were saying; I only saw that my father did not seem to believe the news, the boatman tried to confirm its veracity, my father still could not believe it, with the fervor of sailor folk the boatman almost ripped apart his robe over the chest to prove the truth, my father fell silent and the boatman stomped down onto the bark and took off. Pensively my father turned to me, knocked out his pipe and stuck it in his belt, stroked my cheek and pulled my head close. That was what I liked best, it made me all cheerful, and thus we returned home. There the rice pudding was already steaming on the table, a few guests had gathered, wine was just being poured into the goblets. Without paying attention to this, still on the threshold, my father began to report what he had heard. Of course, I have no recollection of the exact words, but due to the extraordinariness of the circumstances that were compelling even for a child, its meaning left such a deep impression on me that I dare to repeat a version of its wording. I do so because the wording was very characteristic of the popular view. So my father said something like this:

Once, on a winter afternoon, after various business hassles, my business – every merchant knows such time – seemed so repulsive to me that I decided to close it for the day right away, although it was still early in the day in bright winter light. Such decisions of free will always have good consequences,

---

An Old Document

It is as if a lot had been neglected in the defense of our fatherland. We have not worried about it until now and have gone about our work, but the events of recent times have been alarming to us.

I have a cobbler's workshop in the square in front of the imperial palace. As soon as I open my shop at dawn, I already see the entrances of all the streets converging here occupied by armed men. But they are not our soldiers but apparently nomads from the north. In a way that is incomprehensible to me, they pushed into the capital, which is really quite far from the border. At any rate, they are here, and it seems that there are more each morning.

As is their nature, they camp out in the open air, for they detest houses. They busy themselves with whetting their swords, sharpening their arrows, exercising on horseback. They have literally turned this peaceful, scrupulously clean square into a stable. We sometimes try to come out of our shops and, at least, clear away the worst of the filth, but it happens less and less often, for the effort is futile and we risk being run over by their wild horses or injured by their whips.

It is impossible to talk to the nomads. They do not know our language, why, they barely have their own. Among themselves they communicate like jackdaws. This call of the jackdaw can be heard again and again. Our way of life, our institutions are incomprehensible to them, and they are indifferent to them. As a result they are averse to any kind of sign language as well. You may dislocate your jaws and wriggle your hands out of their joints, they still have not understood you and will never understand you. They often grimace; then the whites of their eyes roll up and froth pours from their mouths, but by so doing they neither try to tell us something nor even scare us; they do it because it is their way. They take whatever they need. One cannot say that they use force. Rather than having them touch you, you step aside and leave everything to them.

They have taken many a good piece from my supplies as well. I cannot really complain, since I have seen, for example, how the butcher across from me is faring. No sooner does he bring his wares inside than everything is snatched away from him and devoured by the nomads. Even their horses eat meat, often a horseman lies next to his horse, and they both feed off the same piece of meat, everyone on one end. The butcher is frightened and does not dare stop his meat deliveries. We understand him, collect some money among us and support him. If the nomads did not get meat, who knows what they might think to do, but then who knows what they will think of doing even if they do get their daily meat. Recently the butcher thought he could at least save himself the trouble of slaughtering and brought in a live ox one morning. He must never do this again. I lay for about an hour flat on the floor, all the way in the back of my workshop, and heaped all my clothes, blankets, and cushions on top of me, only to keep from hearing the ox bellowing, pounced upon from all sides by the nomads tearing out pieces of its warm flesh with their teeth. It had been quiet for a long time when I dared to go outside; like drunkards around a wine cask they lay there wearily around the remainders of the ox.

It was precisely then that I thought I saw the emperor himself in a window of his palace; otherwise he never comes to the outer chambers, he only lives in the innermost garden, but this time he stood, or so it seemed, at a window and, with his head bent down, gazed upon the hustle and bustle in front of his palace.

"What's going to happen?" we all ask ourselves. "How long will we endure this burden and suffering? The imperial palace attracted them here but does not know how to drive them away again. The gate stays locked; the guard, that used to march in or out ceremoniously, remains behind the barred windows. We, the artisans and business owners, are entrusted with the salvation of our fatherland, but we are not up to such a task; and we never boasted of being able to do it either. It is a misunderstanding, and it will be our demise."

This (perhaps all too Europeanizing) translation of a few old Chinese manuscript pages has been provided by a friend of the campaign. It is a fragment. There is no hope of finding the continuation.

(   )

In the following there are a few more pages that are too damaged indeed to infer anything particular from them.

It was in the summer, a hot day. On the way home with my sister, I passed the gate to an estate. I don't know whether she knocked on the gate out of mischief or absentmindedness, or whether she just shook her fist at it and didn't knock at all. A hundred steps further on, where the country road veered off to the left, a village began. We did not know the village, but people came right out of the first house and waved to us, amiably but in warning, terrified themselves, bent with terror. They pointed toward the estate we had passed and reminded us of the knock on the door. The estate owners would sue us; the investigation would begin at once. I was very calm and also calmed down my sister. She probably had not even knocked at all, and if she had, nowhere in the world would this be cause for a lawsuit. I also tried to make this understood to the people around us; they listened to me, but withheld their opinion. Later they said that not only my sister, but I too, as her brother, would be charged. I nodded with a smile. We all gazed back at the estate as though watching a distant smoke cloud and waiting for the flame. And sure enough, we soon saw horsemen riding through the wide-open gate; dust rose, enveloping everything, only the tips of the high lances were flashing. And no sooner had the troop disappeared inside the estate than it seemed to have turned the horses around and was on its way to us. I pushed my sister aside, I would clear it up by myself; she refused to leave me behind, I said she should at least change and appear before the gentlemen in a nicer dress. Eventually she did as told and set out on her long way home. Presently the horsemen were next to us, asking for my sister from their horses down; she isn't here at the moment, was the anxious reply, but would come later. The reply was received almost with indifference; it seemed above all important that I had been found. They were mainly two gentlemen, the judge, a younger, lively man, and his quiet assistant, named Assmann. I was ordered to enter the farmhouse living room. Slowly, rocking my head, adjusting my suspenders, I started walking under the gentlemen's keen eyes. I still almost thought that a word would be sufficient to free me, the city man, from this peasant folk, even with honor. But when I had crossed the threshold to the room, the judge who had jumped up and was already expecting me, said: "I feel sorry for this man." It was beyond all doubt that he was not referring to my present state but to that which was to happen to me. The room looked more like a prison cell than a farmhouse living room. Large stone flags, dark gray bare wall, somewhere an iron ring cemented into the wall, in the center something that was half plank bed, half operating table.

———

Would I be able to savor any other air than that of the prison? That is the great question, or, rather, it would be if I had any prospects of being released.

I am Latude, the old prisoner

Just after taking office, but before granting amnesty as is customary, the young prince visited a prison. Among other things he inquired, as had been expected, about the man who had been in this prison the longest. It was someone who had murdered his wife, had been sentenced to life in prison and had now completed his twenty-third year. The prince wanted to see him; he was lead into the cell; as a precaution the prisoner had been placed in chains for the day.

The prisoner was in chains. I went into his cell, locked it and said: You are an old prisoner

---

When I got home in the evening, I found a large an overly large egg in the middle of the room. It was almost as high as the table and bulged accordingly. It quietly rocked back and forth. I was very curious, took the egg between my legs and carefully cut it in two with my pocketknife. It was already hatched. The crumpling shell fell apart and out leapt a stork-like, still featherless bird flapping the air with its too-short wings. "What do you want in our world?" I felt like asking, squatted down in front of the bird and gazed into his anxiously blinking eyes. But he left me, and hopped along the walls, half fluttering, as though on sore feet. "One helps the other," I thought, set my dinner out on the table and beckoned to the bird who was just drilling his beak between my few books on the other side. He immediately came over, apparently feeling more at home, sat down on a chair, began to sniff the sandwich which I had placed in front of him with his whooping breath, but merely skewered it up and flung it back to me. "A mistake," I thought, "of course, one does not leap out of an egg to start eating cold cut right away. Some female experience would be useful here." And I scrutinized him to see whether I might be able to divine his food preferences from the outside. "If he belongs to the stork family," I suddenly thought, "he probably likes fish. Now, I'm even ready to get fish for him. But not for nothing. My means don't allow me to keep a pet bird. So if I make such sacrifices, I want an equivalent, life-sustaining service in return. He is a stork, so when he is fully grown and fattened with my fish, he may take me with him to southern climes. I have always longed to travel there, and I have only refrained from it for lack of stork wings." I immediately brought paper and ink, dipped the bird's beak in the ink, and, without the bird putting up any resistance, wrote the following: "I, stork-like bird, undertake to carry you on my back to southern climes, provided that you feed me fish, frogs, and worms (I added the last two foods because they are cheap) until I can fly." I then wiped off his beak and held the paper in front of the bird's eyes once more before folding it and placing it in my billfold. But afterward I went to get fish right away; I had to pay dearly for it, but the merchant promised to have spoiled fish and plenty of worms ready for me from now on at a cheaper price. Perhaps the trip south would not be all that expensive. And I was glad to see how the bird savored what I had brought for him. The fish were gulped down with a gurgle, filling his little reddish belly. Day by day, surpassing human children, the bird made progress in his development. True, the unbearable stench of the rotten fish never left my room anymore, and it wasn't easy to find the bird's waste and get rid of it, also the winter cold and the rise in coal prices prohibited the airing out that was so necessary – no matter, come spring, I would swim towards the glorious south in light air. The wings grew, became covered with feathers, the muscles grew stronger; it was time to practice flying. Unfortunately there was no mother stork; had the bird not been so willing, my instruction surely would not have been enough. But he apparently realized that he had to compensate for my deficient teaching by paying close attention and exerting the greatest effort. We started with the armchair flight. I climbed up, he followed, I jumped off with my arms spread, he fluttered after me. Later we proceeded to the table, and eventually to the wardrobe, but all flights were systematically repeated many times.

The Pest

The pest lived in the forest. In a long abandoned hut from the time of the old charcoal burner. Upon entering, one notices only the lingering smell of mildew, nothing else. Smaller than the smallest mouse, invisible even to the eye brought very close, the pest presses itself into a corner. There's nothing, nothing at all to notice; the forest calmly rustles through the empty window-hole. How lonely it is here, and how perfectly this suits you. You will sleep here in this corner. Why not in the forest where the air flows freely? Because you're already here, secure in a hut despite the fact that the door was long since broken off its hinges and carried away. But you still feel around in the air as though you wanted to pull the door shut; then you lie down.

Finally I jumped up from the table and shattered the lamp with a punch. At once a servant entered with a lantern, bowed and held the door open for me. I rushed out of my room down the stairs, the servant behind me. Downstairs a second servant put a fur around me; since I just submitted to him doing so, he did even more, turned up my fur collar and buttoned it at my throat. It was necessary; the cold was brutal. I mounted the spacious sleigh waiting for me, was tucked in snugly under many blankets, and, with a clear ring of the bell, the ride began. "Friedrich," I heard someone whisper from the corner. "You're here, Alma," I said and held out my thickly gloved right hand. Another few words of delight about the encounter, then we fell silent, for the breakneck ride took our breath away. Dozing, I had almost forgotten about my fellow traveler when we stopped in front of an inn. The innkeeper stood by the carriage door, my servants to his side, everyone with craning necks prepared to take orders from me. But I bent forward and simply called out: "What are you standing here for, keep going, keep going, don't stop!" And with a stick that I found next to me I poked the driver

––––––––––

21

My business rests entirely on my shoulders. Two ladies with typewriters and account books in the front room, my room with desk, cash box, conference table, club chair, and telephone, that is my entire work equipment. So easy to manage; so easy to run. I'm young, and business is rolling in front of me; I'm not complaining. I'm not complaining. A young man has rented the small vacant apartment next door since the New Year, which I, uncleverly, hesitated too long to rent. A room with a front room as well and a kitchen to boot. I could have well used the room and front room; my two ladies do sometimes feel overburdened – but what use would I have for the kitchen. This petty doubt was the reason that I let him snatch the apartment from me. Now the young man is sitting there. Harras is his name. What he actually does there, I don't know. On the door it only says "Harras, Bureau." I've made inquiries, I've been told that it was a business similar to mine. One could not exactly warn against granting credit, for here was an ambitious young man whose business might have a future, but one could also not advise in favor of giving credit, for, by all appearances, there were presently no assets. The usual information given when one doesn't know anything. Sometimes I run into Harras on the stairs; he must always been in an extraordinary rush, he virtually scurries past me, I have not even really seen him yet, he holds his office key ready in his hand, in a heartbeat he has opened the door, has slipped inside like a rat's tail, and I stand again in front of the plate "Harras, Bureau," which I have read a lot more often than it deserves. Those wretchedly thin walls that betray the honest working man, but cover the dishonest. My telephone is mounted on the wall that separates me from my neighbor, but I only point this out as an ironic fact: even if it were hanging on the opposite wall, one could hear it in the neighboring apartment. I have stopped saying my customer's names on the telephone, but it doesn't take much to divine the names from characteristic, yet unavoidable turns in the conversation. Sometimes, the earpiece to my ear, spurred on by nervousness, I dance around the telephone on my tiptoes, and still can't prevent secrets from being divulged. Thus, naturally, my business decisions on the telephone become less certain, my voice shaky. What does Harras do while I'm on the phone? If I truly wanted to exaggerate – which one often needs to do to get clear about something – I could say: Harras doesn't need a telephone, he uses mine; he has pushed his couch against the wall and listens, whereas I, when the telephone rings, have to walk there, take down my customer's wishes, make serious decisions, perform large-scale persuasions, and most of all involuntarily give a report to Harras through the wall. Perhaps he doesn't even wait for the end of the conversation, but gets up after the point in the conversation has been reached that has given him sufficient insight into the case, scurries through the city as his custom, and before I have even hung up my earpiece, he may already be working against me.

A Crossbreed

I have a peculiar pet, half kitten, half lamb. I inherited it from my father's estate, but it developed only during my time; it used to be much more lamb than kitten, but now it has the same amount of both. The cat's head and claws, the lamb's size and shape, the eyes of both, flickering and gentle, the fur soft and clinging to the body, the movements both jumping and slinking; it curls up and purrs in the sunshine on the windowsill, on the meadow it runs likes mad and can hardly be caught, it flees from cats, wants to attack lambs, in a moonlit night the eaves are its favorite path, it cannot meow and abhors rats, it can lie in wait next to the chicken coop for hours on end, yet it has never taken advantage of an opportunity for murder, I feed it sweet milk, which it stomachs best and sucks in long draughts through its predator's teeth. Of course, it's a great spectacle for children. Sunday morning is visiting hour; I have the little creature on my lap, and the children of the entire neighborhood stand around me. They ask the strangest questions that no one can possibly answer. I don't make much of an effort but content myself with showing them what I have, without further explanations. Sometimes the children bring along cats, once they even brought two lambs; but contrary to their expectation there were no scenes of recognition; the animals gazed at one another calmly out of their animal eyes and seemed to mutually accept their existence as a divine fact.

On my lap the animal knows neither fear nor hunting instinct. Snuggled up against me, it feels most comfortable. It sticks with the family that raised it. This is probably not some extraordinary faithfulness but the true instinct of the animal, which certainly has innumerable kin on earth but perhaps not a single close blood relative, and to whom the protection it has found with us is sacred. Sometimes I have to laugh when it sniffs around me, twines between my legs and is inseparable from me. That's not enough: as it is lamb and cat, it almost wants to be a dog as well. I seriously believe something like this. It has both kinds of unrest in itself, that of the cat and that of the lamb, as different as they are. This is why its skin is too tight for it. Perhaps the butcher's knife would be deliverance for the animal, but since it was a bequest I have to deny it that.

A little boy has a cat as his only bequest from his father and, through it, he became the mayor of London. What will I become through my pet, my bequest? Where does this enormous city extend?

The written and handed-down history of the world frequently utterly fails, but while the human power of augury is often misleading, it does lead, does not let one down. Thus, the records of the Seven Wonders of the World for example have always been accompanied by rumors that there had existed yet an Eighth Wonder of the World, and about this Eighth Wonder several different, perhaps contradictory statements had been made, whose uncertainty was explained by the obscurity of those old times.

"Ladies and gentleman, you will," this is more or less how the European-clad Arab addressed the group of travelers who were hardly listening but, practically ducked, contemplating the incredible structure rising in front of them on the bare stone floor, "You will certainly admit that my agency by far surpasses all other travel agencies, even the ones that are justifiably old and famous. Whereas, as is the old hackneyed custom, the competition takes their clients to the Seven Wonders of the World of the history books, our company shows you the Eighth Wonder."

No, no,

Some say he is a hypocrite, others say it only appears that way. My parents know his father; when he was visiting us last Sunday, I straight-out asked about the son. Now the old gentleman is very clever: it is hard to get the better of him and I lack all cunning for such attacks. The conversation was lively, but barely had I brought up my question that it became quiet. My father nervously began to play with his beard, my mother stood up to check on the tea, but the old gentleman gazed at me smiling out of his blue eyes and had tilted his wrinkled pale face with the very white hair to the side. "Oh, the boy," he said and turned his gaze to the table lamp that was already shining on this early winter evening. "Have you ever spoken to him?" he then asked. "No," I said, "but I've heard a lot about him and I would very much like to talk to him if he would receive me."

"What is it? What is it?" I called out in my bed, still bogged down by sleep, and held my arms upward. Then I got up, far from conscious of the present; I felt as if I had to push aside a few people who were in my way, did the necessary hand motions and then finally came to the open window.

A carpet spreading at your feet,
A canopy flapping at your head,

Helpless, a barn in spring, a consumptive in spring,

The music is playing the old song "Begin you heroes of the arena,"

Begin you heroes of the arena,
begin the game,

Begin you heroes of the arena,
begin the game.

Sometimes it happens, the reasons for it can often hardly be guessed at, that the greatest bullfighter chooses as his arena a dilapidated stadium in a remote little town, the name of which, up to that time, his Madrid audience hardly knew. A stadium, neglected for centuries, here overgrown with grass, playground for children, there searing with bare stones, resting place for lizards and snakes. Long dismantled up on the edges, stone quarry for all the houses around, now just a small basin holding barely five hundred people. No outbuildings, especially no stables, but, worst of all, the railway hasn't been extended up to here, a three-hour coach ride, a seven-hour walk to the next train stop.

"How is it, Hunter Gracchus, so you have been traveling on this old boat for centuries?"

"About fifteen hundred years."

"And just in this boat?"

"Just in this bark. Bark is the correct name, you know. You don't know anything about seamanship?"

"No, I've just started dealing with it today, since I know about you, since I got on your boat."

"No excuses. I'm from a landlocked area myself. Was no seaman, didn't want to be one; mountains and forests were my joy and happiness, and now – the oldest seaman, Hunter Gracchus patron saint of sailors, Hunter Gracchus worshipped by the cabin boy who wrings his hands up there in the crow's nest, frightened on a stormy night. Don't laugh."

"Why would I laugh? No, certainly not. With a pounding heart I stood in front of your cabin door, with a pounding heart I entered. Your friendly disposition puts me somewhat at ease, but I'll never forget whose guest I am."

"Certainly, you're right. Whatever it may be, Hunter Gracchus, that's me. Why don't you have some of that wine, I don't know the brand, but it is sweet and heavy, the patron takes good care of me."

"Please, not now, I'm too nervous. Perhaps later, if you let me stay here for that long. Who's the patron?"

"The owner of the bark. Such patrons are really extraordinary people. I just don't understand them. I don't mean their language, even though, naturally, I often don't understand their language either. But that's just as an aside. I've learned enough languages in the course of the centuries, and I could be the interpreter between the ancestors and today's patrons. But I don't understand the way these patrons think. Perhaps you can explain it to me."

"I'm not very hopeful. How should I be able to explain anything to you, when I'm just a babbling child compared to you."

"Don't be like that, once and for all. Do me the favor and act a little manlier, more confident. What do I do with the shadow of a guest. I blow him out the hatch onto the lake. I need various explanations. You, who goes out and about outside, you can give them to me. But if you sit here at my table shivering and self-deluded, forgetting what little you do know, in that case you can send yourself packing right away. I say it the way I mean it."

"There is some truth in what you say. In fact, I do have a thing or two on you. So I will try to force myself. Ask me."

"Better, much better, now you exaggerate in the other sense and think up some superiorities. You must understand me correctly. I'm a person like you but more impatient by the several centuries that I am older than you. So, we wanted to talk about patrons. Listen. And have some wine to hone your mind. Drink without any inhibition. A lot. There's still a whole shipload left."

"Gracchus, this is an excellent wine. Long live the patron."

"Too bad, he died today. He was a good man, and he passed away peacefully. Well-bred adult children stood at his deathbed; his wife fainted at the foot of the bed, but his last thought was of me. A good man, from Hamburg."

"Good heavens, from Hamburg, and you here in the south know that he died today."

"Why? Why wouldn't I know when my patron has died. You are quite clueless after all."

"Are you trying to insult me?"

"No, not at all, I can't help it. But you shouldn't be so astonished and have more wine. Concerning the patrons, the thing is the following: the bark was not originally owned by a human."

"Gracchus, I have one request. First tell me briefly the whole story, how things stand with you. To tell you the truth: I really don't know anything. Of course, for you these things are self-evident, and as is your nature you presume that the whole world knows about them. But in a short human life – for life *is* short, Gracchus, try to wrap your mind around it – in this short life one has one's hands full to raise oneself and one's family. As interesting as the Hunter Gracchus is – and this is my conviction not groveling – one doesn't have time to think or inquire or even worry about him. Perhaps on one's deathbed, like your man from Hamburg, I don't know. That is when the hard-working man may have time to relax for once, and when, through his idling thoughts, there wanders the green Hunter Gracchus at some point. But other than that, as I said: I didn't know anything about you, I was in the harbor on business, saw the barque, the gangplank was lying ready, I walked across – but now I would like to know something about you, the whole story."

"Ah, the whole story. The old, old stories. All the books are full of them, teachers draw them on the board in all the schools, mothers are dreaming of them while their children drink from their breasts – and you, man, are sitting here and asking me for the whole story. You must have had an exquisitely dissolute youth."

"That may be, just as it is true for anyone's youth. But I think you would benefit very much from going out and looking at the world a bit. As strange as it may seem to you, and now I almost wonder about it myself, but the fact of the matter is that you are not the talk of town, people speak of many things but you're not one of them, the world goes round, and you go on your journey, but up to this day I never once noticed that the two of you had crossed paths."

"Those may be your observations, my dear friend; others have made other observations. There are only two possibilities here. Either you're hiding the fact that you know about me and you do so with a specific intention. In that case, let me tell you candidly: You're on the wrong track. Or: you really do think you can't remember me because you confuse my story with another. In that case, let me tell you this: I am – No I can't, everyone knows, and why should I of all people tell you! It's been such a long time. Ask the historians! With gaping mouths they sit in their rooms gazing at things long past and describing them incessantly. Go to them and then come back. It's been such a long time. How am I supposed to store all that in this overflowing mind."

"Wait, Gracchus, I'll make it easier on you, I'll ask you. Where do you hail from?"

"From the Black Forest, as is universally known."

"From the Black Forest, of course. And it was there that you hunted in about the fourth century."

"Man, do you know the Black Forest?"

"I don't."

"You really don't know anything. The boatman's little child knows more than you, he truly does, a lot more. Just who made you come in here. What a disaster. Your initial modesty was all too well founded, indeed. You're a void I'm filling with wine. So you don't even know the Black Forest. I hunted there until my twenty-fifth year. If the chamois hadn't tempted me – well, now you know – I would have had a long and good hunter's life, but the chamois tempted me, and I fell to my death on the rocks. Don't ask me any more. Here I am, dead, dead, dead. I don't know why I'm here. Was loaded on to the death bark at the time, as is proper, a pathetic corpse, three, four chores were done about me as with everyone, why make exceptions for the Hunter Gracchus, everything was all right, I lay in the bark stretched out,

---

We all know Rotpeter, just as half the world knows him. But when he came to our town on a tour, I decided to get to know him more closely, in person. It isn't hard to be admitted. In large cities where everyone, ingenious, just longs to see celebrities breathe up close, there may be difficulties, but in our town one contents oneself with marveling at things marvelous from the parquet. Thus, the bellboy told me that I had been the only one whose visit had been announced so far. Mr. Busenau, the impresario, gave me a very warm welcome. I had not expected him to be such a modest, almost timid man. He sat in the hall of Rotpeter's apartment eating an omelet. Although it was morning, he already sat there in his evening tailcoat, in which he appeared at the performances. As soon as he saw me, the unknown insignificant guest, he, recipient of the highest awards, king of animal trainers, honorary doctor of the great universities, – jumped up, shook my hands, urged me to sit down, wiped his spoon on a tablecloth and offered it to me in the most friendly manner so as to finish up his omelet with it. He wouldn't accept that I declined with thanks and was about to start feeding me himself. I had trouble calming him down and fending him off with his plate and spoon. "It is very kind of you to have come," he said then with a strong foreign accent. "Really kind. Also, you've come at the right time, because Rotpeter cannot always, unfortunately, not always receive company. He is often reluctant to see people; then no one, whoever he may be, will be admitted, even I, even I am only permitted to deal with him in business matters so to speak, on stage. But right after the show I must disappear, he goes home by himself, locks himself in his room and usually stays that way until the following evening. He always has a large picnic hamper full of fruit in his bedroom; that is what he lives on during such days. But, of course, I can't leave him unsupervised, so I rent an apartment opposite his and watch him from behind curtains."

"As I sit opposite you here, Rotpeter, hearing you talk, drinking to your health, I honestly completely forget – whether you take this as a compliment or not, but it is the honest truth – that you're a chimpanzee. Just little by little, as I force myself out of my thoughts back to reality, my eyes show me once more whose guest I am."

"Yes."

"You're suddenly so quiet, why is that? Just now you were telling me some amazingly accurate opinions about our town, and now you're so quiet."

"Quiet?"

"Is anything wrong? Should I call the trainer? Perhaps you're accustomed to having a meal at this hour?"

"No, no. It's all right again. I can tell you what it was, too. Sometimes, I'm overcome with such disgust for humans that I can barely contain my nausea. Of course, this has nothing to do with the individual person, nothing with your kind presence. It's against all humans. This is nothing unusual either; should you for example continuously live with apes, you would certainly have similar episodes, no matter how much you control yourself. As such, it is not the odor of the fellow humans that I find so revolting but the human odor that I have taken on and which mingles with the odor from my old home. Just smell for yourself! Right here on my chest! Put your nose deeper into the fur! Deeper, I said."

"Unfortunately, I can't smell anything in particular. The ordinary scent of a well-groomed body, nothing else. The nose of a city person, however, is not authoritative here. You, of course, smell thousands of things that will blow right past us."

"Used to, dear sir, used to. That's over."

"Since you brought it up yourself, I dare to ask: How long have you been living among us then?"

"Five years, it will be five years on the fifth of August."

"An enormous feat. To cast off apehood in five years and gallop through the entire human evolution. Truly, no one has done this before. You're in a league of your own."

"It's a lot, I know, and sometimes it's even beyond me. But in quiet moments, my assessment is less exuberant. Do you know how I was captured?"

"I've read everything that's been printed about you. You were shot and then captured."

"Yes, I took two bullets, one here in my cheek, the wound was of course much larger than the scar is now, and another shot below the hip. I'll take off my trousers so you can see that scar as well. This was the point of entry, this was the critical, deep wound, I fell from the tree and when I came to I was in a cage in steerage."

"In a cage! In steerage! It's one thing to read about it, and a different thing altogether to hear you tell it yourself."

"And still different to have lived it, sir. Until then, I had not known what it means: to have no way out. It was not a four-sided barred cage, rather it was three walls affixed to a crate; the crate was the fourth wall. The whole contraption was so low that I couldn't stand upright, and so narrow that I couldn't even sit down. All I could do was squat with bent knees. In my fury, I didn't' want to see anyone and remained facing the crate; so I lay there in wait with trembling knees for days and nights, and the bars cut into me in the back. Confining wild animals in such a way in the very beginning is considered advantageous, and from my experience I cannot deny that this is really the case from a human point of view. But the human point of view didn't matter to me at the time. I had the crate in front of me. Open the wall of boards, bite a hole through it, squeeze through a gap which in reality barely allows you to gaze through it, and which you welcome with a blissful howl of ignorance when you first discover it. Where do you want to go? Behind the board the forest begins,

---

It was summer, we were lying in the grass, we were tired, evening came, let us lie here. Stay lying down

---

My two hands began to fight. They shut the book I had been reading and pushed it aside so that it wouldn't be in the way. They saluted me and appointed me their referee. And instantly they had interlaced fingers and were speeding along the edge of the table, now to the right, now to the left, depending on the predominance of the one or the other. I didn't take my eyes off them. If they are my hands, I have to be a fair referee; otherwise I'll saddle myself with the pain of a wrong decision. But my job isn't easy; in the dark, between my palms, various tricks are played that I cannot let go unnoticed; therefore I press my chin against the table, and nothing escapes me now. All my life I have favored my right hand, without meaning any harm to the left one. Had the left hand only ever said something, being the indulgent and righteous person I am, I would have stopped the abuse at once. But it didn't make a sound, it hung down on me, and, while the right hand was, say, swinging my hat in the street, my left hand was anxiously feeling my thigh. This was a poor preparation for the fight now in progress. How do you, left wrist, intend to push against this mighty right hand over the long term? How can your girlish fingers hold up against the clasp of the five other ones? It doesn't seem like a fight to me anymore, but rather the natural downfall of the left hand. Now it has been pushed into the utmost left corner of the table, with the right hand shifting up and down regularly like a motor piston against it. If, in view of this distress, I didn't have the redeeming idea that those are my own hands fighting and that I can pull them away from each other with a slight jolt and thereby end both battle and distress – if I didn't have this thought, the left hand would have been broken out of its joint and hurled down from the table, and then perhaps the right one in its intemperance as the winner might have struck me in my own observant face like a five-headed hellhound. Instead the two of them are now lying on top of one another, the right hand stroking the back of the left, and I, the dishonest referee, am nodding in approval.

Esteemed Gentlemen of the Academy!

You grant me the honor of asking me to submit to the Academy a report on my apish past.

Unfortunately I cannot comply with your request as such. Nearly five years separate me from apehood, a time period, perhaps short if measured with a calendar, but infinitely long to gallop through as I have done, accompanied for parts of the way by exquisite people, advice, applause and orchestral music, but ultimately alone, for any company, to stay with the metaphor, stayed far in front of the barrier. This achievement would have been impossible had I stubbornly clung to my origin, the memories of my youth. But precisely renouncing any stubbornness was the highest priority I had given myself; free ape as I was, I submitted myself to this yoke. In doing so, however, my memories, for their part, closed themselves off to me more and more. If, at first, my return was still possible, had the humans been willing, through the entire gateway that the skies form above the earth, it became lower and narrower as my development was forced forward; I felt more comfortable and more enclosed in the human world; the storm from my past that blew after me and made me shiver in the back let up; today it is just a light breeze cooling my heels, and the hole in the distance through which it comes and through which I once came, has grown so small that I, even if my strength and willpower were at all sufficient to go back there, would have to flay my fur off my body to get through. To be frank, as much as I like choosing metaphors for these things, well, to be frank: Your apehood, gentlemen, insofar as something of the like lies behind you, cannot be any more distant to you than mine. Anyone walking this earth is tickled on his heel; the small chimpanzee as much as the great Achilles.

In the narrowest sense, however, I may be able to answer your request, after all, and I do so with great joy. The first thing I learned was: to give a handshake; a handshake suggests sincerity; today, that I am at the top of my career, may that first handshake be complemented by sincere words. They will not impart anything fundamentally new to the Academy and will fall far short of what I was required to do and which for the life of me I cannot do – at least it should give you a sense of the trajectory on which a former ape has penetrated the human world and has become established there.

Yet, I couldn't even say the the little I will say if I were not completely sure of myself and had not unshakably consolidated my position at all the great variety theaters of the civilized world.

I hail from the Gold Coast. As to how I was captured, I have to rely on the reports of strangers. A hunting expedition of the Hagenbeck company – it so happens that I have emptied many good bottles of red wine with its leaders since – was lying hidden in the shrubs by the shore, when I ran to the watering place amid a troop of apes. There were shots, I was the only one who was hit; I took two shots, one in my cheek, a slight wound but it left a large shaven red scar, which earned me the ghastly, absolutely unsuitable name Rotpeter – Red Peter, which must have been invented by an ape, as though the only difference between me and the recently croaked ape named Peter, who was known here and there and trained, was a red mark on my cheek. This just as an aside. The second shot hit me below the hip. It was severe; it is the reason why I still have a slight limp today. I recently read in an essay of one of the ten thousand bloodhounds that rant and rave about me in the newspapers that my ape nature was not yet completely suppressed; proved by the fact that I have a predilection to take off my trousers to show off the entrance wound of that shot whenever

I have visitors. That guy should have every one of the fingers of his writing hand blown away. I can let my trousers down in front of whomever I please; one won't find anything there but well-groomed fur and the scar after a – let us choose a specific word for a specific purpose here that should not be misconstrued – the scar after a malicious shot. Everything is clear and evident, there is nothing to hide; when it comes to the truth, every high-minded person sheds his most sophisticated manners. If, however, that writer were to take off his pants when he has visitors that would be regarded as something completely different and I will accept it as a sign of sanity that he doesn't. But then he should also leave me alone with his sensitivities.

After those shots I came to – and this is where my own memory gradually begins – in a cage in steerage of the Hagenbeck steamship. It was not a four-sided barred cage, rather only three walls had been affixed to a crate so that the crate formed the fourth wall. The whole contraption was too low to stand up in and too narrow to sit down. Hence, I squatted with bent, constantly trembling knees, and since at first I probably did not want to see anyone and only stay in the dark the whole time, I turned toward the crate, while the bars of the cage were cutting into the flesh in my back. This way of confining wild animals at the beginning has recently been considered advantageous, and from my own experience I cannot deny today that, from a human point of view, this is actually the case.

At that point, for the first time in my life, I had no way out, at least straight ahead of me there was no way out, straight ahead of me there was the crate, board firmly connected to board. Well, there was a gap running between the boards which, when I first discovered it, I greeted with a blissful howl of ignorance, but this gap was by far not wide enough to even push my tail through and all my ape power could not widen it.

As I was told later, I must have made remarkably little noise, from which it was concluded that I would either die soon or that, in case I managed to survived the first critical period, I would be very trainable. I survived this period. Muffled sobbing, painful flea hunts, wearily licking a coconut, tapping my skull against the crate wall, poking out my tongue when anyone came near me – these were the first occupations in my new life. But the whole time merely that one feeling: no way out. Of course, today I have only human words to sketch out the apish feelings I had then and I therefore misrepresent them, but even if can no longer get at the old ape truth, it is at least in the spirit of my description, there is no doubt about that. I wanted a way out.

I had had so many ways out so far, and now I had none. I was stuck. Had I been nailed down, my freedom of movement would not have been any smaller. Why was that? Scratch your flesh raw between your toes, you will not find a reason. Press your back against the iron bar sliding up and down until it almost splits you in two, and you will not find a reason. I had no way out, but I had to find one, I couldn't live without one. Always against that crate wall – I would invariably have croaked. But for Hagenbeck, apes belong against the crate wall – well, so I stopped being an ape. A clear, beautiful train of thought that I must have somehow hatched in my gut, for apes think with their gut.

I fear that you may not understand exactly what I mean by a way out. I use the phrase in its most common and fullest sense. I deliberately don't say freedom. I don't mean this great feeling of freedom all around. As an ape I may have known it, and I've met people who long for it. But as far as I am concerned, I didn't demand freedom, not then and not now. By the way: humans all too often deceive themselves about freedom. And just as freedom counts among the loftiest feelings, the corresponding delusion is one of the loftiest as well. In the variety theaters I have often seen a pair of acrobats perform on the trapeze up under the ceiling before my act. They swung, they rocked, they jumped, they floated into each other's arms, one carried the other by the hair with his teeth. "That too is human freedom," I thought, "hubris in motion." You mockery of holy nature! No building would withstand the laughter of apedom at this sight.

No, it wasn't freedom I wanted. Just a way out. No matter where I had come, I did not want to be confined by a crate wall or the like, but have a way out, right, left, wherever, I did not make any other demands, should the way out be a deception as well, the demand was small, the deception would not be greater. Move on, only to move on, anything but stand still with arms raised, pressed against a crate wall.

Today I see clearly: without the utmost inner peace I would never have succeeded. And, in fact, I may owe everything I've become to the peace that came over me after my first few days there on the ship. This peace, in turn, I probably owe to the people on the ship. They're good people, in spite of everything. To this day I like to remember the sound of their heavy steps reverberating in my doze. They had a habit of going about everything extremely slowly. If one of them wanted to rub his eyes, he raised his hand like a suspended weight. Their jokes were crude but hearty. Their laughter was always mixed in with a cough that sounded alarming but meant nothing. They always had something in their mouths to spit out, and they didn't care where they spat. They were always complaining that my fleas were jumping on to them but they were never seriously angry with me for it; they just knew that fleas thrive in my fur and that fleas are jumpers; they put up with that. When they were off duty, a few of them sometimes sat in a semicircle around me; they rarely talked but just cooed at one another; smoked their pipes stretched out on crates; slapped their knees as soon as I made the slightest movement, and now and again one took a stick and tickled me where I liked being tickled. If I were invited to join a voyage on that ship today, I would surely decline the invitation, but it is just as sure that those aren't all ugly memories that I would be indulging in steerage.

The peace I acquired among those men prevented me most of all from any attempt to escape. Now, in retrospect, it seems as if I had at least sensed that I would have to find a way out if I wanted to live, but that this way out could not be achieved by escaping. I no longer know if escape was possible but I believe it was; it should always be possible for an ape to escape. With my teeth as they are today I have to be careful even with ordinary nut cracking, but at the time I should have been able to bite through the door lock over time. I didn't. What would have been gained if I had. As soon as I stuck out my head, I would have been captured again and locked into an even worse cage, or I could have fled unnoticed to other animals such as the boa constrictors opposite me and would have breathed my last breath in their embraces or I would have even succeeded to steal onto the upper deck and jump overboard, then I would have bobbed on the ocean for a while and then drowned. Acts of desperation. I didn't reckon in such a human manner but, informed by my environment, I behaved as if I had reckoned.

I didn't reckon, but I observed everything calmly. I saw those men walk up and down, always the same faces, the same movements; it often seemed to me as if they were only one man. So this man or those men were walking unrestrained. A grand goal dawned upon me. No one promised me that, if I became like them, the cage would be opened. Such promises are not made for seemingly impossible fulfillments. But if the fulfillment is achieved, the promises appear after the fact exactly where one had looked for them before. Now there was nothing about those men as such that really appealed to me. If I were a follower of that above-mentioned freedom, I certainly would have preferred the ocean to the way out that opened up to me in the eyes of those humans.

22

She stood at the window and looked down onto the quiet street. Behind her in the small room, her husband lay dressed on the bed, sleeping. A neighbor came in, looked around and left again. When the streetlights were lit down in the street, she left the window and began her preparations for making coffee

---

A miserable horse cart on the country roads, themselves brimming with misery. Grandmother mother and three children lay in the straw under the low roof of the wagon. The father with a fourth child to his left and the reins in his right hand steered the staggering horse ahead. When they came to the city gate

---

A. What is tormenting you so?
B. Everything is incomprehensible to me. I don't understand a thing.

I should be very content. I'm a civil servant with the municipality. How nice it is to be a civil servant with the municipality. Little work, sufficient salary, a lot of spare time, excessive renown everywhere in town. When I keenly imagine the situation of a municipal civil servant, I can't help but envy him. And now I am it, a municipal civil servant – and if I could, I would feed all this honor to the office cat wandering from room to room every morning to collect leftovers after the morning snack

---

I don't know any way out

Lower I cannot

If I were to die some time soon or become entirely unable to live – this is a strong possibility, since I coughed up blood during the last two nights – I may say that I tore myself apart. If my father used to say in wild but empty threats: I will tear you apart like a fish – in reality he did not even lay a finger on me – the threat is now coming true independently of him. The world – F. is only its representative – and my Ego tear my body apart in an insoluble conflict.

Do you believe? I don't know.

I was supposed to study in the big city. My aunt expected me at the train station. Once when I had visited the city with my father, I had seen her. I barely recognized her now.

A hideous face up in the air vent

Help me!	Help yourself
You are leaving me?	Yes
What have I done to you?	Nothing

K. Quiet. I'm starting today. You've been serving me for seven years. Been well paid, lavished with gifts. You have a lakeside mansion as well. Now that should be sufficient, even though I don't want to put down your services at all, least in this moment. Not at all; they were good. For exactly that reason I will pay you a thousand gold florins today because I'm dismissing you. Do you have any objections?

N. Dismissed?

K. Yes yes, but you must get over that point. So I'm dismissing you. I'm tired of you. You bore me, not much, but still a little. And since one has to endure so much boredom from everyone else, but especially when it comes to the jester one really isn't all that strict – that's why.

N. So cruel!?

K. Yes. Or may be not, after all. You are, as I said, expelled by me now. If you don't agree with me and find yourself entertaining, then

You raven, I said, you old unlucky bird, what are you constantly doing in my way. Wherever I go, you sit and ruffle your few feathers. What a nuisance!

Yes, he said and, his head lowered, walked up and down in front of me like a teacher lecturing, it's true, it's almost uncomfortable for me myself. Why, I ask myself

---

The forest and the river – they swam past me as I swam in the water

---

Just let me go!
Where do you want to go?
They're waiting outside.
Who's waiting?
I don't know.
So you lied.
I didn't.

He had finally come to the city where he was to study. A room had been found, the suitcase unpacked, a countryman who had been living there for some time led him through the streets. Entirely by accident, the famous local curiosities depicted in all the textbooks arose at the end of a street that opened up to the side. The view took his breath away, but the countryman just pointed over there with his arm

---

You old rascal what about we clean things up for a change?
No no, I would very much resist that.
I don't doubt it. Nonetheless you will have to be eliminated.
I will go get my relatives.
I expected that, too. They, too, will have to be thrown against the wall.

Where do you come from?
Leave me alone.
You make it easy for yourself. Tramps are not allowed to talk like this. We have

a right to ask what kind of people come to rest here.

I'm Heracles.

A curious name to go by. The more important it is for me to find out where you're from.

You boring questioner, don't you know who Heracles is.

Good heavens! The great demigod Heracles, that is you? Just one more word!

Yes:

> Silence.

Do you know the park guard?

Yes, sure.

Don't you also think that he's crazy?

Whatever it is that pulls me out from between the two millstones that crush me otherwise, provided it doesn't involve all too much physical pain, I experience it as a boon.

---

just but coarse

The dream of the sick woman whom I serve in the ambulance and who beats me at my request.

The small verandah laid out flat in the sun, the weir gurgles peacefully and evermore

---

Nothing is keeping me.

Open the doors and windows

The roads vast and empty

K. was a great conjurer. His repertoire was somewhat monotonous, but due to the indubitability of his performance it was an attraction over and over again. I still remember exactly the show when I saw him for the first time, even though it has been twenty years and I was a very young boy at the time. He came to our small town without prior announcement and gave the show on the very evening of his arrival. In the great dining hall of our hotel, some space had been left around a table in the center – that was all there was in terms of theatrical setup. In my memory, the room was overcrowded, but to a child, any room appears to be overcrowded where there are a few lights shining, the hubbub of adult voices can be heard, a waiter walking back and forth and so on; also, I didn't know why so many people should have come to this seemingly precipitated show, but of course this putative overcrowdedness of the hall surely played decisively into the overall impression I had of the performance.

Whatever I touch, decomposes

The year of mourning was over
The wings of the birds were limp.
The moon revealed itself in cool nights
Almond and olive trees had ripened long ago

The boon of the years

The toll collector

He sat over the accounts. Great columns. Sometimes he turned away from them and placed his face in his hand. What did the accounts yield? Dull, dull accounts

---

Why do you want

Yesterday I went to the management offices for the first time. Our nightshift elected me shop steward, and since the construction and filling of our lamps is inadequate, I was supposed to insist that those defects be remedied. I was directed to the office in charge, I knocked and entered. A tender young man, very pale, smiled at me from his large desk. He nodded his head very much, too much. I didn't know whether I was supposed to sit down; there were an armchair, but I thought that perhaps I shouldn't sit on my first visit right away, and so I told my tale standing up. But apparently it was precisely this modesty that caused difficulties for the young man, for he had to turn his head around and upward to me, if he didn't want to move his armchair, and he didn't want to. But then he couldn't turn his neck all the way, although he was perfectly willing, and thus looked up halfway at the ceiling at an angle as I was talking; I involuntarily did the same. When I was finished, he slowly stood up, patted me on the shoulders, and said: Well, well – well, well, and pushed me into the next room where a gentleman with an unkempt large beard had apparently been expecting us, for there was no sign of any kind of work to be seen on his desk, whereas an open glass door led into a small garden with an abundance of flowers and shrubs. A short piece of information consisting of a few words, whispered to him by the young man, is sufficient for the gentleman to grasp our multiple complaints. He stood up at once and said: Well my dear – he stalled, and since I thought he wished to know my name, I opened my mouth to introduce myself once again, but he cut me off: Yes, yes, it's all right, it's all right, I know you quite well – now your request is certainly justified, I and the gentlemen in management are the last ones who wouldn't acknowledge that. The well-being of the people, believe me, is closer to our hearts than the well-being of the factory. Why wouldn't it be? The factory can be set up again, it only costs money, to the devil with the money, but if a man perishes, it is not only a man who perishes; there is a widow, the children who survive him. Oh my goodness! Therefore every new proposition to introduce new security, new relief, new conveniences and luxuries, is very welcome to us. Whoever comes to us with that, is our man. You leave us your suggestions, we will consider them thoroughly, if any other little splendid innovation can be attached to it, we will be sure not to withhold it, and by the time everything is finished you will get your new lamps. But tell your people down there: We will not rest until we have turned your mining gallery into a salon, and if you don't eventually perish in patent leather boots than not at all. And with that we bid you goodbye!

It was a very large evening party, and I didn't know anyone. I therefore decided to be completely quiet at first, then slowly figure out the people whom I might best approach, and then insert myself into the remaining party with their help. The one-windowed room was small enough, but there were about twenty people. I stood at the open window, following the example of the others who took cigarettes from one of the small side tables, and smoked in peace. Unfortunately, even though I was paying attention, I didn't understand what was being discussed. At one point it seemed to me that there was talk of a man and two women, but then again of a woman and two men, but since they were only talking about the same three people, it could only be owed to my own slowness that I was unable to even handle the few people in question, much less so, of course, the story of those people. The question that was raised, that seemed to be beyond all doubt, was whether the behavior of those three people or at least of one of the three people was morally acceptable or not. But nobody spoke at any length about the story itself anymore, which was known to everyone.

Evening by the river. A boat in the water. Sun setting into the clouds

---

He collapsed in front of me. I'm telling you, he collapsed in front of me, as closely as this table is close to me against which I'm pressing. Are you insane? I yelled. It was long past midnight, I was coming from a party, felt like walking by myself a bit, and now this man had collapsed right in front of me. I couldn't lift this giant; I didn't want to leave him lying there either in that deserted area where no one was to be seen wide and far.

I have three dogs: Hold Him, Seize Him, and Nevermore. Hold Him and Seize Him are ordinary small ratter dogs, and no one would ever take notice of them if they were alone, but then there is Nevermore. Nevermore is a mongrel Great Dane and looks the way even centuries of the most meticulous breeding could never have produced. Nevermore is a gypsy,

Dreams were cascading over me; I was lying in my bed, tired and hopeless

---

I lay ill. Because it was a severe illness, the straw bedding of my two roommates had been carried outside, and I was alone day and night.

I was gravely ill, and since I didn't have any visitors, those sick visits that I would have loved to avoid if it had been in my power may be the first

---

As long as I had been healthy, no one had worried about me. That was quite all right with me in general, so I don't want to complain after the fact, I just want to stress the difference: As soon as I fell ill, the sick visits started, have continued almost without interruption and haven't ceased until today.

Hopeless was going around the Cape of Good Hope in a small boat. It was early in the morning, a stiff breeze was blowing; Hopeless set a small sail and peacefully leaned back. What was there to fear in this small boat with its tiny shallow draft, gliding over all the reefs in those dangerous waters with the nimbleness of a living being.

The life of a poor student is so difficult,

All my spare hours – there aren't very many of them, but all too many I have to spend sleeping against my will, to be able to stand my hunger–

All my spare hours, I spend with Nevermore. On a daybed à la Madame Récamier, I have no idea how this piece of furniture made it up into my garret room; perhaps it meant to go into a closet and, since it was too strained already, decided to stay in my room.

Nevermore is of the opinion that things can't go on like this and that some way out needs to be found. I am basically of the same opinion, but I pretend otherwise. He runs to and fro in the room, occasionally jumps onto the armchair, with his teeth tugs at the piece of sausage I put out for him, with his paw flicks it to me and takes up his circular run again

A. What you have decided to do is a difficult endeavor, no matter how you look at it. There are of course even more difficult ones. Climbing the Mont Blanc is more difficult. But your cause requires a lot of strength after all. Do you feel this inside of you?
B. No. I can't say that. I feel a void inside of me but no strength.

———————

A. What you have decided to do is a very difficult and dangerous endeavor, no matter from which angle one may look at it. However, one also shouldn't overrate it, for there are even more difficult and dangerous ones. And particularly where one doesn't suspect it and therefore one goes into completely innocent and unprepared. This is my opinion, but of course I wish to neither discourage nor dismiss your plans. Not at all. Undoubtedly, your cause requires a lot of strength and is truly worth the exertion. But do you actually feel this strength inside of you?

———————

I rode in through the south gate. Attached to the gate, there is a large inn where I wanted to spend the night. I led my mule into the stable, which was almost overcrowded with mounts, but I managed to find a safe place. Then I climbed onto one of the loggias, spread out my blanket and lay down to sleep

———————

Dear Mr. Rotpeter,
I read the report you wrote for our Academy of Sciences with great interest, even with a pounding heart. This is no surprise, since I was your first teacher, for whom you found such friendly words. Perhaps, upon some reflection, you may have omitted mentioning my stay in the sanatorium, but I realize that due to the distinctive candor of your report you could not suppress this tiny detail, even though it compromises me somewhat, since it happened to occur to you as you were writing it down. But this is not really what I wish to talk about here; I am writing about something else.

Passed in vain! And the two mourners were standing over there,

---

The night is the only time for effective training.

Sweet snake, why do you stay so distant, come closer, still closer, enough, no further, stay there. Ah, for you there are no boundaries. How am I to get you under my control, if you don't recognize any boundaries. It will be a tough job. I start by asking you to coil yourself. I said coil, and you stretch. Don't you understand me? You don't understand me. I'm speaking very clearly, though: Coil! No, you don't grasp it. Well, I'll show you with this stick here. First you have to form a large circle, then on its inside a second one and so forth. When you hold up your little head in the end, lower it slowly according to the tune I'll be blowing on my flute, and when I fall silent, be quiet as well with your head inside the innermost circle.

I was led to my horse, but I was still very weak. I saw the slender animal shivering with the fever of life

---

This isn't my horse, I said, when the servant of the inn led a horse in front of me in the morning. Your horse was the only one in our stable last night, the servant said and looked at me with a smile, or, if I so wished, with a defiant smile. No, I said, this isn't my horse. The fur sack dropped from my hands, I turned and went up to the room I had just left.

A. Was he here?

B. He just left.

A. I suspected it. How was he clad?

B. Light gray suit, quite ordinary. A golden watch chain across his vest.

A. Was he in a good mood?

B. There was nothing to suggest anything extraordinary. We talked about business.

A. Where did he go?

B. He said, he had to go to the bank.

A. Thanks very, very much.

B. Thanks?

A. exits

B. tidies a few things in the room.

Porter: They are here.

B. Please.

Bride, V. M. B.

B. A warm, warm welcome

The countess has been photographed; she is standing on the great lawn in front of the palace with her daughter and her son

[23]

The little one,

I usually trust my driver with everything. When we came to a tall white wall slowly vaulting sideways and above, when we ceased to go forward, groped the wall as were driving along it, and the driver eventually said: It's a forehead.

I encountered Artur at the front door yesterday morning; he said he was on his way to see me, but since I had now come myself we went up to his room together. We had cigarettes and liquor and talked about occasional

We had set up a little fishing operation, built a wood cabin by the sea

---

Strangers recognize me. I could barely squeeze my way through the aisle of the overcrowded car with my small handbag. Then from a semi-dark compartment what seemed to be a complete stranger called me and offered me his seat

---

Strangers recognize me. Recently on a small trip I could barely squeeze through the aisle of the overcrowded car with my handbag

Once, due to a mistake, a coffin lay at our place for a whole night. The day of the funeral had incorrectly been

---

Once a coffin with a corpse lay at our place for a whole night – I don't remember the reason. For us, the gravedigger's children, there was nothing strange about coffins; when we went to sleep we hardly thought about the fact that there was a corpse in the same room.

When I woke up in the night, there was an open coffin lying in the middle of the room. From my bed I could see an old man with a divided long white beard lying in there

It was a quiet gloomy day. Wilted grass bordered the three steps leading up to the front door. On the top there stood a man and looked at a carriage that slowly went up the slope and stopped in front of the house.

---

shift of terminology
Catholicism (even without divorce)
militarism of conviction
coquetry
German irony

---

militarism ———— office

---

agreement in the preliminary impulse

---

militarism does not mean a caste (as with the Hereros), but possibility success of mechanization of war, if necessary as militarism of conviction

---

Austria proof of military's peacefulness (active officers, great despite lack of hatred)

---

power of conviction directed against the reader

---

the rise of the royalist party in a dependent clause
dependent clause means of sophistic rhetoric

however various reasons for lack of hatred in workers and royalists are missing

---

subtleties of revenge idea educational tool of nouveau esprit

---

difficulties of generalizing like I generalize laborers of love at first

---

work as joy
inaccessible to psychologists

---

about retirees,　　America only touched upon
enslavement of the consumer

---

admonishment to the Catholics to become more powerful

Jews good

---

for Austria as well
Austria's art of the administration

---

preposterousness re: Kant

---

nausea after too much psychology. If one has good legs and is admitted to psychology, he can cover distances in a short time and in a zigzag like in no other field. One is dumbfounded at that

---

pleonexia?

prophecy of their original sin

---

about the merchant

Catholic center

love of England
how does he explain it

I'm standing on a desolate piece of ground. Why I wasn't placed in a better land, I don't know. Am I not worth it? One must not say that. No shrub can thrive more abundantly than I anywhere.

On Jewish Theater

I will not dwell on numbers and statistics; I will leave those to the historians of Jewish theater. My intention is quite simple: to present a few pages of memories of Jewish theater with its plays, its actors, its audiences as I have seen, learned, and practiced it in more than ten years, or, to put it another way, to lift the curtain and show off the wound. Only when the disease is known can a remedy be found and perhaps a true Jewish theater created.

For my devout Hasidic parents in Warsaw, the theater, of course, was "treyf," no different from "chazzer." Still – on Purim, when my cousin Haskel would stick a large black beard on top of his small blond beard, put on the caftan the wrong way and play a funny Jewish merchant, I as a young child could not tear my eyes off him; he was my favorite cousin, I could not stop thinking about him. And, at eight years old, I already imitated my cousin Haskel at the cheder. Whenever the rebbe was not in, we played theater at the cheder; I was the manager, director, everything, even the thrashing I got from the rebbe was the greatest one. But that did not bother us, the rebbe thrashed, and yet we thought

227

up new theater plays every day, and the whole year it was only hoping and praying: Purim may come, and I should be allowed to watch my cousin Haskel in his masquerade. That I, once I was grown up, would put on masks and sing and dance at every Purim like my cousin Haskel seemed only natural to me. But I had not the faintest idea that people wear masks outside of Purim, and that there are many more such artists like my cousin Haskel.

We encountered one another on the path. Where are you going, I asked. To Brunnersdorf, he said.

A river divided the city.

Eventually there was only one other man at the inn besides me. The innkeeper wanted to close up and asked me to pay. "There is another man sitting there," I said, morosely, because I realized that it was time to go, but I didn't feel like leaving or going anywhere at all. "That is the problem," the innkeeper said, "I don't know how to communicate with the man. Do you want to help me?" "Hello," I called through my cupped hands, but the man didn't budge and quietly kept looking sideways into his beer glass

---

"The Count will see you now," the servant said with a bow and opened the high glass door with a silent jerk. The Count came hurrying toward me, half flying, from his desk that stood by the open window. We gazed into each other's eyes; the Count's vacant stare startled me.

We were going down the quiet river in a boat

It was already late at night when I rang at the gate. It took a long time until, evidently from the depths of the manor, the castellan emerged and opened up

---

I was lying on the ground in front of a wall, writhing with pain, feeling that I wanted to burrow myself into the moist soil. The hunter was standing next to me and lightly pushed his foot into the small of my back. A magnificent catch, he said to the beater who was cutting open my collar and overcoat in order to feel me. Tired of me and eager for new deeds, the dogs were running up against the wall in vain. Then a carriage came, my hands and legs tied up, I was thrown across the rear seat next to the gentleman, so that my head and arms were hanging outside the carriage. The journey was brisk, dying of thirst with my mouth open I sucked in the swirled up dust; now and then I felt the gentleman's joyous hand on my calves

---

What am I carrying on my shoulders? What ghosts drape around me?

It was a stormy night, I saw the little ghost crawl out of the shrubs

---

The gate slammed shut, I stood eye to eye with him

A pale tangle around her head, black burning eye, lips pulled to and fro

---

He had finally surmounted the last wall, he was cro

Everyone into the room,

A dim light issued from that mountain
a dim light

A lamp burst, a stranger entered with a new light, I rose, my family with me, we greeted him, it went unnoticed

---

The robbers had tied me up, and there I lay close to the chief's fire.

The trumpet sounded clearly, and we gathered

Barren fields, barren ground, behind fogs the pale green of the moon. Low walls around the fields

---

He leaves the house, finds himself in the street, a horse is waiting, a servant is holding the stirrup, the ride goes through the resounding barren land

---

Isaac Löwy

On Jewish Theater.

I will not dwell on numbers and statistics in what follows; I will leave those to the historians of Jewish theater. My intention is quite simple: to present a few pages of memories of Jewish theater with its plays, its actors, its audiences as I have seen, learned, and practiced it in more than ten years, or, to put it another way, to lift the curtain and show off the wound. Only when the disease is known can a remedy be found and perhaps a true Jewish theater created.

1.

For my devout Hasidic parents in Warsaw, the theater, of course, was "treyf," no different from "chazzer." Only on Purim there was theater, for then my cousin Haskel would stick a large black beard on top of his small blond beard, put on the caftan the wrong way and play a funny Jewish merchant – as a young child I could not take my eyes off him. Of all my cousins, he was my favorite; I could not stop thinking about him, and, as soon as I turned eight years old, I played theater in the cheder like my cousin Haskel. Whenever the rebbe was not in, there was theater in the cheder; I was the manager, director, in short everything, and the thrashing I would get from the rebbe was the greatest, too. But that did not bother us, the rebbe thrashed, and yet we thought up new theater plays every day. And the whole year, we were just hoping and praying that Purim may come and that I should be allowed to watch my cousin Haskel masquerade. That, once I was grown up, I would put on masks and sing and dance like my cousin Haskel – there was no question about that for me.

But I had not the faintest idea that people wear masks outside of Purim, and that there are many more such artists like my cousin Haskel. Until I once heard from Isruel Feldsher's boy that there truly was such a thing as the theater where one acts and sings and wears masks, and every night, not just on Purim, and that there are such theaters in Warsaw as well, and that his father had taken him along several times. This news – I was about ten years old at the time – virtually electrified me. A secret, previously unsuspected desire took hold of me. I counted the days that would have to pass until I was grown up and I could finally see the theater myself. At the time, I did not even know that the theater was a forbidden and sinful thing.

I soon found out that opposite City Hall there was the "Grand Theater," the best, the most beautiful in all of Warsaw, in the whole world, really. From that time on, merely the exterior view of the building when I passed it positively blinded me. But once, when I inquired at home when we would finally go to the Grand Theater, I was shouted at: a Jewish child must not know anything about theater; it was not allowed; theater is only for the Goyim and for sinners. This answer was enough for me, I did not ask any more, but I could not stop thinking about it, and I was very afraid that I would surely have to commit this sin at some point, and, when I was older, would have to go to the theater after all.

Once, when I went past the Grand Theater with two cousins on the evening after Yom Kippur, there were a lot of people on the theater gallery and I could not take my eyes off this "impure" theater, my cousin Mayer asked me: "Would you want to be up there, too?" I stayed silent. He probably didn't like my silence and therefore added: "Now, child, there is not a single Jew there – heaven forbid! On the evening right after Yom Kippur, even the worst Jew wouldn't go to the theater." I concluded from this that no Jew went to the theater after the close of the Holy Yom Kippur, but that many Jews did go to there on ordinary nights throughout the year.

In the fourteenth year of my life, I went to the Grand Theater for the first time. As little as I had learned of the local language, I was able to read the bills, and so I read there one day that the Huguenots would be performed. I had already heard about Huguenots in the "klaus," also the play was by a Jew "Mayer Beer" – and so I gave myself permission, bought a ticket, and in the evening I was in the theater for the first time in my life.

What I saw and felt is beside the point, just this: I became convinced that they sang much better there than cousin Haskel did and that the costumes were much more beautiful than his as well. And I brought home yet another surprise: I had already known the ballet music from the Huguenots for a long time, because the tunes were sung at the "klaus." Friday night for Lecha Dodi. And I couldn't understand how it was possible that they were playing at the Grand Theater that which had been sung at the "klaus" for such a long time.

From then on, I became a frequent visitor to the opera. The only thing was, I had to think of buying a collar and a pair of cuffs for the performance and throw them into the Vistula on the way home. My parents were not allowed to see these things; while I was feeding on William Tell and Aida, my parents were of the firm belief that I was sitting in the klaus over the folios of the Talmud, studying the Holy Scripture.

2.

Some time later, I learned that there was a Jewish Theater as well. As much as I would have liked to go there, I didn't dare to, because it would have been all too easy for my parents to find me out. I frequently went to the opera at the Grand Theater, and later to the Polish Drama Theater as well. At the latter I saw Schiller's "The Robbers" for the first time. It surprised me very much that it should be possible to play theater so beautifully without song and music – I never would have thought it – and strangely enough I was not angry with Franz, rather he made the greatest impression on me; I wanted to play him rather than Karl.

Of all my comrades at the klaus, I was the only one who had dared to go to the theater. Otherwise, we the boys at the klaus had already filled up on all the "enlightened books:" this was when I read Shakespeare, Schiller, Lord Byron for the first time. In terms of Yiddish literature, however, all I was able to get my hands on were the great crime mysteries shipped from America in a language half German, half Yiddish.

A short time went by, but I couldn't stop thinking about it: a Jewish Theater in Warsaw, and I should not go see it? And so I took the risk, I risked everything for a ticket, and I went to the Jewish Theater.

The experience completely transformed me. Even before the beginning of the play, I felt completely different than among "the other ones." Most of all, no gentlemen in tailcoats, no ladies in low necklines, no Polish, no Russian, only Jews of all kinds, long clad, short clad, women and girls, in conventional dress. And everyone spoke loudly and openly in their mother tongue; no one took notice of me in my long little caftan, and I didn't feel embarrassed at all.

A tragic comedy was played with song and dance, in six acts and ten scenes: *Baal-Teshuva* by Shumor. They didn't start precisely at eight as at the Polish Theater but not until around ten and ended long after midnight. The lover of............ and the villain spoke "High German," and I was amazed that all of a sudden – without knowing a thing about the German language – I was able to understand such excellent German so well. Only the comedians and the soubrette spoke Yiddish.

All in all I liked it better than the opera, the drama theater, and the operetta all taken together. First of all it was in Yiddish, if German Yiddish, but still Yiddish, a better, more beautiful Yiddish, and second everything came together, drama, tragedy, song, comedy, dance – life! The whole night I barely slept due to my excitement; my heart was telling me that I should serve at the temple of Jewish art one day, that I should become a Jewish actor.

But the next day in the afternoon, my father sent the children to the next room, and only told my mother and me to stay. Instinctively, I felt that a "kasha" was being cooked up for me. The father is no longer seated; he walks to and fro in the room; his hand on his small black beard, he doesn't speak to me but to my mother: "You should know this: he's getting worse and worse every day, yesterday he was seen at the Jewish Theater." Startled, my mother folds her hands, my father, all pale, continues do walk to and fro in the room, my heart hurts, I sit like a convict, I can't stand seeing my dear, devout parents in pain. I don't remember today what I said at the time, I only know that, after several minutes of oppressive silence, my father turned his large black eyes on me and said: "My child, just think, this will take you far, very far" – and he was right.

AFTERWORD

The chronology of texts in this volume results from the caesura in Kafka's biography marked by the flare-up of his pulmonary disease in the summer of 1917, as well as his stay in the country brought on by it (autumn 1917 to spring 1918). The present volume comprises the texts Kafka wrote up to autumn 1917 – with the exception of the two novels *The Man Who Disappeared* and *The Trial,* as well as everything passed on in his journals. In terms of content, it corresponds in part to the volumes *Description of a Struggle: Novellas, Sketches, Aphorisms from the Estate* (third edition, 1954) and *Wedding Preparations in the Country and Other Prose Writings from the Estate* (1953) within the last of Brod's Kafka editions. On the other hand, it consists of – apart from a number of smaller, heretofore unpublished texts and text snippets – the first drafts of several stories published by Kafka himself, which are included in *Printings during his Lifetime* in the shape and configurations of the printings.

All of the texts are presented in chronological order according to the author's manuscripts, in such a manner that even the textual sequence and the textual contexts of the original document – i.e. of Kafka's notebooks, sheaves (convolutes), and individual papers – are preserved. Brief indications on all documents, numbered from [1] to [24] can be found in the table of contents.

The presentation of the texts themselves is based on Kafka's manuscripts in their last discernible state. In two cases – for documents [12] and [24] – the presentation had to be based on copies in someone else's hand. The character of the manuscripts, which is occasionally far from polished, has been preserved throughout: emendations were made only where readability would have been severely hampered.

Some items appear strikingly differently in this edition compared to their habitual form owed to the previous printing history. The texts published here are – as already suggested – not only printed in their original shape but also within their original contexts in the manuscripts: what appears together in the manuscripts, has thus been left together. Max Brod, however, followed a different path – at a time when it was the objective to introduce Kafka's posthumous writings for the first time at all. Having published the three great posthumous novels in the twenties, he proceeded to select those from the entirety of the shorter posthumous texts that he considered "completed or at least completed to a certain degree" and publish them as independent pieces – complete with titles, which he had to come up with himself, for the most part. The first selection Brod put together in this manner was published in 1931, under the title *The Construction of the Great Wall of China*, and in the following served as a foundation for the more extensive selections which he published, in various forms, under the title *Description of a Struggle* – last in 1954, within his last complete edition. In his presentation of all the texts included in those volumes Brod remained true to his intention professed as early as 1931 to "present a readable entity as close as possible to Kafka's supposed intentions" each time. To this end he frequently considered it necessary to reorganize the remaining manuscripts, join thematically kindred fragments, fuse competing versions, and even restore passages that the author had crossed out. The texts that Brod thought all too fragmentary to be presented as quasi-polished individual pieces were brought to print only in the 1953 volume *Wedding Preparations in the Country*, a collection of all "other" posthumous texts. In summary, one can say that Brod's classification of the texts according to the criterion of their "artistic unity and accomplishment" has been undone so that the context of the genesis of a text heretofore concealed is now obvious for the first time.

The present text corpus, however, conveys a very incomplete picture of all of Kafka's writings during the time period in question. As far as his literary attempts in the time up to 1911 are concerned, the by far greater part appears not to have survived. Thus the "few thousand lines" sent to his friend Oskar Pollak at the end of 1912 as well as the "about 200" pages of an "entirely unusable" version of *The Man Who Disappeared*, for example, must be considered lost. The number of pages the author must have discarded can be gauged by a journal entry from 17 December 1910: "That I put aside and crossed out so much, why, almost everything I have written this year, at any rate, has kept me very much from writing. It is a mountain after all, 5 times as much as I have ever written..." On 11 March 1912 he notes that he burned "many old, disgusting papers"; presumably the only extensive literary texts preserved from the early years – namely the two versions of "Description of a Struggle" and the fragments of the so-called "Wedding Preparations in the Country" – escaped this fate only because he had already passed them onto Max Brod. As far as the later period up to autumn 1917 is concerned, it must also be pointed out that a great number of Kafka's literary sketches and fragments only survived in his journals, which he also used as workbooks. Therefore, according to the editorial principles of the edition, they are printed in the volume *Journals*, which may be consulted for comparison.

Some of the texts presented here were composed on special occasions and may be difficult to understand without the respective context. In conclusion a few brief explanations on those texts:

[3] "One cannot say...": Kafka reacts to an article by Max Brod, which appeared under the title "On Aesthetics" in the weekly *Die Gegenwart* ("The Present") on 17 and 24 February 1906 respectively.

[7] "This choice should be thoroughly welcomed...": Kafka composed this official speech in 1909 to commend the promotion of his former section head, Dr. Robert Marschner, to leading manager of the Arbeiter-Unfall-Versicherungs-Anstalt on behalf of the staff.

[10] "Samuel knows at least...": This is a sketch of the introduction of the travel journal novel *Richard and Samuel* that he and Max Brod were planning to write together, of which only the first chapter – under the title "The First Long Railroad Journey (Prague-Zurich)" – was published in 1912.

[11] "What a sight it is...": For this review of *Heinrich von Kleist's Anecdotes* (ed. by Julius Bab, Leipzig: Rowohlt, 1911), no evidence of publication has been found.

[12] "Before you hear the first few verses by Jewish poets from Eastern Europe...": Kafka organized an evening of readings for the Eastern Jewish actor Yitzchak Loevy in Prague, which took place on 18 February 1912 and which he opened with an introductory speech.

[24] "On Jewish Theater": This text is Kafka's edited version of a never completed essay by Yitzchak Loevy, which was to be published in the monthly journal *Der Jude* ("The Jew"). On 20 July 1917, Kafka writes to then-editor Martin Buber on the subject: "Would you care to receive for the coming *Jew* an essay stemming from personal experience on the situation, i.e. the distress, i.e. the spiritual distress (the actual distress is almost broken with the conditioning of long years), thus the spiritual distress of Jargon acting?". In a letter to Max Brod on 28 September 1917, he gives the following example for the difficulties of the editing process: "In the audience at the Polish theater he sees as opposed to that at the Jewish theater: tuxedoed gentlemen and negligeed ladies. There is no way of putting it any more exquisitely but the German language resists it."

Translator's Note:
This being the first English edition of an entire volume of Kafka's *Posthumous Writings and Fragments*, the translation preserves the unpolished, imperfect, spontaneous nature of the original. The occasional missing question mark or period to mark the end of a sentence, the inconsistent use of verb tenses, awkward wordings, and run-on sentences are therefore intentional, attempting to replicate the idiosyncrasies of Kafka's writing.